# COLLECTION 13

Kristy and her friends love babysitting and when her mum can't find a babysitter for Kristy's little brother one day, Kristy has a great idea. Why doesn't she set up a babysitting club? That way parents can make a single phone call and reach a team of babysitting experts. And if one baby-sitter is already busy another one can take the job. So together with her friends, Claudia, Mary Anne and Stacey, Kristy starts THE BABYSITTERS CLUB. And although things don't *always* go according to plan, they have a lot of fun on the way!

*Catch up with the very latest adventures of the Babysitters Club in these great new stories:*

*And coming soon. . .*

## COLLECTION 13

**Book 37**
DAWN AND THE OLDER BOY

**Book 38**
KRISTY'S MYSTERY ADMIRER

**Book 39**
POOR MALLORY

# Ann M. Martin

Scholastic Children's Books,
Commonwealth House, 1–19 New Oxford Street,
London, WC1A 1NU, UK
A division of Scholastic Ltd
London ~ New York ~ Toronto ~ Sydney ~ Auckland ~
Mexico City ~ New Delhi ~ Hong Kong

*Dawn and the Older Boy*
First published in the US by Scholastic Inc., 1990
First published in the UK by Scholastic Ltd, 1992
*Kristy's Mystery Admirer*
*Poor Mallory!*
First published in the US by Scholastic Inc., 1990
First published in the UK by Scholastic Ltd, 1993

First published in this edition by Scholastic Ltd, 1999

Text copyright © Ann M. Martin, 1990
THE BABY-SITTERS CLUB is a registered trademark of Scholastic
Inc.

ISBN 0 439 01181 7

Typeset by M Rules
Printed by Cox & Wyman Ltd, Reading, Berks.

1 2 3 4 5 6 7 8 9 10

# CONTENTS

# DAWN AND THE
# OLDER BOY

The author gratefully acknowledges
Mary Lou Kelly
for her help in
preparing this manuscript.

# 1st CHAPTER

"I don't think orange is your colour," Claudia Kishi said thoughtfully. "You're more the peaches-and-cream type, with your light skin and blonde hair."

"Mmm, I think you're right." I stared at myself in the mirror and reached for a tissue. The orange lipstick had to go. I looked as if I'd just kissed a pumpkin.

"Try this," Claudia went on, handing me a tube of gooey pink lip gloss. It reminded me of used bubble gum.

Claudia caught the expression on my face and burst out laughing. "Trust me, Dawn. It will look fantastic on you."

Claudia is an artist and can see shapes and colours in a way that nobody else can. It's a good thing that she's creative because she's not the world's best pupil. (She's a terrible speller.) And just to make things worse, she has an incredibly brainy older

5

sister called Janine. Janine is the type of girl who sits around doing quadratic equations for *fun*. Honest.

But back to the story. I glanced around Kristy Thomas's bedroom and saw that all six of my friends were experimenting with lipstick and nail varnish. A few of them, like Stacey McGill, were even trying out new hairstyles. It was a sort of mass "make over", and there was a lot of giggling going on. (And some of the "befores" looked better than the "afters", if you know what I mean.)

I think I should stop right here and introduce everybody before I tell you anything else about the sleepover at Kristy's. First of all, all seven of us are members of the Babysitters Club (or BSC), which I'll explain about later. My name is Dawn Schafer, and I am the alternate officer of the club. I live in Stoneybrook, Connecticut, and I'm thirteen years old. My friends all say I *look* like a California girl with my long blonde hair and sparkly blue eyes. This makes sense since I lived in California before my parents got divorced and my mum and my brother Jeff and I moved to Stoneybrook. Now Jeff lives in California again with my father (he just wasn't happy in Connecticut), and sometimes I go back to visit. What else would you like to know? Well, I love the outdoors, I'm a vegetarian, and I try to eat a healthy diet. (Unlike

Claudia, who thinks Dime Bars are nature's perfect food.)

Claudia is a beautiful, dramatic-looking Japanese-American who loves exotic clothes. (She's also the vice-chairman of the BSC.) Claudia's one of those people who can wear anything and get away with it. Today, for example, she had stuck to two colours: black and white. Black cotton bib overalls over a white cotton polo neck with a shiny black patent leather belt looped around her waist. Black suede ankle boots and white cotton socks. Long black hair swept off her face with giant white plastic combs. Anyone else would look like a penguin in that get-up, but Claudia looked great.

"What do you think?" she asked, holding up a white hoop earring next to her face. "Too much?"

I nodded. "Maybe just a little." The earring was the size of a doorknob.

"Hey, Dawn, will you have a look at my hair?" asked Mary Anne. Mary Anne Spier is my stepsister (my mother married Richard, her father) and she's also my best friend. Mary Anne is a lot less daring with clothes and make-up than I am, but she has grown up quite a bit in the past year.

When I first met Mary Anne, she looked like a little girl. She was wearing little-girl clothes and, worst of all, she was wearing her brown hair in two long plaits. Awful! When I got to know her better, I realized

7

that she's really sweet and very sensitive, and that she dressed like that because her father chose all her clothes. Mary Anne's mother died when Mary Anne was just a baby, so her father has always been very protective of her. Luckily, he's loosened up a lot since he married my mum, and Mary Anne dresses like a normal thirteen-year-old now. And she even has a steady boyfriend. She's the only one of us BSC members who can say that. Her boyfriend's called Logan Bruno, and he's part of the club, too. Mary Anne is the club secretary.

"What's the problem?" I asked, rushing over to her side of the room. The minute the words were out of my mouth, I knew the answer.

Stacey McGill (a real New York girl) was busily "scrunching" Mary Anne's long brown hair into a tangled mane that trailed down her back. Very hip, very in, but not very "Mary Anne". I thought it looked fantastic, but I knew that Mary Anne wasn't happy with it. Mary Anne usually wears her hair in a smooth style; she's used to seeing herself in a certain way. (I should explain that Mary Anne would never complain to Stacey, because she doesn't like to hurt anyone's feelings.)

"Honestly, Mary Anne, if you'd just keep your hands out of the way, this would go a lot quicker." Stacey had scrunched her own hair into a cloud of blonde curls and was trying for the same effect with my stepsister.

Mary Anne shot me a desperate look in the mirror, just as Stacey gave a final pat to her hair and said pointedly, "doesn't she look great?"

I was on the spot. "I think it's a nice change," I began. "Of course, you wouldn't have to wear it like that every day."

"She should. It's a big improvement," Stacey said flatly. Stacey McGill, the club treasurer, is very fashion-conscious and always wears the newest, trendiest clothes. She's sophisticated, like Claudia (who happens to be her best friend), and she has boyfriends sometimes, but no steady ones. She's an only child and grew up in New York City until her father's company transferred him to Connecticut. The McGills had lived in Stoneybrook for a year when her father was sent *back* to New York. We all said tearful goodbyes to Stacey and wondered if we would ever see her again. About a year later, Stacey's parents got divorced, and Stacey and her mum returned to Connecticut. Talk about a complicated life! Stacey still seems like a New York girl at heart (just like I'm a California girl at heart) and she visits her father in New York whenever she can.

Just to add to Stacey's problems, she's got a severe form of diabetes. She's very careful about what she eats and knows how to give herself insulin injections every day. Diabetes is something she has to live with, but at least she can keep it under control. The main thing she has to remember is not to eat sweets. Just imagine a life without sugar and sweets, and you'll get the idea. At first, we tried not to have biscuits or things lying around where she could see them, but we discovered that Stacey has a lot of self-control. She doesn't eat those things because she knows she could get really ill.

"Well, it's finished," Stacey said. She put down the brush and reached for an apple. The rest of us were munching on fudge (except for me – too unhealthy), but that's off-limits for Stacey, of course.

"I appreciate it, I really do," Mary Anne said earnestly. I knew that Mary Anne would never wear her hair that way again, but she managed to look as if she were thrilled with her new style.

"I'll be happy to do it for you anytime," Stacey said. "The thing to remember is to use just a little bit of gel and—" She stopped talking suddenly and sat down on Kristy's bed.

"Are you okay?" asked Kristy. (Kristy Thomas is the chairman of the Babysitters Club, and she's a take-charge sort of person.)

"I'm fine," Stacey said lightly. She put her hand up to her forehead, just for a second, as though she had a headache.

"You look a bit pale," Kristy said, peering at her. I remembered that Stacey hadn't felt well for the past few days.

"Hey, I'm fine. Really." Stacey bounced right back on her feet and picked up her hairbrush. "I think I'm a little dizzy from all the hairspray," she said with a smile. "Maybe we should get some air in here."

"Good idea." As usual, Kristy took command of the situation and marched over to the nearest window. Sometimes I get a bit annoyed because Kristy tends to be bossy (wait till you see her at a club meeting, and you'll understand), but I have to admit she really gets things done. It's funny, because in some ways, Kristy seems younger than thirteen. She has no interest in clothes and make-up and practically lives in her favourite outfit: a sweatshirt, faded jeans and trainers. But in other ways, she seems very mature and is exactly the kind of person you would want to have around in an emergency.

Kristy has an interesting family. She has three brothers – Sam and Charlie, who are at high school, and David Michael, who's only seven. For a long time, Mrs Thomas supported the family all by herself, because her husband had walked out one day and never come back. It was very hard on everyone, but Mrs Thomas managed to get a good job and keep the family together. Then (and this is the wonderful part) she met a millionaire called Watson Brewer and they married and the Thomases moved across town into his mansion! It sounds like something out of a film, doesn't it? Watson Brewer has two children, Karen, who's just turned seven, and Andrew, who's four, so Kristy found herself with a new brother and sister. (They only live with their father every other weekend and for two weeks during the summer, though.) Things got even *more* interesting after that because the Brewers adopted an adorable little Vietnamese girl whom they called Emily. By now Kristy's family was beginning to look like the Brady Bunch, so Nannie, Kristy's grandmother, moved in to help. Kristy loves her new family, and since she's terrific with kids, she's a big help with her younger brothers and sisters.

Okay, now I need to tell you about the two junior officers of the BSC, Mallory Pike and Jessica Ramsey. While the rest of us are eighth-graders at Stoneybrook Middle School, they are eleven and in the sixth grade at SMS. They're very different, but they're best friends.

Actually, Mal and Jessi have a couple of things in common. They're both the oldest in their families (that can have some good points and some bad points). And they share some interests.

Let's start with Mal. Mal comes from an *enormous* family. She has seven brothers and sisters, including a set of identical triplets (boys). She's very creative and loves to read and write and draw. Her ambition in life is to write and illustrate children's books, and I think she'd do a wonderful job.

Jessi has an eight-year-old sister named Becca (short for Rebecca) and a baby brother named Squirt. Squirt? That's right. His real name is John Philip Ramsey Jr, but he was so tiny when he was born that the nurses in the hospital nicknamed him Squirt.

Jessi also likes reading (she and Mal both love horse stories), but her real talent is quite different from Mallory's. Jessi wants to be a professional dancer and has studied ballet for years. It takes a lot of skill and hard work to get roles in major ballets and to perform in front of hundreds of people, but Jessi's got what it takes. She doesn't even get stage fright. (I know I'd be scared stiff if I had to do something like that.)

Another difference between Jessi and Mal – Jessi is black and Mal is white.

I have a lot more things I want to tell you about my friends (especially about my step-sister, Mary Anne, and the really romantic way our parents got together), but I'll have to save that for later. Stay tuned!

## 2nd CHAPTER

At eleven o'clock the following morning, Mary Anne tapped me on the shoulder.

"Dawn, wake up," she said urgently. "It's practically lunchtime!"

I snuggled deeper into my sleeping bag and buried my face in the pillow. "Uh-huh," I mumbled. What was Mary Anne getting all steamed up about? *Nobody* bounces out of bed the morning after a sleepover, and besides, we hadn't turned out the lights till three am. No wonder I felt like a zombie.

But Mary Anne wouldn't give up. She sat down next to me. "I think we should all get up right this minute," she said firmly. "We've already wasted half the day!"

"Stop talking," Stacey muttered from her sleeping bag. "Some people are trying to sleep."

"I know you are," Mary Anne apologized.

14

"But I think the Brewers expect us to turn up for breakfast. We shouldn't be lounging around in bed all morning when they're trying to feed sixteen in the kitchen." I hated to admit it, but I decided Mary Anne was probably right. I also thought that my stepsister was the only person in the whole world who would worry about something like that.

"Mmm, I think I smell bacon cooking," Mal said. She wriggled off her lilo and stretched. "I agree with Mary Anne. We should all go downstairs."

Jessi gave a gigantic yawn. I've decided to have breakfast in bed," she said sleepily. "Just leave a tray outside the door for me."

"Ha! Fat chance!" Claudia yelled, tossing a pillow at her. "If we get up, *you* get up."

Mary Anne yanked open the curtains, and the room was flooded with harsh yellow sunlight. Everybody *really* woke up after that, including Kristy, who had burrowed like a mole under her fluffy pink quilt.

"Hey, Kristy," Stacey asked, "do we have to get dressed to go down to breakfast?"

"On a Saturday morning? Are you kidding?" Kristy grinned and jammed her feet into a pair of fat furry slippers. "That's the great part about weekends. You can wear whatever you like, and Mum and Watson won't care. Honest."

Claudia glanced in the mirror. Her hair was a mass of tangles and her mascara had smudged over her cheekbones in two dark shadows. She looked like someone straight out of *Night of the Living Dead*.

"Claudia, you look awful," Kristy said cheerfully.

"You don't look so terrific yourself," Claudia retorted. She wasn't in the least bit offended because the truth is we *all* looked awful.

"I know. Isn't it fun?" Kristy grabbed her favourite baseball cap (the one with the collie on it) and plunked it on her head. "But who's going to see us at breakfast except for Karen and Nannie and Mum and everyone?"

A few minutes later we had our answer. Who was going to see us? Only the most gorgeous guy in the whole world!

Talk about having a panic attack. All seven of us had trooped downstairs, looking our absolute worst, when we realized there were *boys* sitting around the kitchen table! Two of them were Kristy's older brothers, Charlie and Sam, and the other looked like a film star. Sandy brown hair, deep blue eyes, and a smile that I knew I would never forget. Claudia was in front of me, and she skidded to a stop just like the Road Runner in that Saturday morning cartoon programme. Naturally, I bumped into her, and she lurched against the back of Sam's chair.

"Oh, Claudia. Hi there." He glanced at Kristy. "I figured you were going to sleep all day." Sam took a quick peek at the rest of us, and his jaw dropped open. Why hadn't we taken a few extra minutes to brush our hair and put on some make-up? (Or at least take off the old make-up?) I know I looked terrible. I have very fair skin and, as I've said, my hair is so blonde it's practically white. Can you imagine what I look like first thing in the morning, especially with mascara smudges under my eyes?

I tried to duck behind Stacey, who immediately caught on and started inching her way back towards the hallway.

"Hey, don't run away," Charlie teased her. "Kristy, I want you and your friends to meet someone." He waved a hand at the fantastic-looking boy at the table. "Travis, meet my sister and the rest of the Babysitters Club. Travis has just moved to Stoneybrook," he went on.

Travis half rose out of his chair and smiled at everyone. (He could afford to be cheerful. He looked terrific, and the rest of us were wrecks.) The other kids in the family were at the table with him. Emily was spooning up cornflakes with David Michael, Karen and Andrew, but I barely looked at them. I couldn't take my eyes off Travis (and I couldn't stop wishing I were invisible)! Why did I have to look my absolute worst?

Travis was too polite to look shocked, though, and I thought I would drop through

17

the floor when he reached across the table and shook my hand! No one my age shakes hands (do they?), but somehow it seemed just right when Travis did it.

I could feel a little ripple of excitement go through the group, even though most of us were busily staring at our toes and wishing we were on another planet. There was this incredibly long silence while everyone waited for someone else to think of something to say, and Travis and I just stood and stared at each other.

Without thinking, I blurted out the first words that came into my head. "Is that muesli you're eating?" Not the brightest remark in the world, but you have to realize that this was a crisis situation. Think how you would feel if you happened to be wearing a tattered old nightdress and a three-sizes-too-big bathrobe at a time like this. It was enough to make anyone tongue-tied.

"That's right," Travis said easily. "It's practically the state food in California." *He was from California!* "Why don't you join us?" He gestured to an empty seat beside him, and it was all I could do not to throw myself into it. Then I remembered my shiny face (and morning breath) and decided against it.

"Oh, we'll get something to eat later," I said, trying to sound totally calm and in command of the situation. (I wasn't in control at all, and my heart was beating like a rabbit's.)

"Breakfast is the most important meal of the day," he said teasingly.

"I know that," I replied, nodding. If he wanted to talk about nutrition, that was fine with me. Mum and I are fanatics about eating healthy food, and we even make our own breakfast cereal.

Kristy, as usual, took charge. "I really think we should be heading back upstairs," she said firmly.

"Yeah, that's right." Claudia was stepping sideways towards the door.

"Without having breakfast?" Sam said, looking amused, as if he knew exactly what we were up to.

Claudia shrugged and pushed her long black hair out of her face. "Well, actually, we . . . uh, left our electric curlers switched on in the bathroom."

"Oh, that's right," Mary Anne piped up. (I should tell you that Mary Anne is a *terrible* liar.) "Gosh," she added, "if we don't get back upstairs straight away, the curlers might overheat and burn the house down." Charlie sniggered and even Travis looked amused.

Without another word, all seven of us stampeded towards the door. I had time for one last look at Travis, and when his blue eyes homed in on mine, I felt a funny little flutter in my chest.

Upstairs, I had a quick shower and spent the next hour fiddling with my hair and make-up. I decided that I wanted to look casual (but gorgeous!) and finally settled on a pale blue ten-button top with my favourite jeans. (Not that I had much choice, since I'd only packed for an overnight stay.)

When we went back downstairs it was almost twelve o'clock, and guess what? The boys were still there! I couldn't believe my luck. I made *sure* that Travis noticed me and slid on to the bench next to him.

"You must be starving," he said, pushing a bowl of fruit towards me.

"Ravenous," I replied, taking a tiny bite of an apple. Who could think about food at a time like this?

"Hey, Travis," Charlie spoke up, "have I mentioned that you and Dawn have some-thing in common? She's from California, too."

"Really? That's fantastic." Travis looked as if he'd been waiting all his life for this bit of information. "Do you miss the ocean? We lived right on the ocean, and I used to go for long walks on the beach every night after dinner."

"You *did*? We didn't live on the ocean, but I used to go for long walks, too." I was so excited I nearly dropped my apple. Have you ever met someone and felt as if you've always known that person? That was the way I felt about Travis.

"There's a place just above Malibu," Travis began, "and when the sun sets, it looks as if it's dropping right into the ocean."

"I know. I went there once." I felt almost giddy. Travis and I talked non-stop for the next half hour and I have *never* met anyone whose feelings were so close to my own. We could have been twins.

"You know, you should always wear blue," Travis said, gently touching my sleeve. "It brings out the colour of your eyes. Just like the ocean. . ."

What an unbelievable morning! I couldn't get Travis off my mind for the rest of the day, and I practically drove Mary Anne insane talking about him.

"Mary Anne, do you believe in love at first sight?" I asked her the minute we were back home.

"I think so," she said slowly. "Look at your mother and my father. I think they fell in love at first sight at high school. It's just that it took them all this time to get together."

Remember that romantic story I promised to tell you about our parents? This is it. My mum went out with Mary Anne's father at high school (we didn't know this when I first moved to Stoneybrook) and they went steady. They were madly in love with each other – but now comes the sad part. My grandparents (my mum's mother and father)

21

disapproved of Mary Anne's father and didn't want my mum to keep seeing him. My mum comes from a wealthy family, and I suppose they always thought she would marry someone rich. I'm glad to say that the story has a happy ending. My mum and Richard *did* find each other again (with a little help from Mary Anne and me), and now they're happily married and we all live in my house.

I had to ask another question. "Mary Anne," I said, "don't you think Travis is the most gorgeous boy you've ever seen?"

"Travis?" She looked at me suspiciously. "Dawn, you're not going to get some kind of hopeless crush on him, are you?"

A hopeless crush! I was insulted. "Of course not," I said stiffly. "I just think he's very . . . attractive."

"Oh, well, yes," Mary Anne said. "I do, too. Of course, *I* think *Logan* is gorgeous." She paused. We know each other so well that she could read my mind. "Dawn," she said, "He's at *high* school!"

"I know that."

"And even if you like him, it doesn't mean he's going to ask you out or anything."

"Right." I changed the subject then, but my mind kept racing along the same channels. I had found the one boy in the world for me, and his name was Travis.

# 3rd
# CHAPTER

A lot of kids hate Mondays, but I don't mind them. Why? Because Monday is the first meeting of the week for the Babysitters Club. I know you're probably wondering about the club and how it works, so I'm going to fill you in on our last meeting. It took place the Monday after the sleepover, and if you're guessing that I was still thinking about Travis, you're absolutely right.

I should begin by telling you that we meet on Mondays, Wednesdays and Fridays, and that we start *promptly* at five-thirty. And that means on the dot! Kristy Thomas, our chairman, is a stickler for being on time (and for a lot of other rules as well). We meet for half an hour, until six o'clock.

I rushed into Claudia's bedroom about two minutes late (due to a sitting job), and got an icy glare from Kristy. She was sitting in her director's chair, as usual, and made a big drama out of looking at Claud's digital clock, the official BSC timekeeper. She didn't say anything, but she gave her head a little shake, and I knew she was annoyed.

"Sorry," I said, stepping between Mallory and Jessi, and setting myself on Claud's bed between Claud and Mary Anne. Mal and Jessi were smiling at each other, and I knew that they were trying not to giggle at some private joke. Since they're a couple of years younger than the rest of us, you'd think that Kristy would bend the rules a little for them. No way! Whoever said rules are made to be broken has never met Kristy Thomas.

You're probably curious about why we meet in Claudia's bedroom. That's easy – Claudia is the only one of us with her own phone and personal phone number. And a phone is very important when you're running an organization like the BSC. Why did I call it an organization? Because it's partly a club and partly a business.

Maybe I'd better slow down and tell you how it all started. One day, before Kristy's mother had married Watson, when Kristy still lived opposite Claudia and next door to Mary Anne, she noticed that her mother was phoning all over town, trying to find a babysitter for David Michael, Kristy's little brother. Kristy had a brainwave. Why not form a babysitters club – an organization that parents could phone to reach several sitters at once.

This is the way our club works. My friends and I meet three times a week, as I've mentioned, and anyone who wants a babysitter can phone us at those times – and reach *seven* sitters. It's wonderful for the parents and great for us. We sometimes have more jobs than we can handle (which is why we have a couple of backup babysitters), and everything is done on a very professional basis.

We have elected officers, we collect subs money, and we keep very accurate records of who sits when and how much money they make. We also write down our babysitting "experiences" in a notebook. This information is very helpful to all the club members and gives us tips about what to expect from the kids.

You already know that Kristy Thomas is the chairman, and I'd say that she is perfect for the job. Even though she does tend to be a little bit bossy, I have to admit that she keeps the club running well. (Also, let's face it. I can't really think of anyone else in the club who would want to be chairman. It's a *lot* of responsibility. Besides, the club was Kristy's idea.)

Claudia Kishi is our vice-chairman. We felt it was only fair since we use her room three times a week, use her phone and eat her junk food.

Mary Anne is the secretary, and she looks after the record book. Don't get confused. The record book is different from the notebook. The record book is like a giant appointment book. Mary Anne schedules every single babysitting job, and since she's very good at details, she actually *enjoys* doing this. She also keeps track of clients' names, addresses and phone numbers, and the rates our clients pay. Mary Anne could tell you anything about our schedules — the date of Jessi's next dance class, or when Mal is due to have her brace checked at the dentist's. She *never* makes mistakes, and as far as I know, has never mixed up a babysitting appointment. That job would drive me straight up the wall, but Mary Anne loves it.

Stacey McGill is the club treasurer because she's practically a genius with numbers. She keeps track of who makes what (each of us keeps the money we make, though; we don't split it with the group), but it's good to know how things stand. Stacey is also responsible for collecting subs from everyone each Monday. The subs are pretty low, and the money is well spent, but it's still hard to get people to part with money. Actually, the subs are important for several reasons. We help Claudia pay her phone bill, and we pay Charlie, Kristy's older brother, to drive her to and from the meetings, since she lives in a different neighbourhood, now that her mother has married Watson. We also use the money to restock our Kid-Kits (I'll explain later), and if there's any money left over, we blow it on fun things like pizza parties.

Not to be snide or anything, but as alternate officer, I think I have the most interesting job in the BSC. I get to fill in for any club member who can't attend a meeting. Since Kristy is such a stickler for attendance, that hardly ever happens, but I've been the vice-chairman and the secretary, and I was club treasurer while Stacey was back in New York. I like being able to try all the different jobs.

Mal and Jessi are our junior officers because they're not allowed to babysit at night yet, unless it's for their own brothers and sisters. Still, they're both *very* responsible and are a big help to us in the club by taking on a lot of the after-school jobs.

Finally, we have two associate members, Shannon Kilbourne and Logan Bruno – Mary Anne's boyfriend! Shannon and Logan don't come to our regular meetings, but we know we can call on them in a crisis when we really get swamped with jobs. They're both good babysitters.

Anyway, back to the meeting. We were discussing club business, but my mind was filled with Travis. I was *dying* to ask Kristy if she'd seen him again, but I couldn't think of any way of slipping it into the conversation.

Kristy must have noticed that I was a million miles away because she suddenly said, "How about you, Dawn? Do you need some more crayons or Magic Markers for your Kid-Kit?"

It took me a minute to come back to earth.

"Uh, no, but I'd like to buy a few more colouring books."

This is what a Kid-Kit is. We've each made our own. It's a decorated cardboard box filled with our old toys, books and games, and we take it with us when we babysit. The kids love them, and the kits are part of what makes our club so special. For some reason, someone else's old toys are much more interesting than your own. However, although the toys and games last for ever, certain items, like crayons and colouring books, need to be replaced from time to time. We use money from the treasury for this.

My mind was racing, though, trying to fit Travis into the conversation, and a minute later, I got my chance. Kristy mentioned that Charlie would be a bit late picking her up at Claudia's.

"Oh, really? Is he out somewhere with Travis?" I asked, trying to sound ultra-casual.

Kristy gave me a funny look. "No, he's at the dentist having a filling done."

"Oh, that doesn't sound like much fun."
I tried to laugh, but it didn't quite come off. "So how's he doing, anyway?" I asked.

Kristy rolled her eyes. "I'm sure he's fine. It was a very small filling. Now if we can get back to business—"

"I don't mean Charlie," I said quickly. "I mean Travis." *Everybody* was looking at me now, and I knew I was probably giving the whole thing away by being so persistent.

Kristy shrugged. "How should I know?" She glanced down at the notebook, all set to talk about Charlotte Johanssen, who is one of our favourite sitting charges.

"You mean Travis hasn't been back to your house?" The words just tumbled out.

Kristy looked at me suspiciously. "Maybe once or twice," she said vaguely. "I think he came over to play basketball yesterday."

"You *think*?" How could she not know a thing like that?

"There were a lot of boys playing basketball in the drive," she snapped. "Now we really need to. . ."

I blocked out the rest of what Kristy was saying. Item one: Travis may or may not have been back to her house. Item two: Travis *probably* hadn't mentioned me, at least not to Kristy. (But maybe to one of her brothers? I couldn't be sure.) I really hadn't found out very much in this conversation, but at least it was fun to talk about Travis. I just liked hearing his name!

29

The phone rang just then, and Kristy grabbed it. "Good afternoon, Babysitters Club." Kristy listened for a few moments, jotted down some notes, and promised to get back to the caller. I should explain that everyone is "equal" in our club. Just because you answer the phone doesn't mean you can take the job for yourself (although this has happened a few times). Instead, you are supposed to write down the details of the job, discuss it with the club members, let Mary Anne check the record book, and *then* call the client back. It's a good system.

"That was Mrs Hobart," Kristy said, looking round the group. "She needs a sitter for Johnny, Mathew and James next Saturday because Ben is taking Mal to the cinema."

Six of us gasped, and Mal turned an interesting shade of pink.

"Is that true?" I asked. "You and Ben are going out together?" I should mention that the Hobarts are an Australian family who moved into Mary Anne's old house across the street. There are four boys in the family, all with reddish-gold hair and Aussie accents. Ben Hobart, the oldest in the family, is Mal's age and a really nice boy.

"I wouldn't call it going out together," Mal said. She looked a little flustered, and I knew she wasn't thrilled at being the centre of attention. "We're just going to see a film."

"Sounds like going out to me," I teased her. Naturally, my mind went to Travis. I'd give *anything* to go to see a film with him, and I wouldn't care if anyone called it going out or not.

"Let's get back to business," Kristy said crisply. "Who's available on Saturday?" Mary Anne scanned the record book, and it turned out that Jessi was free.

She nodded to Kristy, who already had her hand on the phone. "Tell her I'll be there," Jessi piped up. "The Hobarts are great."

The meeting broke up shortly after that, and Mary Anne and I cycled home in the fading sunlight. I couldn't help but think about Mal and her date-that-wasn't-really-a-date. I tried to imagine what it would be like to go out with Travis. What if he just phoned me up out of the blue and asked me out? What if he asked me out for pizza or a film? What would I do, what would I say, what would I wear? I was thinking so hard, I nearly rode into the gutter.

"Dawn, wake up!" Mary Anne said. "You're in another world."

I tightened my grip on the handlebars and tried to look serious. It was hard, though, because I really *was* in another world. A world filled with just two people – myself and Travis.

# 4th
# CHAPTER

Have you ever had a funny feeling that something exciting is going to happen to you? That's how I felt during the next few days, except I wasn't sure if it was going to be wonderful-exciting or awful-exciting. (Once I just *knew* that I was going to have an exciting day, and that was the day Claudia broke her leg. So it's better not to get your hopes up too high when that feeling hits you.)

The feeling was pretty strong by the weekend, though. At about ten o'clock on a sunny Saturday morning, Mary Anne and I were raking the leaves in the front garden while our parents were out shopping. We have a really *enormous* lawn, and when it's covered with leaves, it seems as big as a football field. But before you picture the garden, I'd better tell you about our house. When Mum and I moved to Stoneybrook after the divorce, we didn't buy an ordinary house like most people. Instead, we bought a colonial farmhouse that's over *two hundred* years old. I love it. It has lots of little rooms, and the doorways are so low that tall people have to duck under them. Mum says people used to be shorter in the 1700s. Anyway, it also has a smokehouse, a barn and an *outhouse*. If you like spooky old houses, then you'd love this one, because it's even got a secret passage. There's a long dark tunnel that leads from my bedroom to the barn, and we think that it was probably part of the Underground Railroad, which helped slaves escape from the South before and during the Civil War. It's exactly like something out of a ghost story. (I'm a big fan of ghost stories, in case you hadn't guessed.)

But back to that Saturday morning. Mary Anne and I had got up early and pulled on our oldest jeans, ready to tackle the front garden. Even with two people raking, it was like attacking an iceberg with a toothpick, but we were making some progress. I was wearing my Walkman, lost in my own world, when Mary Anne grabbed me by the arm.

"Look, look!" she mouthed. She pushed me around so I faced the drive, and my stomach did a somersault. A dark blue Chevy was pulling up in front of our house, and a moment later, a terrific-looking boy got out. Not just *any* terrific-looking boy, though. *Travis.*

"Ohmigosh!" I whispered to Mary Anne, pulling off my headphones. "What am I going to do?" I felt as if someone had just yanked the lawn out from under my feet, and I nearly dropped the rake.

"You're going to say hello to him," Mary Anne said calmly. (It was easy for her to be calm, because she didn't feel the same way about him that I did.)

By now, Travis was strolling towards us, and without thinking, I brushed my hair out of my eyes. Unfortunately, I also left a big black smudge on my face, but I didn't realize it.

"What will I say? How do I look?" I asked desperately. Mary Anne smiled and didn't answer me. She was already waving hello to Travis and heading back towards the house. I know she was giving us the chance to talk privately (Mary Anne is *always* tactful), but suddenly, I didn't want her to leave. I was afraid to be alone with Travis, afraid that I would make an idiot out of myself. (Also, Richard and my mum have very strict rules about us having boys over when they're not at home. Boys are not allowed in the house. Full stop.)

"Hi there," Travis said, walking up to me. (He certainly wasn't nervous.) He looked fantastic in a pair of jeans faded to just the right blue-white shade, and a heavy, new SHS (Stoneybrook High School) jacket.

"I didn't know you could drive," I blurted out. What a brilliant remark. For some reason, whenever I was with Travis, I seemed to lose the power of reasonable speech.

He shrugged, not the least bit embarrassed. "I've been driving since the day I turned sixteen."

I should explain that it's legal to drive at sixteen in Connecticut, but I don't know anyone who really starts driving at that age. Charlie Thomas' parents, and a lot of others I know, make their kids wait until they're *seventeen* before they can drive alone. Some parents even make their kids wait until they're seventeen just to take the driving test.

"Um, I like your car." This wasn't the world's most fascinating remark, either, but it was the best I could do under the circumstances.

"Thanks." Travis looked pleased, and we automatically started walking back towards the house. I waited about fifteen seconds for him to say something (it seemed like fifteen hours) and finally asked him if he'd like some lemonade.

"Maybe later," he said, turning on that thousand-kilowatt smile. "Why don't we sit out here and talk for a while." He touched my elbow and gestured to the front step.

"Sure." I gulped. So Travis really *had* come over just to talk to me. You're probably wondering why I didn't know this all along. I suppose I did, but I couldn't believe it. I nearly asked him what he wanted to talk about but caught myself just in time. I decided it was time to stop making stupid remarks and try to start a real conversation. Before I had a chance to open my mouth again, he beat me to it.

"Fifty thousand miles on her, but you'd never know it," he said, pointing to the Chevy.

I nodded, not sure how to respond. Was fifty thousand miles good or bad? It sounded like a *lot* of miles, but as I don't drive, I'm not really up on things like this. I decided to play it safe. "It's good that your parents let you borrow it," I said.

Travis laughed. "Borrow it? She's all mine. I can drive her whenever I want." He paused and pulled out a packet of sugar-free chewing gum. After offering me a stick (I refused – the last thing I wanted to do was get gum stuck to my teeth during an important conservation) he went on. "I have to pay for the petrol and the insurance."

I nodded again. I was beginning to feel like one of those doll heads that bob up and down in the back windows of cars. "It looks very . . . shiny," I said finally.

Travis beamed and I knew I'd said the right thing. "Three coats of Super-Gloss," he said proudly. "You see, Dawn, the whole trick is to dry the car thoroughly in between each coat. A lot of people don't take the time, and that's why they get water spots."

"Oh," I said appreciatively. I had never thought about water spots before, but Travis made them sound almost interesting. "I'll have to remember that."

"And always use an old terry towel. It doesn't scratch the finish, but it gives you a nice shine. That's extremely important." I smiled and tried to look encouraging.

We could probably have talked about cars a little more, but Travis abruptly changed the subject. "So tell me, how do you like Stoneybrook Middle School?"

"Oh, I think it's great," I began. "All my friends are there—"

"That's nice," he cut in. "I make friends easily, too. A lot of people think it's hard to change schools, but not for me. I make friends wherever I go."

"So do you like Stoneybrook High—"

"You bet!" Travis said enthusiastically. "The first day I was there, I was invited to join five clubs. Five!" He ticked them off on his fingers. "The debating club, the drama club, the pep club, the computer club . . . oh, yeah, and the Latin club."

"That's nice," I said weakly. The Latin club didn't surprise me a bit – I was pretty sure it was all girls.

"And once they found out I play football and tennis" (Travis shook his head in mock amazement) "they drafted me on the spot."

"Wow!" That was all I could manage before Travis revved up again. I had never met anyone so energetic. (Or so talented, or so good-looking. . .)

"It was really funny," he added, "but the next day, Coach Higgins and Coach Reilly both turned up at the same time. One wanted me for basketball and the other wanted me for football." He laughed. "It was like a tug-of-war."

"I can imagine." I laughed a little to show I was getting into the spirit of things.

"Well, that's enough about me," he said suddenly. "Let's talk about you." He pulled out a small white box. "I've brought you something."

*A present?* I nearly fainted. Even my daydreams hadn't prepared me for this. "What is it?" I cried.

"Open it up and see." Travis grinned at me. "I think you're going to like it."

My first present from Travis. My hands were shaking as I untied the bow. "A necklace!" I lifted a string of beautiful blue beads out of the box.

"There's more," Travis said. I found two hair combs nestled in the tissue paper. They were deep blue, like the beads.

"But it's not my birthday or anything," I protested.

Travis leaned forward and gently lowered the necklace over my head. "When I

38

saw this, it just made me think of you. That's all. It's the same shade as your eyes."

"It is?" I felt ridiculously pleased.

"Definitely. And I had a special reason for buying the combs. I saw a girl on TV who had her hair swept back at the sides, like this." He lifted my fine blonde hair and tucked it behind my ears. "This is a much better style for you. It brings out the colour of your eyes and your cheek-bones. I think you should try it."

"I suppose I could," I said, flustered. "Usually, I just brush my hair and wear it straight. It's so long."

"Oh, yeah. That's another thing I wanted to mention." Travis picked up a strand of hair and looked at it critically. "When's the last time you got your hair cut?"

"Cut? I never get it cut. Well, sometimes I have the ends trimmed a little."

Travis gave me a very serious look. "I think you should lose a few inches, maybe three or four. It will give your hair more lift, you know?"

"Maybe," I said doubtfully. I like my hair the way it is – very long and fine. Whenever I try a new style, I usually hate it and just go back to wearing it straight.

"I'm not talking about anything drastic," Travis went on, "just a sort of trim. You could ask the hairdresser or someone to shape it up if you want." He laid his hand very gently over mine, just for a second. "Think about it, okay? For me."

*For me*! I nearly slid off the step. I knew that Travis must be really interested in me or he never would have gone to all this trouble.

"Of course I will," I told him.

He grinned and stood up. "I've got to run. My mum wants me to go shopping for her."

"Thanks for the necklace and the combs—" I began awkwardly.

"That's okay," Travis interrupted, heading towards the car. "But remember, I want to see you in that new hairstyle." He started the engine, waved goodbye, and headed down the street.

I stood rooted to the spot with a silly grin on my face. Travis liked me!

I could have stood there daydreaming for ever, but I didn't want to waste a minute. I picked up the combs and dashed inside the house.

"Mary Anne!" I yelled, thundering up the stairs. "Get a brush and some scissors. We've got work to do!"

# 5th CHAPTER

Saturday

I never know what to expect when I sit for the Hobarts, and this time I got an even bigger surprise than usual. The kids asked me to watch them rehearse a play! And guess what. James, who is only eight years old, wrote it all by himself. He made sure that everybody got a part, and Chewy, believe it or not, was the star! It was great! I'll tell you more about it at our next meeting.

Jessi's babysitting job with the Hobarts turned out to be one of the best afternoons of her life. Who would think that putting on a play with five kids (the three Hobart boys and two of the Perkins girls) could be so much fun?

When the Hobarts first moved into the neighbourhood, naturally everyone was very curious about them. Some of the kids said that the Hobarts talked just like Crocodile Dundee, so we decided to see for ourselves. What did we find? Four boys, all with red hair and great accents! But a few kids actually *made fun* of the way the Hobarts talked, and we thought this was incredibly rude. After all, maybe the Hobarts thought *we* sounded funny with our American accents.

But back to Jessi's babysitting job. Mrs Hobart asked her to come over at two o'clock on Saturday afternoon. She and her husband were going out shopping and they needed someone to watch the three youngest boys, James, aged eight; Mathew, aged six and Johnny, who's only four. Ben, the oldest boy, is in my class, so he obviously didn't need a sitter. And anyway, he was taking Mal to the cinema that afternoon.

The three younger boys were playing outside when Myriah and Gabbie Perkins ran over to say hello.

"Hi, Jessi Ramsey," Gabbie yelled. Gabbie is two and a half and calls most people by their full names. She's got two sisters, Myriah, who's almost six, and Laura, who's just a baby. The Perkinses moved into Bradford Court when they bought Kristy's old house. They have given the BSC lots of business, and we love to sit for them.

All three girls are great, and Myriah is especially theatrical. She can sing and dance (tap *and* ballet), and is even into gymnastics. Since Jessi is a dancer, she feels that she's got a lot in common with her. Jessi says she's always impressed when little kids can get up and perform, because she knows how hard it is to face an audience. Myriah can sing "On the Good Ship Lollipop," and she knows "Tomorrow" from *Annie* by heart. A lot of kids love to sing, but Myriah's really good at it. She's just like someone you'd see on TV. When she sings, she knows every word. She's right on pitch and she even gets the timing right.

Anyway, when the Perkins girls ran over, they didn't come alone. They brought their dog with them. Chewbacca is a huge black Labrador who's extremely friendly. (Sometimes *too* friendly!) He looks like a small bear but acts like a puppy.

"Chewbacca, stop that!" Myriah shouted. Chewbacca was running in circles, trampling the Hobarts' flower beds. "He's just had a bath," she explained, "and that always makes him crazy."

43

"Bring him over to the patio," Jessi said. "Let's all sit at the picnic table and play a game."

"What kind of game?" Mathew asked. He still has a trace of an Australian accent. "Something fun?"

"Definitely something fun." Jessi looked at Chewbacca. Playing Frisbee was out. Chewbacca had already chomped his way through three of them.

"Let's have a rehearsal," Myriah suggested. "That's my favourite thing to do in the whole world."

"A rehearsal?" Jessi said blankly. "I was thinking of playing 'I Packed My Grandmother's Trunk'—" She was immediately out-voted.

"No, we want to rehearse! James and Mathew yelled. "We'll show you our play." I should tell you that the Hobart kids are very interested in drama, and Mathew was given the lead in his school play.

"You're putting on a play?" Jessi asked.

"An original one," James said proudly. "I'm writing it."

An eight-year-old kid writing a play? Jessi was impressed.

"We've been working on it for a couple of weeks," Myriah piped up. "Do you want to see how far we've got?"

"Of course," Jessi told her. And she saw the perfect opportunity to send Chewbacca back to his own house. "But don't you think you'd better take Chewy home first? You could leave him on the porch so he won't interrupt the rehearsal."

"No, Chewbacca has to stay," Myriah replied. "Mummy says we have to keep him outside till he dries off." She grinned. "Besides, he's our star."

*Oh, no.* Jessi groaned inwardly. Then she poured herself a glass of lemonade and sat back to watch the show. After a few minutes, she found herself getting *really* interested. Even though there was a lot of giggling (and almost everyone forgot some of their lines), the play was good.

The story was very simple. Chewy (the hero) was a lost dog who wandered up and down a busy shopping centre, looking for his owner. Jessi started to point out that dogs aren't usually allowed in shopping centres, but she knew that would spoil the fun.

Myriah had the opening lines. "Hello, doggie," she said abruptly. "Don't you have a home?" She walked up to Chewy and pretended to inspect his neck. "Uh-oh," she said, making a face. "No collar." She rolled her eyes. "Now it's going to be really hard to find your owner." Chewy jumped up and started licking her face. "Down, Chewy," she said sharply. "I mean, down, doggie."

Gabbie cleared her throat, eager to get in on the act. Myriah nodded and started walking across the patio with the dog. "Let's see if any of the people who work in the shopping centre know your owner," she said. "We'll start with the shoe shop."

"Want some shoes?" Gabbie asked. "We've got all kinds – yellow, green and red. And all sizes."

Myriah stopped so suddenly that Chewy stumbled into her. "Not today, thanks," she said very seriously. "I've got a problem. This is a lost dog, and I'm looking for his owner."

"How about some shoes?" Gabbie persisted.

"Hey, Gabbie," James cried. "You're supposed to talk about the dog, not the shoes."

Myriah frowned. "Think hard," she said to Gabbie. "Have you seen his owner?"

"We've got trainers," Gabbie continued. "And cowboy boots—"

Myriah sighed. Gabbie must have forgotten the script. Myriah would just have to make the best of it. "Let's go, doggie," said Myriah. "Maybe your owner stopped off for a slice of pizza." She walked over to the barbecue grill, where Mathew was pretending to throw pizza dough in the air. "Excuse me. . ."

"Not while I'm making the dough," Mathew said. "I can't talk until I get this in the oven."

Myriah looked annoyed. It was obvious

that Mathew was adding some new lines to his script. "Look," she said, "this is an emergency."

Mathew shook his head and refused to look at her. He twirled the imaginary dough in his hand, pretending to toss it high in the sky. Finally he spread some pretend-pizza sauce on it and put it in the oven. Then he wiped his hands on a pretend-apron (a nice touch, Jessi thought) and grinned. "Okay, what do you want?"

Myriah repeated the story about the lost dog while Mathew listened intently. "Afraid I can't help you," he said, twirling another piece of dough.

Jessi was beginning to wonder what Myriah would do next when Zach came tearing round the corner on his bicycle. Zach's a good friend of James, but he's very bossy and is always telling James what to do.

When he saw Myriah leading Chewy around the patio, he came to a stop. "What are you doing?"

"We're rehearsing a play," Myriah said.

"Can I watch?"

"I suppose so," she replied. She waited until Zach had settled himself on a huge tyre, suspended from a rope, and then went on with the play. She had just taken Chewy into a department store, when Zach burst out laughing.

"This is the silliest play I've ever seen," he hooted.

"It is not," James said angrily. "I wrote it."

"You *wrote* it?" Zach laughed so hard, he nearly fell off the swing. "It's terrible!" He jumped off the tyre and headed for his bike. "And what are you doing playing with *girls*, anyway?"

"They're part of the play," James began, his face a bright red.

"I don't believe this," Zachary said, still chuckling. "First you hang around with that retard, Susan Felder, and now you're playing with a group of little kids." (Susan Felder is a handicapped girl whose family lives in the neighbourhood. She goes to a special school, doesn't talk, and doesn't know how to play with other kids.)

Jessi thought it was really mean of Zach to call her a retard and said so.

"Yeah, well, she is," Zach said bluntly. He wasn't even embarrassed. "You know something, James?" he said, swinging on to his bike. "If you really want to be an American, you've got to change. You need to hang around with me and the other boys. You need to spend more time on your skateboard. And you should dump these girls. Oh, yeah. One more thing. Stop calling your mother 'Mummy'."

James just stood there listening, his hands clenched at his sides. Finally he spoke up. "You know what your problem is, Zach?" he said very quietly. "You're

48

just jealous because you're not in the play."

"He probably can't even act," Mathew said, and Jessi giggled.

"I can so!" Zach said hotly. "Maybe I just don't want to hang around with a load of girls!" Zach pedalled as fast as he could down the drive, chanting, "James is a gi-irl, James is a gi-irl!"

James's face fell, and Jessi felt sorry for him.

Nobody said anything for a moment, and then Chewy barked. "I think he's trying to tell us it's time to go back to the play," James said. Everybody laughed. James clapped his hands loudly. "Okay, places everyone. Let's take it from the top."

Jessi felt very proud of him.

# 6th CHAPTER

Last Tuesday I got the biggest shock of my life! You're going to be really surprised when I tell you about it.

School had just finished, and Stacey and I had walked Kristy to her bus. Claudia and Mary Anne were trailing behind us, and everyone was trying to decide what to do next.

"Why don't you come over to my house?" Claudia offered. "Mum's bought a gallon of Pecan Crunch ice cream." She glanced at Stacey. "And there's homemade applesauce, too. The kind with no sugar."

Stacey smiled. "It sounds good, but I've got an English test tomorrow. So have you, Claudia," she added teasingly. "In case you've forgotten."

Claudia groaned and clutched her head in her hands. "You had to remind me!" She turned to me. "How about you, Dawn?"

I shrugged. I never eat ice cream (I like frozen yoghurt better) but I didn't want to sound rude. I was just about to make up some excuse not to go to Claudia's when a car horn tooted behind me. I turned automatically and saw – Travis!

"Ohmigosh!" I muttered under my breath.

Mary Anne spotted him at the same time. "Isn't that—"

"Yes, yes," I said quickly, practically fainting on the spot.

"Look, he's pulling over to the kerb," Stacey said, grabbing my arm. "And he's waving to you."

My mind went blank. What was Travis doing here? Did he really want to see me?

"Go over to the car," Stacey whispered, giving me a little shove. "What are you waiting for?"

What *was* I waiting for? The best-looking boy I'd ever seen in my whole life was offering me a lift, and I was frozen like a statue! I probably would have stood there for ever, except that Stacey jabbed me with her spiral notebook.

"Move!" she ordered.

Travis had already pushed the passenger door open and was flashing his gorgeous smile at me.

"Hop in," he said casually. "Are you on your way home?"

"Yes, but—"

"I've got a better idea," he cut in

smoothly. "How'd you like to go shopping with me? I've got to choose a birthday present for my dad."

I hesitated. Going *anywhere* with Travis would be fantastic, but I knew I should check with Mum first. I shifted from one foot to the other, trying to stall for time. Maybe I could duck back into school and phone her first? But then Travis would think I was a baby! Besides, Mary Anne could always tell Mum and Richard where I was – if she absolutely had to.

Another horn beeped, and Travis patted the front seat of his car. "C'mon," he said urgently. "This is a no-parking zone."

I made up my mind. I dumped my books on the front seat, slid inside, and a minute later we were zipping down the street, with the sounds of hard rock filling the car.

Travis waited till we stopped at a red light to turn to me. "I'm glad you decided to come," he said simply.

I grinned, relaxing a little. "So am I. There's just one thing I should warn you about. I've got to be home by six."

"No problem. We've got plenty of time. I thought we'd hit Surf and Sail first, and then we'll play it by ear." The lights changed and he turned left.

"Surf and Sail?" I repeated.

"It's a sports shop. My dad has had his eye on a new compass for a long time, and they're in the sale this week."

I nodded, happy to be with him. He looked terrific in a blue cotton workshirt and faded jeans. I could hardly *believe* my good luck.

As soon as we stepped into Surf and Sail I knew I was out of my depth. I've been sailing plenty of times, but I don't know a lot about serious boating equipment. Travis stopped in front of a display case filled with compasses, and I decided to speak up. "Travis, I'm afraid I'm not going to be much help to you. Are you *sure* your father wants a compass?"

Travis laughed and slid his arm around me. "I just wanted an excuse to see you today."

"Really?" I felt a little light-headed. Travis chose a compass very quickly, and we were back on the pavement a few minutes later. Now what? I wondered. I was totally confused. (And a little disappointed. I'd been hoping that Travis would take a long time to make up his mind, so we could spend more time together.)

I started for the car, but he grabbed my elbow and steered me towards Burger Bite. "Aren't we going back home?" I asked.

"We've got hours ahead of us. I thought we'd stop for a snack and then do some more shopping."

I've got to tell you that Burger Bite is not my favourite kind of restaurant, and I was surprised that Travis wanted to go there, too, since he'd said once that he likes health food. Still, I was glad to be sitting in a back booth with him. I reached for a menu, but Travis closed his hand over mine. "We don't need that. I come in here all the time."

*But I don't*, I longed to say. Travis was obviously planning on ordering for me. I know some girls like it when a boy takes charge like that, but I like to make up my own mind. Besides, how could Travis possibly know what I felt like eating?

I practically held my breath when the waitress appeared, and wondered if I should mention that I don't eat meat. I lost my nerve at the last minute, but luckily, Travis ordered grilled cheese sandwiches for both of us.

"So," Travis said when the waitress had left. "What's been happening with you today?"

"Not much, how about you?" I still felt a bit tongue-tied with Travis and decided it was easier to let him keep the conversation going. He *always* seemed to have something to talk about.

"I tried out for track today," he said earnestly. "You wouldn't believe what happened. I was the first guy the coach picked. I suppose all that running I did in California paid off. . ." I let Travis's words drift over me, thinking how wonderful it was to be sitting there with him. If I had to describe the ideal boy, it would be Travis.

Tall, good-looking, with a fantastic smile and a great personality. And he liked me even though he was three years older than I was.

When the sandwiches arrived a few minutes later, he had moved on to another topic, football. "You see, Coach Larson was demonstrating an intricate play for us," he said, looking into my eyes. He took a bite of sandwich and moved a salt shaker next to the napkin holder. "The quarterback ran down to the twenty-yard line like this. . ." I watched, caught up in the sound of his voice. "And then the tight end zigzagged over here. . ." He picked up a ketchup bottle and plonked it down next to the sugar bowl. "Bingo! Right over the line for a touchdown."

"That's amazing," I said, trying to look impressed.

"And you know what?" he added, sliding the pepper shaker across the table. "I was the only one there who knew what he was talking about."

"That's wonderful. You really know a lot about football."

Travis grinned. "What can I tell you?" He wolfed down the rest of his sandwich and I hurried to keep up with him.

It was almost four by the time we left Burger Bite, and I was starting to feel a little edgy. I knew Mum wouldn't be too pleased if she found out that I'd spent the afternoon with Travis (but I also knew that she and Richard wouldn't get home for another two hours). So I was safe, at least for the moment.

We walked around in town, and Travis surprised me (as usual) by leading me to the jewellery shop. "I saw some pierced earrings in here that would look great on you," he said. He led me to a display counter and spun an earring tree with his thumb. "Good! They're still here." He lifted a pair of delicate silver earrings off the tree and held them out to me. "Do you like them?"

They were perfect. Tiny butterflies in flight. "I love them," I said softly.

Travis held them up to my ear and smiled. "I knew they'd be right for you."

"I'll wear them under the stars," I promised him. (I should explain that I wear two earrings in each ear.)

"No," Travis said flatly. "You should wear them up higher. Just get another hole pierced in your ear."

"Three holes? I don't know," I said doubtfully. I remembered that I'd had to persuade Mum to let me get my ears pierced in the first place.

Travis laughed. "It's no big deal. All the girls in California wear them that way. It would look really cool on you."

"I'll have to think about it," I said, trying to sound casual.

"There's nothing to it," Travis answered.

We were standing side by side at the cash desk. "They could probably do it for you now."

"No!" I was starting to feel a little panicky. I could just imagine Mum's reaction if I did something like that without asking her.

I felt relieved when we left the jewellery shop a few minutes later and headed back to the car, even though I knew that Travis was a tiny bit annoyed with me.

"Thanks for the earrings," I told him, trying to smooth things over.

"I'm glad you like them." He squeezed my arm. I knew I would never, *ever* forget this moment.

My happiness didn't last long though, because when I got home I had the surprise of my life. Mum and Richard were waiting for me in the kitchen.

"You're home early," I said casually, tossing my books on the kitchen table.

"You're home late," Mum answered, frowning a little. She was cutting up vegetables for a salad.

"Um, not really." I nibbled on a carrot, stalling for time. I could tell that Mum and Richard were *both* annoyed with me. What an ending to a perfect day!

"Mary Anne said you went shopping with someone called Travis," Mum went on. "I'd like you to tell me about it." Mum can be *really* direct when she wants to.

I had to tell them the truth.

"I ran into Travis after school," I said. "He's a friend of mine, and he asked me if I'd like to drive into town with him—"

"Drive? You went in his car?" Richard interrupted.

"Well, yes. He had to buy a birthday present for his father," I said quickly.

"Who is this Travis?" Mum said. "And how come he can drive?"

"He's old enough to drive," I told her. "He's sixteen."

Wrong move. Richard looked furious, and Mum looked upset.

"Let me get this straight," Richard said slowly. "You went out with a sixteen-year-old in a car? A boy we don't know? You had no business going off like that without asking us first."

I shrugged. This was getting complicated. (And deep down, I had the nagging feeling that Mum was right.)

"Look, why don't we just forget the whole thing and make dinner? I'll help you," I said, reaching for the salad bowl.

"There's no way we're going to forget this," Mum said. "No one's going to eat anything until we get this sorted out."

I knew from the look on her face that she meant business. I was really in for it.

# 7th CHAPTER

Mary Anne wandered into the kitchen and stopped dead in her tracks when she saw me. She had "uh-oh" written all over her face. She took her time opening a tin of cat food for Tigger, her kitten, and I knew she was listening to every word. If only she hadn't told Mum and Richard that I'd been out with Travis!

"We've got a problem here," Richard said flatly. He motioned for me to sit down at the kitchen table.

"I didn't think you would get this upset," I began, but Richard held his hand up.

"You showed very poor judgment, Dawn," he said sternly.

"I know it looks that way, but—"

"I'm very disappointed in you," Mum said. She sat down opposite me. I felt as if I was being attacked from all sides!

"If you met Travis, you'd really like

him," I protested. I stared at my hands, not knowing where to begin. "He's really a nice boy."

Mum stared at Richard. "I'm sure he is, but that's not the point."

Mary Anne took a quick peek over her shoulder and went back to feeding Tigger. I couldn't believe all the trouble she'd got me into.

"Then what's wrong with him?"

"For one thing, he's too old for you," Richard said bluntly. "He's sixteen and you're only thirteen. What could you possibly have in common?"

"Well, we're both from California. We're interested in the same things." I glanced at Mum, wondering if she would agree with me. She should be able to understand how I felt. Even though I love my friends in Connecticut, I miss my friends in California. So does she.

"And another thing," Mum said, "we've never even met this boy. Did you know he was going to pick you up at school today?"

I shrugged. "Nope. That's just the way Travis is. He likes to do things on the spur of the moment. He's impulsive." *And fun and exciting*, I wanted to add.

"If he really liked you," Richard said, "he would make plans to see you. He'd visit you here at the house and meet the rest of your family."

I sighed. Richard is very serious about

being a good stepfather, but sometimes he just worries too much. I wish he would calm down a little and be more like Mum.

"Travis *does* like me," I said. "You wouldn't believe all the presents he's given me. First a necklace and hair combs, and today he bought me some earrings in town."

"I'm not so sure I like that idea," Mum said slowly. "You hardly know him, and he's showering you with presents. Something just isn't right."

I glanced at Mary Anne, who had finished feeding Tigger and was slipping out of the kitchen. I couldn't *wait* to talk to her alone! None of this would have happened if she had kept her mouth shut.

"It's no mystery," I said, scraping my chair back and standing up. "Travis gave me some presents because he likes me. I don't know why you can't understand that." I looked at Mum. "And I *really* want to see him again."

"I know you do, honey," she said, softening a little. "And I'm sure that once we meet him, we'll feel differently."

"You mean you're going to let her continue to see him?" Richard exploded. "I can't believe you're serious."

"Well, maybe we came down a little hard on him," Mum said hesitantly. She cupped her chin in her hands and looked thoughtful. "You know, he really does sound nice—"

"This is ridiculous!" Richard broke in. "We don't know this boy at all."

"Now, Richard," Mum said soothingly. "Maybe we're making too big a deal out of this. As long as Dawn understands that she can't see him without our permission, I don't think there's any problem."

"Of course there's a problem. She shouldn't be seeing him at all. He's too old for her."

They were still arguing when I quietly slipped out of the kitchen. It was obvious that the argument was going to go on for a long time, and there was someone I wanted to talk to: Mary Anne. I found her upstairs, sprawled on her bed, doing her homework.

"Thanks a lot," I told her. "You really got me into trouble with Mum and Richard."

"Oh, Dawn, you know I didn't want to do that," she said, sitting up. "I feel awful that they're angry with you, but I didn't know what else to say."

"Why did you have to tell them anything?" I asked, slamming my books on her desk. "You could have kept your mouth shut."

"But how could I have?" Mary Anne said in a quavery voice. "They asked me if I knew where you were. So I had to tell them the truth. I said you'd gone shopping. With Travis."

I sighed. I knew Mary Anne couldn't have made up a good lie. Besides, I didn't want her lying for me.

"Anyway, you never said it was a secret." Mary Anne's voice shook a little, and her eyes had grown very bright. "Sharon and Dad would have been really worried about you if I'd told them I didn't know where you were."

"I know," I said wearily. I had a feeling Mary Anne was about to start crying.

"You know I wouldn't do anything to hurt you," she said, sniffling. Mary Anne cries *very* easily. I didn't say anything for a moment, and then I realized that Mary Anne was right. It wasn't her fault that I was in such a mess.

"Look," I said, putting my arm around her shoulders, "why don't we just forget about it? There's really nothing else you could have done."

She looked up, her eyes teary. "Do you mean that?"

I nodded and sat down on her bed. "How was your day? I've hardly seen you."

"Logan came round after school," she said, brightening up a little. "He gave me that toy for Tigger, just like he promised."

Logan is one of the most dependable people I know. He and Mary Anne are a lot alike. You can always count on them, and you always know where you stand with them.

"You really like him, don't you?" I said, even though I knew what her answer would be.

"Of course I do." Mary Anne blushed a little. "I suppose that seems silly to you. He's not exciting, like Travis."

"I don't think it's silly. I like Logan."

"He's not full of surprises," Mary Anne said slowly. "But that's okay with me."

I thought about all the problems Travis had caused me today. "Maybe surprises aren't such a good idea after all," I said.

Mum called us for dinner just then, and we didn't have a chance to talk about Logan and Travis any more. I slid into my place at the dining room table and had no idea what to expect. Would Mum and Richard argue all through dinner? Would I get a lecture? Would they criticize Travis?

Luckily, none of these things happened, and dinner went fairly smoothly, considering the circumstances. But Mum and Richard didn't say much during the meal. Mum just stared at a spot over my head, and Richard pretended to be absorbed in his Greek salad. Mary Anne and I exchanged a look now and then, but neither one of us felt much like talking. However, I had the feeling that this wasn't the last I would hear about Travis.

**8th CHAPTER**

Saturday

Today I babysat for my younger brothers and sisters and they had a terrific time outdoors playing one of Karen's favourite games -- "Going Camping." It's easy because it's mostly make-believe. All we used today were an old bedspread, some chairs, a few props, and lots of imagination. Karen supplied plenty of that! The best part is that big kids and little kids can play, and it can go on for hours. I think the only other thing you need is a sunny day, but come to think of it, you could probably move the tent into the living room!

Kristy always likes to give a lot of details about her babysitting jobs because she expects the club members to read the notebook very carefully. It's a great way to learn what other babysitters are doing with their kids, and you can get a lot of good ideas. None of us really likes to write in the notebook, but Kristy takes her job as chairman very seriously, and she tries to set an example for us.

"Going Camping" was the perfect way to entertain her four younger brothers and sisters. Karen has a great imagination and loves any kind of game that involves "let's pretend". David Michael is an easygoing kid who will go along with just about any game you suggest. And Andrew and Emily love to play, full stop!

This is the way Kristy and Karen set up the game. They found an old bedspread upstairs in the linen cupboard. It had belonged to Andrew and was bright yellow with racing cars all over it.

"It doesn't look like a real tent," David Michael said doubtfully when Kristy and Karen brought it downstairs. "It should be dark green, or maybe brown."

"No, this is fine," Kristy said hastily. She knew the kids were getting restless, and she wanted to start things moving as quickly as possible.

"I'll help!" Karen yelled when Kristy

started to drape the bedspread over some garden chairs.

"Make it a *big* tent," David Michael suggested. "Then we can move all our supplies inside." He picked up a brown canvas canteen and a cast-iron frying pan.

"Big ant?" Emily said, puzzled. Emily is learning English quite slowly. The paediatrician says she's language-delayed.

Andrew laughed. "No, big *tent*," he said, pointing to the bedspread. "C'mon inside."

"Wait! Don't go in yet!" Karen said urgently.

Kristy looked startled. "Why not?"

Karen lowered her voice to a whisper. "Because you can't just walk into a tent without looking. You have to check it first for bears. There could be one sleeping inside."

"Bears?" Emily started to look a little worried.

"It's just pretend," Kristy said, taking her hand. Karen is *very* imaginative, and when you set up a pretend situation, she jumps right in. "What should we do?" Kristy asked very seriously. She was still holding on to Emily's hand. She didn't want to squelch Karen's imagination, but she didn't want Emily to be frightened, either.

Karen thought for a moment. "I'll go in first," she said. She picked up a broken torch. "If I'm not back in a few minutes, you'd better call the mountain rescuers."

"Good idea," David Michael told her. "I think I can signal them. It's a good thing I know Morse code." He scrambled through a cigar box filled with toys and picked out a set of fake teeth. He clicked the teeth together a few times. "We're lucky this is still working."

"I want to do Morse code! I want to do Morse code!" Andrew shouted.

"Sssh," Karen said. "You'll wake up the bear if he's sleeping inside. Do you know how angry they get if you wake them up when they're hibernating? That's all we need!"

"Sorry," Andrew said, clapping his hand over his mouth. "Please can I do Morse code?" he whispered.

David Michael handed him the plastic teeth. "Just remember that SOS is three short, three long, and three short. You got it?" He clicked the teeth together to show him.

"I've got it."

"Places everyone," Karen said. "I'm going in now. Andrew, are you ready?"

"I'm ready with my teeth. I mean the Morse code!"

"David Michael?"

"I'm standing by with the—" He spotted a pile of branches nearby. "The bonfire!"

"Why do we need a bonfire?" Kristy asked.

David Michael rolled his eyes. "In case

the Morse code doesn't work. I can always light the bonfire and use smoke signals to get the mountain ranger."

"Oh, right. Good idea." Kristy smiled to herself. The kids were *really* getting into it. She could hardly wait to tell the BSC members this at the next club meeting.

"Me, too! Me, too! Me, too!" Emily said, tugging at Karen's T-shirt.

"She wants something to do," Kristy said. "Let's give her a job."

"I know. You can wish me luck. I have a very dangerous job ahead of me," Karen said seriously. She walked over to Emily and shook hands. "Say 'Good luck'," she prompted.

"Good luck," Emily said, smiling. Kristy had no idea if she knew what "good luck" meant, but she knew Emily was happy to be included.

"Here goes," Karen said dramatically. She took a deep breath and crawled inside the tent. Everyone else crouched down and waited outside, ready to run, if necessary. A few moments passed, and then Karen reappeared. "It's all safe," she said. "There are no bears inside. At least not right this minute."

"What do you mean, right this minute?" David Michael asked.

Karen looked over her shoulders as if she expected a bear to appear at any moment. "I don't want to scare anyone," she said slowly, "but I have to warn you that I found a pot of honey inside."

"Honey!" Andrew clapped his hands over his mouth.

Karen nodded. "And you know what that means," she said, looking round the group.

"What does it mean?" David Michael looked blank.

Karen nudged him. "It means there must have been a *bear* in there."

"Oh, right." David Michael scuffed the dirt with his toe and looked a little embarrassed. "So what do we do now?"

"Well, I think we should all go into the tent," Karen said, holding the flap open. "But make sure you rig up a bear alert outside for us."

"A bear alert?" David Michael brightened. "That's a great idea. You go in and I'll make one."

Kristy trooped inside with the younger kids, and for a minute everyone was quiet. It was pretty hot and uncomfortable in the tent, and she wondered what Karen was going to come up with next. Luckily she didn't have to wait long.

Emily was yawning when Karen grabbed Kristy's arm. "Did you feel that?"

"Feel what?" Kristy asked.

"The ground just shook," Karen said, looking at each of the kids. "I think we're in for an earthquake."

"No!" Andrew screamed. "What should we do?"

"Let's all hold hands," Karen said calmly. "That way nobody will be swept away when it happens again."

Emily glanced at Kristy, her eyes wide as saucers, and Kristy scooped her on to her lap. "Don't worry, Emily," she said, holding her very tightly. "I'm not going to let anything happen to you."

"There it goes again," Karen said. She fell against the side of the tent, and Andrew did the same thing. "Hold on tight, everybody!"

"Wait a minute," Andrew yelled. "What about David Michael? He's outside making that stupid bear alert!"

"We'll have to help him," Karen said firmly. "Andrew, rescue David Michael."

Andrew looked impressed. "Wow!"

"Open the flap of the tent *very* carefully and peep outside. The minute you see him, tell him to get in here."

"Okay." Andrew crawled to the edge of the tent and lifted the bedspread. "David Michael! David Michael!" he whispered. "Come inside. I've got to rescue you." He crawled back inside. "He's not there!"

"Are you sure?" Karen asked.

"I'm sure!"

Karen sighed. "This is much worse than I thought."

"Do you think the earthquake got him?" Andrew asked.

"No, I think . . . Morbidda Destiny got him!"

Kristy tried not to laugh. Morbidda Destiny is the old lady who lives next door. Her real name is Mrs Porter, but Karen is convinced that she's a witch. She lives in an old Victorian house with gables and turrets, and she even keeps a broomstick on the front porch.

"Now what will we do?" asked Andrew.

Karen looked stumped. "I don't know. Morbidda Destiny has special powers. She could turn David Michael into a witch if she wanted to, or she might make him drink a magic potion."

"No!"

Karen nodded. "She might even make boy stew out of him."

"Ugh! Gross," Andrew muttered. "How can we save him?"

"Let me think," Karen said, just as the tent flap opened and David Michael crawled in.

"The bear alert is in place," he said, scooting over to Kristy. "You'll all be safe."

"Are you okay?" Karen asked him. "We thought Morbidda Destiny had got you."

David Michael laughed. "Of course I'm okay."

Karen looked at him suspiciously, as if he really might be a newt or a toad pretending to be David Michael. "I suppose so. Where were you when Andrew called you?"

"I was hiding," he said teasingly. "I knew you'd think that Morbidda Destiny had kidnapped me, and I wanted to see what you'd do about it."

"Well, it wasn't funny," Karen said sternly. Andrew started telling David Michael about the earthquake, and Karen sat down next to Kristy. "You know what I think?" she whispered in Kristy's ear. "I think Morbidda Destiny really *did* get him and made him say that he was hiding!"

"Do you really think so?" asked Kristy.

Karen nodded. "Witches have their ways," she said mysteriously.

# 9th CHAPTER

"You've got to give Chewy a doggie treat or he's going to ruin the play!" Myriah cried.

It was a Thursday afternoon, and I was babysitting for the three younger Hobart kids while Ben was at the dentist. Mathew, James and Johnny were in the back garden rehearsing their play with Myriah and Gabbie Perkins.

"We can give him a dog biscuit if you want," I suggested, "but I don't think it'll help." Chewbacca, the hero of the play, was tearing around and around the garden. I've never seen a dog with less acting ability. He was supposed to act sad and lonely (according to the script James wrote), but he was running round in circles, yapping and wagging his tail. Every once in a while he'd snap at an imaginary fly.

"Come here, Chewy," I said wearily. "Let's see if this calms you down." I popped a doggie treat into his mouth. He immediately sat up on his hind legs and begged for more.

"I told you it wouldn't help," James said. "That dog can't act."

"He can!" Myriah put her arms around Chewy's furry neck. "He just doesn't feel like it."

"Let's take it from the top. Start the shopping centre scene again," James ordered. "Does everybody remember what they're supposed to do?" He glanced at his notes. "Gabbie, you own a shoe shop."

"Shoes, shoes," she sang. I put my fingers to my lips to remind her to be quiet, and she grinned at me.

"Mathew, you work in the pizza place, and Johnny, you work in a pet shop."

"I want to work in a pet shop!" said Gabbie. "Pets for sale! Pets for sale! We have rabbits, gerbils and hamsters. Maybe even cats and dogs. . ."

"No, Gabbie," James said quietly. "You stay in your shoe shop and sell shoes. You have a very important part in the play." Gabbie beamed. That was the best thing that James could have said to her.

"Now can we *please* begin?" James said.

"Shoe sale! Shoe sale!" Gabbie chanted. "Come and buy some shoes. We have special offers today."

"Myriah, you can make your entrance now," James said. "Quiet, everybody." He sat down next to me at the picnic table. Nobody moved. "Myriah, what are you waiting for?" he yelled.

She stared at him, her hand on Chewy's neck. "We're waiting for you to cue us," she said. "That's the way they do it in films. You're supposed to say, "And . . . action!""

James rolled his eyes. "All right, all right," he muttered. "And . . . action!"

I smiled.

The scene started smoothly. Myriah was talking softly to Chewy, asking if he was lost, when suddenly earsplitting rock music filled the air.

"Who turned on that radio?" James demanded. He jumped up and raced over to Mathew, who was sitting in a red wagon. "Mathew, what do you think you're doing?" He reached into the wagon and pulled out a small radio. "You're ruining the scene. We can't hear Myriah's lines."

Matthew shrugged. "I'm playing music in my pizza parlour."

Myriah frowned. "Mathew, you can't make any noise when someone else is saying their lines. That's the first thing you have to learn when you put on a play."

"But I don't have anything to do. Nobody gave me any lines."

"You have lines in the next scene," James told him. "Look, all you have to do right now is stay in your place and act as if you're making pizzas."

"I know what I could do," Matthew said. "If you give me my radio back, I could listen to music through my headphones."

James hesitated. "I suppose that would be okay. Just make sure you pay attention so you don't miss your cue. Myriah's going to visit all the shops in the arcade, and you're the second place she goes."

Myriah shifted impatiently. "Can we start again now? Chewy's getting restless."

"Okay," James said. I could tell he was getting annoyed at all the interruptions. "Places everyone."

"You're at it again? I don't believe it!" exclaimed a voice.

I turned to see Zach steering his bike towards the picnic table, where James and I were sitting. "I thought you'd had enough of this baby stuff the other day."

"It's not baby stuff," Myriah said, insulted. "We're putting on a real play."

"Yeah, yeah." Zach plopped himself down next to James and punched him playfully in the arm. " So, how about a game of football?"

"He can't leave rehearsal," Myriah said. "We're right in the middle of a very important scene."

"I bet!" Zach snorted. "What kind of a play has a *dog* in it? You must be doing *Annie*."

"No. I've already told you. It's a play I wrote myself," James said shyly. Zach doubled up with laughter and nearly fell off the picnic bench.

"I know, I know." He socked James again, this time on the shoulder. "When are you going to grow up and do some boy stuff?"

"Boy stuff?"

Zach leaned close to him. "You know, football, skateboarding, things like that."

"I play a lot of sports," James said stiffly. I could tell he was embarrassed because two little spots of colour had appeared on his cheeks.

"You could have fooled me!" Zach hooted. "Every time I see you, you're hanging around with a group of girls." He paused. "You know, you're never going to be popular at this rate. The kids at school still think you're weird."

"Weird?"

Zach nodded. "Can you blame them? You don't talk properly, you don't go out with the boys, and worst of all, you hang around with girls."

James hung his head and looked sheepish. "I don't want anybody to think I'm weird."

"Well, of course you don't," Zach said, slapping him on the back. "But you can change all that. Just start doing things differently. And you can start right now."

"I can?"

"Sure." Zach stood up and got on his bike. "Come back to my house and we'll kick a football around. Then we'll watch a new horror film I've just hired. Oh, yeah, and we'll practise talking real American." He released the kickstand on his bike, ready to go. "Sound good?"

James hesitated, and then tossed his script on the picnic table. "You're on!" he said.

"James," Myriah wailed. "What about the play?"

James shook his head and didn't answer. He was already on the way to the garage for his bike.

"Now what will we do?" Mathew asked. "We can't put on the play without James."

"We'll think of something else to do," I promised him. I watched as Zach and James pedalled down the drive. Why did James let Zach talk to him like that? And why did he want to change his whole personality to please Zach? James was a great kid, just the way he was. Zach had no business telling him how to talk or how to act. Why did James let him get away with it? None of it made any sense to me, and I was *very* disappointed in James.

# 10th CHAPTER

Kristy had dropped a bombshell and didn't even know it. It all started at our Monday afternoon BSC meeting in Claudia's room. Jessi mentioned Jackie Rodowsky, the "walking disaster", and everyone started telling funny stories about him. In case you don't know, Jackie is a really sweet seven-year-old with flaming red hair and freckles. He's also accident-prone.

"Do you remember the day I took Jackie to the pool?" Kristy said. "First he got stung by a bee, and then he got lost and almost gave me a heart attack. My brother Sam told one of the girls in his class about it, and she said she saw the whole thing. She was working as a lifeguard that day."

"Really? Who was it?" Mary Anne asked.

"I don't know her name, but she's this *fantastic*-looking girl who's captain of the swimming team at Stoneybrook High

School." Kristy picked up her clipboard, ready to get back to business. "Sam says she's the reason Travis tried out for swimming along with all his other sports. I hear he's really crazy about her. They've been going out together for weeks."

I looked up from the club notebook in total shock. Travis was going out with someone? Travis was *crazy* about someone? How could that be possible? He was interested in *me*! I could feel my cheeks burning, and I wondered if anyone else had noticed. I started thumbing through a *Seventeen* magazine, hoping Kristy wouldn't get annoyed with me.

The club meeting went on as usual and a few minutes later, I actually managed to take a phone call from Dr Johanssen, who needed a sitter for Charlotte. My voice sounded a little shaky, but I wrote down all the details about the job and promised to call her back.

"Now, who gets the job?" Kristy asked brightly, as Mary Anne checked the record book.

I returned to the *Seventeen* magazine, dying for the meeting to be over. What was going on with Travis? Could Kristy be mistaken? I couldn't wait to get home and work everything out in my head.

Unfortunately, Mum asked me to make a salad the minute I walked through the door. It was the last thing in the world I felt like doing, but what could I say? Mary Anne made spaghetti, Mum made the sauce (meatless), Richard made garlic bread, and before I knew it, all four of us were eating dinner together.

I was there, but I wasn't there. Does that make sense? I was sitting at the dining room table, passing the salad and half listening to Mary Anne talk about school, but my mind was a million miles away. I could have been on another planet! My brain was churning, trying to come up with an explanation for what Kristy had said about Travis.

I hated to admit it, but there just weren't that many possibilities. I didn't really think that Kristy had made a mistake, because she had seemed so definite about it. She had mentioned Travis by name (and how many Travises could there be at SHS?).

Then I let my mind play a little game. Maybe there was a weird reason for Travis's behaviour. Maybe he was just pretending to like this girl. But why? I was stumped. Unless . . . maybe Travis *wanted* to join the swimming team, too, and he thought one way to do it would be to go out with the captain. But wait a minute. Travis was a great athlete (he said so himself), so why would he need to do that? Nothing made sense. There *was* no explanation for the way Travis was acting.

I said so later that evening to Mary Anne, when we were upstairs working hard in my room. (Sometimes we do our home-work together.) That night, Mary Anne was solving maths problems, and I was thinking about Travis.

"You know, it just doesn't make sense," I blurted out.

"What doesn't?" Mary Anne hardly looked up from her book.

"What Kristy said about Travis and that lifeguard!" My voice was so loud it startled her.

"Oh, that." She pushed her papers aside and stared at me.

"Well, what did you think about it?" I said impatiently.

Mary Anne shrugged. "I suppose I didn't think much about it either way. Did it bother you?"

*Did it bother me!* "Yes," I said with clenched teeth. "It bothered me a lot."

Mary Anne sighed. "Then I wish she hadn't brought it up."

"No, I'm glad she did. Maybe this way I can work out what's going on. I don't know why he's taking someone else out. And I'm not sure why he's been paying so much attention to me." I was pacing restlessly back and forth in front of the dressing table.

"Dawn, it's not the end of the world. I wish you weren't so unhappy about it." Sometimes Mary Anne gets really upset over other people's problems, but she's usually a good person to talk to.

"But I thought Travis cared about *me*!"

Mary Anne hesitated. "I'm sure he does. But he can take out anyone he wants to. It's not as if the two of you are going steady. Anyway, she's probably a lot closer to him in age."

"But why is he paying so much attention to me? I thought he really liked me."

"I suppose he likes her, too. There's nothing wrong with that, is there?"

I was all ready to argue, and then I stopped myself. What Mary Anne was saying made sense, even though it hurt to admit it. Travis and I didn't have a formal relationship the way Mary Anne and Logan have. In a way, I envy Mary Anne, because she always knows where she stands with Logan. And he knows where he stands with her. But Travis is the kind of boy who keeps you guessing. He's full of surprises (the lifeguard was a big one!), and I'd have to find a way to handle it.

Later that night, as I turned out my light, the idea came to me in a flash. The best way to find out how Travis felt about this girl was to see the two of them together. And that was exactly what I was going to do.

I got my chance a few days later. It was a sunny Thursday afternoon, and my teacher decided to let our class out ten minutes early. I raced across the school yard. If I hurried, I could just get to SHS before the dismissal bell rang.

The SHS kids were rushing down the broad stone steps of the school as I came tearing round the corner. My heart sank. How would I ever find Travis in this huge mob? I was just trying to decide where to stand to get the best view, when I had an incredible stroke of luck. I spotted Travis pausing in the doorway to put on his sunglasses. He looked terrific in faded jeans and a white T-shirt, and my heart did a little flip-flop. I was dying to run up to him and tell him how glad I was to see him.

But he wasn't alone. He turned round and linked arms with a great-looking girl. Her long red hair tumbled down her back, and she had high cheekbones, just like a model. She was dressed in a white cotton flight suit, exactly the kind of trendy outfit that Claudia or Stacey would wear. I hated her on sight. Then I stopped and reminded myself that it wasn't her fault she was gorgeous, or that Travis liked her.

Travis and the girl headed for the pavement and I held my breath, hoping that Travis didn't have his car. Another stroke of luck. They walked right past the school car park, still arm in arm. They were probably going into town (another shopping trip?) and if I was very careful, I'd be able to follow them. I waited behind a tree until they were a good distance ahead of me.

I had to know what Travis was up to.

# 11th CHAPTER

A few minutes later, I decided I wasn't cut out to be a spy. Do you know how hard it is to follow someone? (I know what you're probably thinking. How can I say that when it looks so easy on television?)

But I had two disasters almost immediately. First, I stepped into a huge puddle, ruining my new shoes, and then I was nearly run over by a dustcart. I was so busy watching Travis that I didn't even notice the lights had changed, and I stepped straight out into the road. How stupid!

I took a deep breath and told myself to calm down. I would never find out the truth about Travis if I were flattened by a lorry. The trick was to stay cool.

I made sure Travis and the girl stayed at least a hundred yards ahead of me. With any luck, I'd be able to blend into the crowd once we got into town. The tricky part was a long stretch of a street with a narrow pavement and very few trees. I knew that if Travis turned round for any reason, he would spot me.

I was being extra cautious when a car horn blasted right behind me. I nearly jumped out of my skin! To my horror, Travis heard it, too. He glanced over his shoulder, and I hardly had time to dart behind a bush. Had he seen me? I had no idea, but I wasn't taking any chances. I crouched behind the bush, feeling a little silly, but afraid to get up. I counted silently to ten and then took up the chase once more.

A few minutes later we reached Stoneybrook town centre. Travis and the girl stopped first at Burger Bite, and I watched them go into a back booth. Would he order for her? I wondered. I took a seat near the front door and peered out from underneath a giant menu. If I scrunched around in my seat, I could see them in the mirror.

They were laughing and talking, and when the girl picked up the menu, Travis put his hand over hers. He winked at her before he gave their order to the waitress. My heart sank. The smiles, the tender looks . . . it was all so familiar. Travis was staring at her as if she were the only girl in the room. He had looked at me in exactly the same way!

I gulped down a lemonade and quietly left the restaurant. My heart was pounding in my chest as I sat on a bench across the street from the Burger Bite. I decided to wait for them to come out and then follow them to their next stop. Why was I doing this? I can't explain it. I just *had* to know what they were going to do next, even though I knew it was going to hurt me.

About half an hour later, they came out arm in arm and headed for the Jewellery Shop. Hamburgers and pierced earrings. Sounds familiar, doesn't it? Travis was taking her to *exactly* the same places he had taken me. I wondered for one crazy moment if Travis would even buy her the same earrings he had bought for me. (Not that it would matter at this point.)

They didn't buy anything, but they wandered up and down the aisles, looking at the jewellery. They kept their heads close together, laughing and talking. Even though I couldn't hear what they were saying, I could see that they were having a terrific time together. Why couldn't I have been the one with Travis? My chest felt so tight, I thought it would explode, but I forced myself to keep watching them. I should have known that things could only get worse.

It was late afternoon when they finally finished their window shopping and headed away from town. I tagged along after them, feeling tired and discouraged. (And very jealous.) There were so many thoughts crowding in my head at once that it was impossible to think clearly. Why was Travis so interested in this girl? Yes, I know she was great-looking, but it had to be more than that. Travis had told me again and again how beautiful my eyes were, and he had even picked out combs for me to wear in my hair. So that must mean that he thought I was pretty good-looking, didn't it? What did she have that I didn't have?

I was trying to sort everything out when Travis and the girl suddenly entered a small park. I barely had time to duck into a bus shelter when the two of them sat down on a bench just a few feet away. Now what?

I didn't have to wait long. I watched in horror as Travis leaned over and *kissed* her! I know I gasped out loud, but both of them were too busy to notice. My hand flew up to my mouth, and I felt hot tears stinging my eyelids. How could this be happening?

I don't know how long they would have stayed in the park, but suddenly a group of little kids sat down next to them. I saw Travis frown and then laughingly pull the redhead to her feet. She laid her head against his shoulder, just for a moment, and then the two of them moved off again, arm in arm. I felt like staying there in the bus shelter and crying my eyes out, but I knew I had to keep going.

After a few yards, they stopped at the cinema and looked at the marquee. The way they were nodding and talking, it was obvious that they were making plans to see a film together. That night? That weekend? I had no way of knowing, but it didn't really matter. All that mattered was that *she* would be with Travis, and I wouldn't. Their fingers were laced tightly together, and I saw the look in Travis's eyes when he smiled at her. He should be smiling that way at *me*.

I had seen enough. It was nearly dusk, and I hurried home, thinking, thinking, thinking. Did Travis like this girl because she was his own age? Was I really too young for him, just like Richard had said? Was Travis annoyed with me because I hadn't taken his advice and had that third hole pierced in my ear? Surely he wouldn't get so annoyed over a little thing like that? No matter how hard I tried to explain things, my mind kept coming back to one point: Travis didn't care about me at all. How could I have been so wrong about him?

I was still *very* upset over Travis when we had our next BSC meeting. I had made up my mind not to say anything to my friends, but somehow everything came pouring out.

We were waiting around for phone calls when Kristy mentioned that Sam and Travis were on the track team together. "I don't know how Travis does it," Kristy said admiringly. "He's playing three different sports this season, and he's even talking about auditioning for the school play."

"He should," Stacey piped up. "Can you imagine how great he'd look on stage? He's gorgeous! He's got the dreamiest eyes I've ever seen."

Stacey (who happens to be a little boy-crazy) was all set to launch into a long description of Travis's smile, when I cut her off.

"Please, can we change the subject?" I pleaded. I jumped up and grabbed my jacket. "If we're just going to sit around and talk about boys, I'm going home. I've got better things to do."

Kristy looked shocked, and Stacey gave me a long look. "Dawn, what's wrong?" she asked.

"Nothing," I snapped. I turned round so that my friends couldn't see the tears that were threatening to spill down my cheeks. "I've just heard enough about Travis, that's all. In fact, I've heard *more* than enough!" I stumbled blindly towards the door to Claudia's room, but Mary Anne stopped me.

"Wait, Dawn," she said softly. "You might as well tell everyone what's going on."

"I don't want to talk about it," I said stiffly.

Mary Anne took my hand and pulled me gently on to Claud's bed. "That's what friends are for, you know. We're all here for each other."

I hesitated. Everyone was looking at me, and they all seemed worried. Maybe it *was* better to get things out into the open.

"I saw Travis with someone else," I said slowly. "Probably the captain of the swimming team. That's why I'm so upset."

Stacey looked puzzled. "Why would that bother you? Unless—" She clapped her hand over her mouth. "Are you going out with him? Oh, wow! When did all this happen?"

I shrugged. "We're not really going out together, but I know he cares about me. I mean, I *thought* he cared about me." I told them about the surprise visit at the house, and the necklace and hair combs. (Also the trip to Burger Bite and the Jewellery Shop.) I left out the part about Mum and Richard being so angry with me.

"That rat," Stacey said angrily after I told them about Travis kissing the girl in the park. "Why did he lead you on like that?"

"He didn't really lead her on," Kristy said. "Don't forget, he never really asked her out. At least, not on a real date."

"Oh, Kristy," Claudia said. "You're being much too practical. If somebody visits you at your house and brings you presents, it's like a date. And if they take you shopping after school, that's like a date, too."

"It is?" Jessi asked. She and Mallory had been following the whole conversation without saying a word.

Claudia unwrapped a Murray Mint and popped it into her mouth. "Well, sort of. At least I think it is."

"I think so, too," Stacey said. "Travis gave Dawn the idea that he liked her, so he's definitely a creep."

I sighed. I was glad that my friends were all taking my side, but I didn't feel much better. My chest ached every time I thought about Travis.

"Don't worry, Dawn," Claudia said. "You'll meet someone a million times nicer than Travis. Someone who *appreciates* you."

I sniffled a little. How could there be anybody nicer than Travis?

"In fact," Mary Anne said, "I think I know just the person."

"You do?" Kristy asked. "Tell us about him."

Mary Anne grinned. "Well, he's fourteen, and he's fantastic-looking. And he's got a great sense of humour, and he's supposed to be *really* nice."

"Supposed to be?" Kristy raised her eyebrows. "Don't you know for sure?

"I'm sure" said Mary Anne. "It's just that I haven't met him yet."

"Who is he?" Jessi asked. "Does he go to SMS?"

"No, he lives outside town." She paused. "He's Logan's cousin. His name is Lewis and he's coming here for a visit soon." She bent down so we were on eye level. "And guess what? He hasn't got a girlfriend."

Mary Anne looked quite pleased with herself. I didn't want to sound ungrateful, but I had no desire to meet Lewis. I didn't care how nice he was or how handsome or funny. I wanted Travis. Why couldn't everyone understand that?

"Isn't it wonderful?" Mary Anne went on, all smiles.

I blew my nose and tried to look interested. There was no point in hurting Mary Anne's feelings, and I could always make up some excuse for not seeing Lewis when he got here.

"Wonderful," I said. "Just wonderful."

# 12th
# CHAPTER

Tuesday

When I sat for the Hobarts today, I walked into the middle of James's play. I was just settling down for a game of Chinese checkers when James announced that it was "show time." He insisted that I see <u>Little Dog Lost</u> (the play he had written). Several of you other BSC members have already seen it, and he wanted me to see it, too. Plus he had an actual audience this time. The play was a big hit!

95

"Please, Mary Anne," Mathew and Myriah chanted together. "We want to do the play for a big audience today. It's really ready."

"I thought we'd play chess," Mary Anne said, "and then make brownies together."

"Brownies! We can have brownies *anytime*," said Myriah. "This is important stuff. This is a play!"

"Please!" Gabbie squealed. "No brownies! No chess! Don't you want everyone to see *Little Dog Lost*?"

"Well, of course," Mary Anne replied. "Of course I do." She knew about the play from reading Kristy's and Jessi's babysitting notes. They had seen it "in rehearsal" and Mary Anne realized that the kids had been working on it a lot since then.

She glanced at James, who was looking very pleased with himself. "Are you ready to do this?"

He nodded. "As ready as we'll ever be. Everybody knows their lines, and if Chewy stays under control, we'll be fine."

Chewy! Mary Anne's heart sank. She had forgotten that Chewy was the star of the play. "Where is Chewy?" Mary Anne asked.

"He's all ready!" Gabbie informed her. "He's waiting in the garage." She looked at James. "We call that offstage."

"I see." Mary Anne watched as Gabbie opened the garage door and Chewy came barrelling across the garden. He acted like a dog who'd been cooped up for five years.

He immediately began running round in circles.

"He's excited," Myriah explained.

"I can see that." Mary Anne gently pushed Chewy off the garden chair he'd jumped on. "Are you sure he'll calm down enough for the play?"

"I know he will," Myriah said, petting him. "I'll put him back in the garage."

Mary Anne doubted that Chewy would calm down but she didn't want to discourage Myriah. "Okay," she said finally, "where do we start?"

"We need to set up chairs for the audience, and then we need to start ringing doorbells." James was suddenly very businesslike as he dragged some folding chairs over to the patio. "This is the stage," he said, motioning to the back garden, "and this is where the audience sits."

"That looks fine, but what did you mean about ringing doorbells?"

"To tell people about the play," said Mathew impatiently.

"We should really have sent out invitations," Myriah said, "but we've been so busy rehearsing, we didn't get round to it." She looked a little worried. "It's not too late to ask people to come, is it?"

"I suppose not." Mary Anne glanced at her watch. It was after three-thirty. "But we'd better get started straight away. How about if I phone Mallory Pike to see if she can bring some of her brothers and sisters?"

"Oh, good!" Myriah clapped her hands together. "And ask Jessi to bring Becca and Squirt."

"The more the better," James said. "The grown-ups can sit on the folding chairs, and the little kids can sit on blankets."

"Are we inviting grown-ups?" asked Mary Anne.

"Of course! Otherwise it won't seem like a real play," James replied.

"Hmm, I suppose you're right." Where could Mary Anne find some real live parents at a moment's notice? she wondered. She thought of Mrs Pike. As far as she knew, Mal's mum was the only one of our clients who might be at home.

A quick phone call to Mrs Pike settled things.

"Of course I'll come, Mary Anne," she said warmly. "Stacey took a couple of kids to the playground, but I'll round them up along with Vanessa and the triplets. I know they'd love to see a play."

Half an hour later, everything was falling into place. Mal (who was babysitting for Charlotte Johannsen) arrived with Charlotte and her best friend, Becca Ramsey. Jessi brought the Newton kids. Stacey arrived a few minutes later with two of the Pike kids – Margo, who's seven, and Claire, who's five.

"Hi, Mary Anne-silly-billy-goo-goo!" Claire shouted. (Claire is going through an extremely silly stage at the moment.)

Mary Anne was helping everyone find seats when Claudia appeared. "I've just heard about the play," Claud whispered. "I'll help seat people if you want to go and help James. He looks as if he's got a problem."

Mary Anne glanced up. James was darting back and forth with a clipboard, barking orders to his actors. "Johnny, I want you to be quiet until it's time for you to say your lines!"

"*Little dog lost,*" he sang softly.

James put his finger to his lips. "No talking," he said sternly.

"I wasn't talking. I was singing," Johnny said, making a face.

James looked as if he wanted to throw his clipboard in the air. Mary Anne touched his shoulder. "I'll make sure the younger kids are in their places," she told him. "Why don't you do something about Chewy? He's making a racket in the garage, and I'm afraid someone's going to let him out."

"Let him out?" Myriah repeated. "Oh, no!" She grabbed a Magic Marker and a piece of paper and told Mary Anne to make a sign that read: STAR'S DRESSING ROOM. KEEP OUT!

Mary Anne smiled. "I think that'll do it," she said.

The audience was settling down and James edged over to Mary Anne.

"Do you think I should say something to the audience?" He looked a little nervous.

Mary Anne nodded. "You'll have to introduce the play. After all, they don't even have programmes."

"I feel a little silly."

"Don't feel silly. And remember to tell everyone that you *wrote* the play."

"Do you think so?"

"Of course. You should be very proud. Not many kids your age could write a play.

James smiled then, and Mary Anne knew he was relaxing a little. A few minutes later, he cleared his throat and stepped in front of the crowd. Mary Anne crossed her fingers as he finished the introduction and took a seat in the front row. It was show time!

Myriah made her entrance like a professional actress. She was wearing one of Mrs Perkins's coats and carrying a large handbag.

"Oh, I just love shopping in the arcade," she said brightly.

"Hi, Myriah-silly-billy-goo-goo!" Claire shouted from the audience.

Myriah frowned but stayed in character. "Where shall I go first?" she said, coming close to the audience. "There are so many shops to choose from."

Mary Anne knew that Chewy was supposed to be on stage by that point, but there was no sign of him. James turned round from the front row and caught her eye. "Get Chewy fast!" he mouthed.

Mary Anne grabbed Johnny Hobart, who didn't have to go on stage for a while. "Quick, Johnny," Mary Anne hissed. "Let Chewy out of the garage."

Johnny stared at her. "I already have," he said solemnly.

"Then where is he?"

Johnny pointed toward the Perkinses' garden, where Chewy was digging an enormous hole in the flower garden.

"Oh, no!" Mary Anne wailed.

"I can whistle for him," Johnny suggested.

"Do it!"

Johnny stuck two fingers in his mouth and made an earsplitting sound. Chewy bounded across the lawn, knocked over Gabbie's "shoe shop", and skidded to a halt at Johnny's feet.

The kids in the audience started laughing, not sure if this was supposed to be part of the show. Mary Anne knew she had to act fast. She grabbed Chewy's collar and pushed him "on stage".

"Go on. Act as though you're lost," she pleaded.

Myriah waited until Chewy raced over to her, and then she sank down to her knees.

"Oh, you poor dog," she cried. "You're lost and looking for your owner." Chewy immediately began licking her face, nearly beside himself with joy. "You must be very . . . sad," she said doubtfully.

Someone in the audience giggled at this line, because Chewy was running in circles and barking. He didn't look in the least bit sad!

Myriah decided to adlib some lines. "Sometimes dogs *act* happy, but they're really sad. And *lost*," she added, in case the little kids in the audience had missed the point.

James signalled to Myriah to begin her walk through the "arcade", and she headed for Gabbie, who was rearranging her shoe shop.

"Shoe sale! Shoe sale!" Gabbie yelled, picking up a decrepit shoe. It was muddy from Chewy's mad dash through the garden. Everybody laughed at her line, and Gabbie looked pleased.

James rolled his eyes. Mary Anne knew the play wasn't turning out at all as he expected, but at least he was getting a lot of laughs. And then *Mary Anne* got a surprise. She was standing at the back of the patio when Zach appeared! He was the last person in the world she wanted to see at the play.

Mary Anne wasn't taking any chances. She showed him to a seat right at the back of the audience, and decided to sit next to him. "It's a great play," she whispered. "Really funny."

"Uh-huh." Zach looked totally unimpressed. He crossed his arms in front of his chest and didn't smile for the next fifteen minutes. Mary Anne couldn't imagine why he had bothered to show up.

The moment the play was over (to wild applause) Zach grabbed James by the arm. "Hey, how about some football?" he said.

"I don't know. I'm a bit busy at the moment," James began.

"C'mon. Drop this baby stuff and let's kick a ball around," said Zach, and James looked completely confused.

Zach pulled James down the drive. Mary Anne didn't know why James let himself be dragged along, or why he didn't speak up. A lot of kids wanted to talk to him about the play, and James was letting Zach ruin his big moment for him. It didn't make sense.

Then Mary Anne thought about Dawn and Travis and got an idea. Dawn would be sure to read the notebook. Maybe this was Mary Anne's chance to tell her some things she'd been thinking about.

*Tuesday (con't)*
*Even though the play went well, I can't stop thinking about James and the way*

he let himself be controlled by Zach. I hate to say it, Dawn, but it made me think of you and Travis. Zach is trying to make James into something Zach wants him to be, and, well, can you see that Travis is doing the same thing with you? You know I'm not saying this to hurt your feelings, but it's something you should really think about. Travis is trying to make you into someone you don't want to be. You're great, just the way you are. Please don't let him change you, and don't hang around any more waiting for him to drop by. That's not your style. Kristy, I hope you're not angry

with me for writing
this in the club note-
book, and Dawn, I
hope you're not angry,
either. But it's easier
for me to write this
than to say it. I hope
you understand. And
I hope you'll see Lewis
when he comes to town.

# 13th
# CHAPTER

You're probably wondering why I would even *want* to see Travis again after that scene in the park. After all, I'd seen him kissing another girl, so what could be left between us? I was tempted to forget the whole thing (and Travis, too) but I couldn't. I wanted Travis to know that I was on to him, and there was only one way I could do that. I'd have to wait until he left school with the girl and follow them again. But this time would be different. This time, I would confront Travis!

What did I hope to accomplish? Well, if nothing else, I would *embarrass* him! I could just imagine how Travis would react when I bumped into him with his girlfriend. Let's see how cool and confident he'd be then!

I got my chance the following Tuesday afternoon. We had a quiz at the end of the day, and our teacher said we could leave as soon as we handed in our papers. What a lucky break! I whizzed through the test, double-checked my answers (it was a multiplechoice test), and left school fifteen minutes early. I had plenty of time to catch Travis as he left SHS.

My heart was pounding as I waited on a bench near the front steps of the school. I was wearing sunglasses, and I kept my head ducked down. I wanted to make sure that I spotted Travis before he recognized me!

Soon the bell rang, and kids came pouring out of the double doors. I saw Travis and caught my breath. He was alone! My mind raced with possibilities. Maybe he'd broken up with the girl. Maybe he'd realized *I* was the girl he'd wanted all along. Maybe the two of us could spend a wonderful afternoon together. Maybe, maybe, maybe. . .

There I was, lost in fantasyland when Sara (Kristy had found out her name for me) appeared on the scene. She darted up to Travis, and he grabbed her in a big bear hug. They hurried down the steps, just inches away from me. (I didn't need the sunglasses after all, because they never even looked at me. They were too wrapped up in each other.) My heart sank, but I was more determined than ever. It was time to catch Travis out.

I decided that the best place to "bump into" them would be in town. That way I could pretend that I was out shopping. (I certainly didn't want Travis to know that I'd waited for him outside his school.)

Travis and Sara walked briskly along, and I kept a hundred metres or so behind them. I didn't feel nervous at all because I was absolutely sure I was doing the right thing. The only question now was, *where* should I run into them?

I got my chance outside the Jewellery Shop. It was a bright, sunny day, and the shop was holding a sale. Customers were jamming the area in front of the shop, looking for bargains, and Travis and Sara had stopped in front of a display rack.

Travis was pointing to a pair of gold hoop earrings, when I positioned myself on the opposite side of the rack. If I waited a few more seconds, he'd be bound to see me. The moment he gave the rack a little spin, we'd be staring right into each other's eyes!

"I really like the silver hoops better," Sara was saying. I remember thinking what a wispy little-girl voice she had, and then it happened. The rack shifted and Travis and I were face-to-face. The moment of truth at last!

I gave him a casual smile, and to my amazement, he *grinned* back at me. "Hi, Dawn," he said in a friendly way. He didn't sound in the least bit embarrassed! I was baffled, but I tried to be cool.

"Hi, Travis. I suppose this is one of your favourite spots." I thought he deserved a little dig. After all, he'd taken *me* to the Jewellery Shop not too long ago, and now he was back in the same spot (with another girl).

He laughed, totally missing the point. "It does look that way, doesn't it?" Sara, who had been paying no attention to the conversation, suddenly held up a pair of heavy gold hoop earrings.

"What do you think, Travis?" she asked, ignoring me. "Are these too big?"

I couldn't resist. "Yes, definitely too big. They look like they should be holding up a shower curtain."

Sara frowned and gave Travis a "who-is-this-person?" look, and he introduced us.

"Dawn is from California, too," he added.

"Really?" Sara gave me a cool smile. "Oh, now I remember," she said, as if a light bulb had switched on inside her head. "Dawn Schafer . . . the little girl you told me about."

*Little girl?* I was steaming. What a nerve. I tried to think of a really stinging comeback, but my mind was a blank. And the next words out of Sara's mouth were even worse. "I'm sure you've turned her into a real beauty, Travis," she murmured.

That did it! "I was already a beauty," I said hotly. I suppose it was a very conceited thing to say, but I didn't care.

Sara and Travis exchanged an amused

look. I have *never* been so embarrassed in my life, and I knew I was making a fool of myself. The only thing to do was get out of there – fast.

"I've got to get home," I muttered.

"Nice to have met you," Sara said. She looked like she was going to burst out laughing the minute my back was turned.

"See you around." Travis grinned at me as if nothing had changed. How could he be so casual when my whole world had turned upside down?

I practically ran all the way home. I felt hurt, angry, upset and *very* foolish. I didn't say a word during dinner and bounded upstairs to my room the minute the dishes were done.

"You're pretty quiet," Mary Anne said. She had come into my room so softly, I hadn't heard her. I was sprawled on my bed, maths book in hand, but my mind was on Travis and Sara.

"I'm thinking," I told her. I looked at her and then looked away.

She sat down at my desk, watching me. "Did you ever see *My Fair Lady*?" she asked. "You know, the film based on the play *Pygmalion*?"

What was she getting at? I sat up in bed, scrunching a pillow behind my head. "I saw it a long time ago. We got it out on video once."

Mary Anne looked pleased. "Then I

suppose you remember the story. You know how proper Professor Higgins turns Eliza Doolittle, the Cockney girl, into his 'fair lady'?"

"Of course. He changed everything about her, the way she walked and talked and even the way she dressed. He wanted to make her into a real lady."

Mary Anne stared at me. "Well," she said slowly, "I never liked that."

I nodded. "Me neither. Eliza should have been allowed to be herself."

"Exactly."

We were both very quiet, and then it hit me. "I get it," I said. "You're talking about Travis and me." Mary Anne didn't answer, and I thought about it a little more. "He wanted to change me and make me into someone else." I hesitated. "But why did he choose *me*? There were dozens of girls he could have picked."

"Who knows? I think he really liked you at first. Or maybe he was interested because you were from California."

I sighed. Everything was falling into place. Travis had never liked me as much as I had liked him. I was simply a "project" for him. I felt a *little* better, having worked out what was going on, but now I had another problem. What should I do next?

Mary Anne must have read my mind. "I think you should confront him," she said. "Tell him exactly what you think."

"I think so, too. It won't be easy. That's what I thought I was going to do today. But I know it's the right thing to do." I smiled at her. "You've been a big help, Mary Anne."

"I'm glad." She hugged me and headed towards the door. "Oh, and Dawn, there's one more thing you need to do."

"What's that?"

She grinned. "Be sure you read the club notebook."

# 14th
# CHAPTER

Now that I'd made up my mind about what to do, I didn't think twice. I didn't make elaborate plans to follow Travis, or think about what I was going to say to him. I just reached for the phone, hoping that the right words would come to me. (Sometimes when you have to say something really hard, it's better not to plan too much.)

"Dawn, how are you?" exclaimed Travis when he picked up the phone.

He acted as if nothing was wrong! His voice was so warm and friendly, I almost lost my cool, but I knew I had to be strong.

"I'm fine," I told him. "In fact, I've always been fine, but it took me a while to realize that."

"Huh?"

I took a deep breath. "You don't get it, do you?" I rushed on. "Well, maybe I can explain it to you."

"Okay, shoot." A tiny note of doubt crept into his voice.

I braced myself for the toughest part of all. "You really hurt me, Travis."

"I *hurt* you?" He sounded incredulous.

"Yes, you did. You told me how to dress, how to do my hair, how to act. You tried to make me into something I'm not."

There was a long pause. "You're right. I don't get it," he said finally. "How could something like that hurt you? You're a great-looking girl, Dawn. I just thought you could use a few suggestions on how to dress and do your hair."

"It was more than a few, but anyway, that's not the point. You can't imagine what a big effect you had on me. I took everything you said to heart." I hesitated, twisting the phone cord around my fingers. "Maybe you can't understand this, Travis, but I practically ran round in circles trying to please you. I tried so hard to be everything you wanted me to be." It's funny, but even as I said the words, I realized that the harder I tried, the more hopeless things had become. I knew now that I could *never* be what Travis wanted (and that I didn't want to be).

Travis gave a little laugh. "Dawn, I really think you're making too much of this. You know, if we could just get together and talk this over, I think you'd see things my way."

"I don't think so," I said quietly.

"You mean you don't want to see me

just because I told you to wear combs in your hair? I can't believe it."

"It's a lot more than that, Travis. Look, I'll give you the perfect example. Remember when you wanted me to get that third hole pierced in my ear? I actually felt guilty because I didn't want to go along with it. I'm just glad I had the brains not to listen to you."

"Dawn, you're making a big deal out of nothing," Travis spluttered. Now he was beginning to sound *really* uncomfortable.

"No, it's true. You've been trying to change me ever since the day you met me," I said, cutting him off. "You wanted to change everything about me. I just didn't see it in the beginning."

"Dawn, this is crazy."

"It's not crazy at all," I said smoothly. "I've had time to think about it, and I've talked things over with Mary Anne. You never liked me for myself, just for what you could make me into. It all makes sense now."

"Look, I never wanted to hurt you, Dawn—"

"Maybe not, but that's what happened. Besides everything else, you led me on. You let me think I was special to you, but you were seeing Sara at the same time." I felt very calm. "Anyway, I think we should just say goodbye now."

"Say goodbye? Are you serious?"

"Very serious," I said softly. "That's why I phoned you tonight, Travis. To say good-bye, and to say that I hope you find the perfect girl for you. She's probably out there somewhere, Travis, but I'm not her. Maybe it's Sara."

Travis started to say something, but I didn't give him a chance. I hung up the receiver very gently and stared out of the window for a few minutes.

It was over. And I knew I'd done the right thing.

The reaction at the next BSC meeting was just what I had hoped for.

"Dawn! I can't believe you did it. I'm so proud of you!" Claudia was beaming. "He really got what was coming to him."

"Travis must have been furious," Stacey chimed in. "I wish I could have been there."

"I'm just happy you're rid of him," Mary Anne said. "You finally realized."

"It took a little help from my friends," I added. "For a while, I thought there was something wrong with *me*."

"Ha! That's probably what he wanted you to think," Kristy said. She tilted her visor back. "I had no idea Travis was such a jerk. He hangs around with my brothers all the time."

Mary Anne looked up from the note-book. "Well, he's probably okay when he's with boys because he's not trying to change them."

Kristy nodded. "I suppose you're right. The main thing is that he's out of Dawn's life for good—" I started to giggle, and Kristy stopped in mid-sentence. "What's so funny?"

"I just thought of something I should have said. I should have told Travis to get his hair trimmed and to get rid of those stone-washed jeans. He could do with a few fashion tips himself!"

"You would have been wasting your breath," Stacey said, examining her nail varnish. "He's so conceited, he probably thinks he's perfect."

I was struggling with a maths problem later that night when Mary Anne came into my room. She looked a little embarrassed, and I wondered why.

"How's it going?" She glanced at my maths book, but I knew she had something else on her mind.

"Okay." I closed the book and spun round in my seat. "I can have a break if you want to talk."

"Well . . . yes," Mary Anne said, settling herself on the bed. I waited while she fumbled in her pocket for a white envelope. "I . . . just wanted to tell you again that I'm really proud of the way you handled Travis."

I smiled at her. "I'm glad. But I bet that isn't why you came in here."

Mary Anne flushed. "Well, I – Okay, I'll be honest with you. I've got something for you." She glanced at the envelope but drew back when I reached for it. "No, wait! Before you read it, I want to explain something."

From the look on Mary Anne's face, I knew it must be something important. And I knew there was no way I could rush Mary Anne. She would tell me in her own good time.

"Do you remember when I told you about Lewis?"

"Lewis?" I drew a blank, and then it hit me. "Oh, yeah. Logan's cousin. What about him?"

"Well, guess what? His visit to Stoney-brook is all planned!"

"Really?" I know Mary Anne expected me to look thrilled, but I just couldn't. My hand edged back to the maths book. I had about a million problems to work on, and Mary Anne was all ready for a long conversation about some boy I didn't even know!

"Don't you get it?" she said finally. "Lewis wants to meet you."

"That's silly," I said, sharpening a new pencil. "He doesn't even know me."

Mary Anne cleared her throat. "That's not exactly true. He, um, knows a *little* bit about you."

118

"How could he?" I was flipping through the book, trying to find my place when I paused and said, "Mary Anne, what have you done?"

She was blushing all the way up to her hair roots. "Now don't get annoyed, Dawn, but Logan and I told Lewis a few things about you. And I sent him a photograph of you."

"What!"

"Please don't get upset. If you just think about it, you'll realize it was a great idea. Logan says Lewis is a really great boy, and I think he's just what you need just now." She was still clutching the white envelope and she handed it to me.

"It's a letter addressed to me," I said, turning it over. "Mary Anne, what's going on?"

"It's from Lewis. Isn't that great? He must have liked your photo and the things Logan and I told him, so he decided to write to you. I *said* he was a great guy."

"Terrific," I muttered, tearing open the envelope. I scanned the first few lines and relaxed a bit. Lewis said that he'd heard a lot about me, and he wanted to meet me. He also said I was very pretty and that we had a lot in common. He didn't sound too bad, but I just wasn't interested in meeting another boy at the moment. Why couldn't Mary Anne understand that?

"Well?" Mary Anne said. She stood next

to me, trying to read over my shoulder. "What do you think?"

I shrugged. "He seems like a pretty nice boy." A photo of a boy with dark brown hair and a nice smile fell out of the envelope. And he's even good-looking."

"Definitely. And he's a lot of fun, too. That's why Logan and I want this to work out." She looked at me very seriously. "You'll see him when he visits, won't you? *Please*, Dawn."

I looked at the photograph again. I didn't feel any sparks the way I had with Travis, but Lewis *did* seem nice. Still, the timing was wrong, all wrong.

"Well?" Mary Anne said impatiently. "Will you see him or won't you?"

I sighed. "I don't know."

"Dawn, puh-*leeze*!"

"Okay, okay. If Lewis wants to take me out when he comes to Stoneybrook, I'll go. I suppose."

"Good!" said Mary Anne. "That's all I wanted to hear."

# 15th CHAPTER

Later, when I was alone in my room, I read Lewis's letter again. (Okay, I'll tell you the truth. I read it *three* more times.) I'm not sure exactly what I was looking for, but I wondered if Lewis was too good to be true. He seemed funny, intelligent, not at all stuck-up, and *nice*. I'll show you what I mean. He started out by describing himself. (We had to do this once in an English lesson, and it was the toughest project I've ever had.)

DEAR DAWN,

I KNOW LOGAN IS GOING TO MAKE ME SOUND LIKE SOME FILM STAR, SO I THOUGHT I'D SEND YOU MY PHOTO. THIS WAY YOU CAN MAKE UP YOUR OWN MIND. I'M FIVE FOOT TEN, AND I HAVE BROWN EYES AND BROWN HAIR. NO MATTER WHAT LOGAN TELLS YOU, GIRLS DO NOT FAINT AT MY FEET.!

WAIT, I TAKE THAT BACK. A GIRL DID
FAINT AT MY FEET ONCE. HER NAME WAS
JENNY O'CONNOR. WE WERE DOING A
SCENE FROM A PLAY CALLED THE GLASS
MENAGERIE AND JENNY HAD THE WORST
CASE OF STAGE FRIGHT I'VE EVER SEEN. THE
CURTAIN WENT UP AND SHE PASSED OUT COLD!

SO MUCH FOR A BIG OPENING NIGHT. I
THOUGHT YOU MIGHT BE INTERESTED IN
ACTING, SINCE YOU'RE FROM THE WEST COAST.
WHENEVER I THINK OF CALIFORNIA, I
THINK OF FILM STARS AND HEALTH FOOD.
BUT I COULD BE WRONG. WHEN I TELL
PEOPLE THAT I'M FROM LOUISVILLE, THEY
ALWAYS THINK THAT I LOVE CHICKEN
AND THAT I HAVE A HOUND DOG NAMED
BEAU! (NEITHER IS TRUE.)

WELL, I BETTER WIND THINGS UP
HERE. I HOPE I HEAR FROM YOU!

'BYE FOR NOW.
LEWIS

Did I write back? Yes. But I took my
time, and I decided to be very casual.

Dear Lewis,
    It was really nice to hear
from you. I can't believe that

122

Logan and Mary Anne sent you
my photo! But you know what?
I'm glad they did, because
now we've met each other.
(Sort of.)

I thought I'd start by
telling you a little bit about
myself. First of all, I love
California, but not because
it's full of film stars. In fact
I've never even met a film
star, even though a couple of
them live near my dad.

You mentioned health food-
I love it! Mum and I are
always trying out new
vegetarian recipes. (Don't gag.
Spinach pie is delicious.)

Am I an actress? No way!
People have always told me I
should go into modelling or
acting, but I know Id get
stage fright, just like your
friend Jenny.

I'd like to tell you a little
about Stoneybrook, but I
have a maths test tomorrow

*(panic time!)*, so I'd better go.
'Bye for now.
Dawn

I read my letter to Lewis twice before sealing the envelope. I wondered if I could have made it more interesting, decided that I couldn't, and finally dropped it in the postbox. Imagine how surprised I was when I got a letter back four days later! Lewis must have written the minute he'd received my letter.

DEAR DAWN,

THIS WILL HAVE TO BE SHORT, AS I HAVE A MATHS TEST, TOO. MATHS ISN'T MY BEST SUBJECT (ENGLISH IS) SO I HAVE TO STUDY EXTRA HARD. I'VE DONE ALL THE PROBLEMS IN THE BOOK THREE TIMES, SO UNLESS I TOTALLY FREAK OUT DURING THE TEST I'LL BE OKAY.

I LIKED HEARING ABOUT CALIFORNIA. I GUESSED THAT YOU WERE INTO HEALTH FOODS (ONE RIGHT ANSWER) AND THAT YOU WANTED TO BE AN ACTRESS (ONE WRONG ANSWER). THAT GIVES ME A

SCORE OF FIFTY. LET'S HOPE I DO BETTER
ON THE TEST TOMORROW.
   SUPPOSE IT'S TIME TO HIT THE BOOKS.
I'M WONDERING WHAT KIND OF THINGS
WE CAN DO IN STONEYBROOK. A FILM?
A CONCERT? A WALK IN THE PARK?
               STAY IN TOUCH. YOUR PAL,
                              LEWIS

It sounded as if Lewis was planning to
spend a lot of time with me when he visited
Logan. Would it be just the two of us, or
would we be doing things with Logan and
Mary Anne? I decided I didn't really want
to see him alone. That would be too much
like a date. But if he wanted to be friends,
that would be okay.

Dear Lewis,
   I worked out what to do
when you visit Logan. How
about a tour of Stoneybrook?
I bet you've never seen a
small New England town. What
do we do for fun? We've got
cinemas and there's a big
shopping arcade, but you have
to drive to get to it. And of

125

course we have pizza parlours.
Do you know I found a place
that sells vegetarian pizza?
It has stir-fried snow peas
and broccoli on it, and it's
great!

> your friend,
> Dawn

In return, Lewis sent me a postcard of Louisville, Kentucky. The picture was of a beautiful boat called *The Belle of Louisville*, and this was the message:

Hi, DAWN,

YOU'RE KIDDING ABOUT THE BROCCOLI PIZZA, RIGHT? (PLEASE SAY YOU ARE!) I LIKE TO TRY NEW THINGS, BUT THAT'S PUSHING IT A LITTLE. STILL, IF YOU SAY IT'S GOOD, I'LL TAKE YOUR WORD FOR IT. I'LL SEE YOU IN STONEYBROOK SOON. I CAN'T WAIT TO MEET YOU. I'M REALLY LOOKING FORWARD TO IT.

> 'BYE, LEWIS

He was looking forward to coming to Stoneybrook. He was looking forward to seeing me. I read the postcard at least half a dozen times and put it in my notebook.

Mary Anne teased me just a little that night when I tucked the postcard into the mirror over my dressing table.

"So you're changing your mind a bit about Lewis?"

"He sounds . . . interesting," I said with a smile.

"Just interesting?"

"Okay, he sounds terrific." I paused. "But I don't want to get my hopes up too much. Remember how mad I was about Travis?"

"Lewis is different," Mary Anne said firmly. "Can't you tell from his letters?"

"I shrugged. "He seems different. He seems nice. And I don't think he wants to change me. We'll probably like each other. Just as friends," I added quickly.

"That's what I'm hoping for." Mary Anne sighed happily and flopped on to my bed. "I want you and Lewis to be great friends. Or maybe even something more," she said with a twinkle in her eye.

"Just friends will be fine."

Mary Anne giggled. "Only time will tell."

# KRISTY'S SECRET
# ADMIRER

For Jennifer and John

# 1st
# CHAPTER

"Concentrate, concentrate," I said softly. Then I raised my voice. "Keep your eye on the ball!" I yelled.

I must have startled Jackie Rodowsky because he swung far too low and missed an easy pitch.

"Strike two!" shouted the umpire.

"Drat," I muttered. I went back to murmuring, "Concentrate, *con*centrate."

It was almost the end of another game between the Krushers and the Bashers. Who are the Krushers and the Bashers? They're softball teams here in Stoneybrook, Connecticut. I am the Krushers' coach. Bart Taylor coaches the Bashers.

I've got a crush on Bart.

Anyway, for the first time in the history of softball games between my Krushers and Bart's Bashers, it looked like the Krushers had a chance of winning. The Krushers are not your average softball team. The players are all kids who are too young or too scared to try out for T-ball or Little League. In other words, as you might have guessed, they aren't great players. (Well, most of them aren't.) One kid ducks every time a ball comes towards him. Most of the kids aren't good hitters. We even have one player who's only *two and a half years old*. We let her use a special ball and bat so she doesn't get hurt, and we have to tell her everything to do. But you know what? She's a pretty good hitter for her age.

Bart's Bashers, on the other hand, are an older, tougher group of kids. (I don't know why they don't just join Little League. Maybe they like having Bart as their coach. I could certainly understand that.) The thing is, the Bashers have always beaten the Krushers easily.

Until now.

Now the score was even, the Krushers had been playing *very* well, the bases were loaded, and it was the bottom of the ninth – with two outs. The only problem was that the Krushers were up, and our batter was Jackie Rodowsky, the walking disaster. Poor Jackie. I love him to bits, but he *is* a walking disaster. He's accident-prone, he has bad luck, and he's not too coordinated.

The pitcher looked nervous, though. After all, the game was tied, and the Bashers had never been beaten by the Krushers.

134

Still, this was the walking disaster at bat. "Come on, come on," I muttered, and gave Jackie the thumbs-up sign.

The pitcher threw the ball, Jackie swung his bat, and – he hit a home run! Four more runs.

"We won! We won!" the Krushers screamed.

I screamed right along with them, even though I knew the Bashers had been playing with handicaps. Their best hitter had the chicken pox, their usual pitcher was out of town for the weekend, and two good players had been disqualified for fighting (with each other).

Still, the Krushers were victorious, and our cheerleaders went wild. "We won! We won! We won!" they couldn't stop yelling. Then they remembered their softball manners and shouted, "Two, four, six, eight! Who do we appreciate? The Bashers! The Bashers! Yea!"

I had a feeling this was the first time our cheerleaders actually meant what they were saying.

Our cheerleaders, by the way, are Vanessa Pike and Haley Braddock, who are nine, and Charlotte Johanssen, who's eight. Haley's brother, Matt, is a Krusher. He's profoundly deaf, but he's one of our best players. We communicate with him using sign language. Several of Vanessa's brothers and sisters (she has *seven*) are on the team, including her littlest sister, Claire, who's five and sometimes throws tantrums, shouting, "Nofe-air! Nofe-air! Nofe-air!" when she thinks she's been wronged.

Anyway, I waited until all of my Krushers had been picked up by mums or dads or sitters or older brothers and sisters, and were heading home joyously, amid surprised and excited cries of "We *beat* the *Bashers*! Honest." And, "We finally won a game!"

Then I looked across the schoolyard to where my big brother Charlie was waiting to drive me and my little brothers and sister home. (Charlie is seventeen, can drive, and has this awful old secondhand car. At least it works.)

Who am I? I'm Kristy Thomas. I'm thirteen and I'm an eighth-grader at Stoneybrook Middle School (SMS). I have three brothers, a stepbrother and stepsister, and an adopted sister. David Michael, my seven-year-old brother, and Karen and Andrew, my stepsister and stepbrother, who are seven and four, are Krushers. Charlie was going to drop Karen and Andrew off at their mother's house and then take David Michael and me home. This was nice of him. We could have walked, but we had an awful lot of equipment.

Charlie and I were just loading the last of it into the back of his car, when a voice said, "Can I walk you home?"

I whirled around. It was Bart.

My heart flip-flopped. It actually felt like it turned over inside my chest. I tried to breathe slowly.

"Charlie?" I asked. "Is that okay with you? You can leave the stuff in the car and I'll help you unload it as soon as I get home."

"No problem," replied Charlie. (He is so good-natured.)

"Okay, see you later, David Michael. Karen and Andrew, I'll see you on Friday afternoon." (Karen and Andrew only live with their dad and my mum and the rest of our family every other weekend. Oh, and for two weeks during the summer. The rest of the time they live with their mother and stepfather.)

"'Bye!" called David Michael, Karen and Andrew, who were still practically hysterical over beating the Bashers.

Charlie drove off in his rattly car, and I looked at Bart. I wasn't sure what to say. Of course, I was ecstatic that we'd beaten his team. On the other hand, we'd *beaten* his *team*. Bart couldn't be feeling too great.

But— "Congratulations," said Bart sincerely. "Your kids certainly have guts. They played really well today."

"Thanks," I replied. I was pleased. Really I was. But all Bart and I ever talked about was softball or our teams.

We walked a little way in silence. I couldn't think of a thing to say. At last Bart said, "Guess what happened in the locker room at school today?" (Bart does not go to SMS. He goes to Stoneybrook Day School, a private school.)

"What?" I asked, shuddering. Did I really want to know what went on in a boy's locker room?

"This guy," Bart began, "got a bit stupid after gym class, and he was clowning around, swinging from the pipes on the ceiling. All of a sudden, this pipe breaks, he falls down on to the benches, and the sprinkler system goes off! Everybody got soaked."

I laughed. "What happened to the kid? Was he hurt?"

"Him? Hurt? Nah. His nickname is Ox. Nothing could hurt him."

"Once," I said, "we were playing field hockey and this girl who is completely uncoordinated took a whack at the ball and it hit the teacher on the head!"

It was Bart's turn to laugh. Then he said, "Somehow I can't picture you in a field hockey kilt."

"They're not so bad," I replied. "The bloomers have changed. The uniforms are much more up-to-date now . . . I wish we could just wear jeans and T-shirts, though. Practically the only time I wear a skirt is when we play field hockey."

"You should wear skirts more often," said Bart.

"Why?" I asked.

Bart shrugged. Then he blushed. "I bet you'd look pretty, that's all."

"I'm not pretty in my Krushers outfit?" I asked. I was just teasing, but Bart blushed even redder. "Come on," I said. "Don't worry about it. I'm just giving you a hard time. So how's school?"

"Fine. The same old stuff."

"Yeah. For me, too."

"How's the Babysitters Club?"

"Great!" (My friends and I have a club that's really a business. We babysit for the families in our neighbourhoods. I'll tell you more about it later.)

"And how are your friends?"

"What is this? A talk show?" I said, laughing.

Bart grinned. "I don't know. I mean, no. I just want to hear about your life . . . instead of softball."

I looked at Bart seriously. "Well, let's see. Mallory's really happy because she's going out with a boy for the first time. Claudia's doing better at school. But I'm a bit worried about Stacey."

"Stacey," repeated Bart. "She's the one with diabetes, right?"

I nodded. "She's never really ill. She just doesn't seem *well* sometimes, if you know what I mean."

Bart nodded.

"How about you?" I asked. "How's everything?"

"Not bad. Kyle gets on my nerves, but I can handle him." (Kyle is Bart's little brother.) "My parents bug me, though. They hate it when my band practises in the basement."

"You have a *band*?" I said in amazement.

"Yup."

"What do you play?"

"Guitar. Electric, acoustic, any kind."

"I didn't know that. So have you had any . . . what are they called?"

"Gigs," supplied Bart. "Yeah, a couple. We could get a lot more, though, if we could find a place to practise. *No one* wants us in their basement."

"What about a garage?"

"The neighbours complain."

"Oh."

Bart and I talked about his band and music and school until, before I knew it, we had reached my house.

Emily, my adopted sister, was sitting on the front steps with Nannie, my grandmother. She came flying out to meet me and gave me a tight hug around the knees.

"Hi, Emily," I said, picking her up. Then I called, "Hi, Nannie!"

Nannie waved to me.

"Well," said Bart, "I'd better get going. I told Mum I'd come home straight after the game. But, um, I'll see you soon, okay?"

"Next game," I said.

"Maybe before that," Bart replied, and he walked off, whistling. I stared after him.

# 2nd CHAPTER

"Hello, Emily-Boo," I said to my little sister. I carried her back to Nannie.

"I heard about the game today," said Nannie immediately. "David Michael was so excited, he could hardly stand it."

"Yeah, the Krushers played pretty well today." I turned to Emily. "Maybe one day you'll be a Krusher too. Do you want to play softball?"

"Yes," replied Emily. (I knew she hadn't understood the question.)

Emily and Nannie and I went inside. Our house is sort of big. Actually, it's a mansion. My stepfather, Watson, is a millionaire. But thank goodness for the big house. When Mum married Watson we moved from our tiny house into his and needed room not just for Watson, my mother, my three brothers and me, but for Karen and Andrew, and now Emily and Nannie. (Nannie is Mum's mother, my special grandmother who doesn't act like a grandmother at all. She goes bowling, wears trousers and has tons of friends.)

Anyway, Nannie began making dinner, so I watched Emily. When the phone rang, I shouted, "I'll get it!"

I picked up the phone in the study. "Hello?"

"Hi, it's me, Shannon."

"Hi!" Shannon lives across the street and she's the first friend I made when I moved into this posh neighbourhood. (Well, we became friends after we stopped hating each other.) We don't see each other much, though, since she goes to Bart's school. She's a member of the Babysitters Club (BSC), but she doesn't come to meetings. (More about that later.)

"How'd the game go?" Shannon wanted to know.

I told her every last detail, and she was almost as excited as I was.

"Maybe I'll come to the next game," she said.

When we got off the phone, I felt happy – and lucky. I have a really nice group of friends in the BSC.

Emily came into the study then to watch *Sesame Street*. (She can't tell the time, but somehow she always knows when the show is on.) I let Bert and Ernie and Big Bird and Cookie Monster fade into the background as I thought about my friends.

My best friend is Mary Anne Spier, the secretary of the club. (I am the chairman.) I used to live next door to her until Mum married Watson. Before I moved to Watson's, Mary Anne and I had grown up together. I lived with my mum and my brothers and my father – until he moved out. But Mary Anne lived with just her father, since her mother died when Mary Anne was really little.

Mr Spier was very strict, bringing Mary Anne up on his own. He made up all these rules for her, but as Mary Anne has grown up, he's relaxed a lot. Maybe because her father was so strict or maybe just because it's her nature, Mary Anne is shy and sensitive and cries easily. (She's just the opposite of me. I'm outgoing and have a big mouth, and it takes a lot to make me cry.) Mary Anne is also romantic and, although she's shy, she's the only one of us to have a steady boyfriend. His name is Logan Bruno, and he's funny and understanding, but I think he and Mary Anne have been having some problems lately.

Believe it or not, Mary Anne and I sort of look alike. We're both short (I'm the shortest in my class), and we both have brown hair and brown eyes. Mary Anne used to dress like a baby, since she had to do whatever her father said, but now that he's loosened up, Mary Anne's clothes have changed from little-girl to, well, not exactly sophisticated, but maybe almost trendy.

In the last few months Mary Anne has gone through some BIG changes, which I'll fill you in on, but first I have to tell you about Dawn Schafer. Dawn is what we call the club's alternate officer, and she is Mary Anne's other best friend. Dawn, her younger brother, Jeff, and her mum moved to Stoneybrook last year when we were in the middle of the seventh grade. They moved because her parents had got a divorce, and Mrs Schafer wanted to come back to the town where she'd grown up. This was fine for her, but not so easy for Dawn and Jeff, who had grown up in California. Dawn misses California but likes Stoneybrook okay. With Jeff, the story was different. He never adjusted to his new home, so after several months he moved back to California to live with his father. Dawn misses that half of her family terribly and visits them as often as she can. However, she now has a new father and a stepsister. And guess who her stepsister is – Mary Anne!

It turned out that Mary Anne's dad and Dawn's mum had been high-school sweethearts, only they'd gone their separate ways after they graduated. Then Mrs Schafer moved back to Stoneybrook, she and Mr Spier began seeing each other again, and after a long time, they got married! So

145

now Dawn has a stepfather, Mary Anne has a stepmother, and it's one big, *usually* happy family. They all (including Tigger, Mary Anne's kitten) live in the colonial farmhouse that Dawn's mum bought when the Schafers moved to Connecticut.

Here are a few more things about Dawn. She's an individualist who stands up for what she believes in, even if no one else believes in it. She's organized (thank goodness, because her mum is exactly the opposite). She and her mum (and Jeff and her dad) *love* health food and don't eat meat. Dawn is gorgeous. She has LONG silky blonde hair. Honest, it's so blonde it's nearly white. She has sparkling blue eyes and she dresses like the individual she is. She wears what she wants to wear. My other friends and I think of it as "California casual". Dawn has *two* holes pierced in each ear. (Mary Anne and I will *never* get our ears pierced.)

The vice-chairman of the club is Claudia Kishi. When Mary Anne and I were still in our old neighbourhood on Bradford Court, we lived across the street from Claudia. So she grew up with us, too. Claudia lives with her parents and her older sister, Janine, who is a genius. It's true. Janine is only at high school, but she gets to take courses at the local college. This is a tragedy where Claudia is concerned. The thing about Claud is that she's bright, but she doesn't *apply* herself, as her teachers are always pointing out. Claud would much rather read a good Nancy Drew book (she's hooked) or work on her art. Usually her art takes priority. (That means that it's more important.) And no wonder. Claudia is a fantastic artist. Her work is incredibly distant. (That's a word my friends and I made up to mean *super*cool.) Claud can sculpt, paint, draw, make collages, you name it. She even makes her own jewellery.

That's another thing. Claudia's clothes. She's a real fashion freak. Talk about distant. Her clothes are *so* distant. Claudia is the most interesting dresser I know. She is always wearing things like Day-Glo hightop trainers, cut-up jeans, off-the-shoulder sweat shirts (sometimes torn) and friendship bracelets. (Her best friend is Stacey McGill, the club treasurer, and Claud plaited friendship bracelets for both of them.)

Claud is exotic-looking. She's Asian and has long black hair that she wears in a million ways, almond-shaped eyes and a complexion I would die for. How come I get spots sometimes and Claud *never* does? Especially since she's addicted to junk food. She hides it all over her room. (Her parents, naturally, don't approve of this.) Also, she has two holes pierced in one ear and one hole in the other.

As I mentioned, the BSC treasurer is

Stacey McGill. Two things about Stacey: 1. She is *the* most distant of all of us. 2. She has had the most problems of all of us (in my opinion).

Stacey originally came from New York City. That's where she grew up, and I think that's why she's so sophisticated. Stacey's clothes are at least as distant as Claudia's, and she gets to have her hair permed and stuff. She has pierced ears, of course, and she is slightly boy-crazy. *But,* her life has not been easy. First, Stacey's father's company transferred him to Stamford, Connecticut, which is not far from Stoneybrook, so Stacey had to leave New York and her friends at the beginning of seventh grade. Then the McGills had only been living here for about a year when Stacey's father was transferred *back* to New York. And not long afterwards, the McGills decided to get a divorce. Not only that, Mrs McGill planned to return to Stoneybrook, while Mr McGill planned to stay in New York with his job. Who was Stacey going to live with? How would she make the decision? It wasn't easy at all, but finally Stacey returned to Stoneybrook and the BSC. Of course, we club members, especially Claudia, were thrilled, but Stacey still feels guilty about leaving her father. She visits New York a lot.

To top things off, as I mentioned before, Stacey has diabetes – a severe form of the illness. What that means is that something in her body called insulin can get out of control if Stacey doesn't stick to a strict no-sweets, calorie-counting diet, give herself injections of insulin (yuck), and monitor her blood. I know this sounds disgusting, but think how Stacey feels. And I have to admit that she hasn't been looking good lately. There's talk of her going to see her special doctor in New York again.

The last two members of the Babysitters Club are younger than the rest of us. They're in the sixth grade at SMS, and we're in the eighth grade. Their names are Mallory Pike and Jessica Ramsey, but they're known as Mal and Jessi. (Mallory, by the way, is someone our club used to sit *for*.) Anyway, Mal and Jessi are best friends, and I can see why. They have a lot in common, although they certainly have their differences, too. First of all, they're both the oldest in their families, except that Mallory has *seven* younger brothers and sisters (she's Claire and Vanessa Pike's big sister), and Jessi has just one younger sister and a baby brother. Becca is eight, and Squirt (whose real name is John Philip Ramsey, Jr) is a toddler. Both Mal and Jessi are at that awful age (eleven) when they want to be more grown-up than their parents will let them be. They *were* recently allowed to get their ears pierced, but Mal has to wear glasses and a brace, so she doesn't feel particularly pretty, and both girls feel that their parents treat them like babies sometimes. Plus, Jessi's mother has just got a job, so with both Mr and Mrs Ramsey working, Jessi's Aunt Cecelia has moved in. Sometimes Jessi feels as if Aunt Cecelia is *her* babysitter. A few more similarities: Mal and Jessi both like reading, especially horse stories, and writing. (Well, Mal likes writing more than Jessi does, but she *did* convince Jessi to keep a journal, which Jessi has been doing faithfully.)

Now for the differences. Mal, the great writer, would like to be an author and illustrator of children's books one day, while Jessi thinks she'd like to be a professional dancer. She's been going to ballet classes for years, dances *en pointe* (that means *on toe*), and has even had leading roles in several ballets, dancing in front of big audiences. She has lessons a couple of times a week at a special school in Stamford, Connecticut. She had to *audition* just to be able to take lessons there.

Furthermore, Jessi and Mal couldn't look less alike if they tried. Jessi is black and Mal is white. Jessi has the long, graceful legs of a dancer, is thin, and has these huge, dark eyes with lashes that I'd like to have as much as I'd like Claudia's complexion. Mal, on the other hand, has unruly red hair, and (as I mentioned before) wears glasses and a brace, so she's not too pleased with her appearance right now. Also, she has freckles, which she can't stand.

Let's see, I might as well finish telling you about me, as long as I'm on the subject of the members of the Babysitters Club. I am active, always on the go and coming up with new ideas. (Some people think I'm bossy.) Can you believe it? I'm the only club member who *still* doesn't wear a bra because I don't need one. I don't care that much about clothes, though, anyway. I'm not trendy and distant like some of my friends. I'm more of a slob. Almost every day I wear jeans, trainers, a T-shirt and a sweater. Those clothes are *comfortable*.

I miss my father. He never phones or writes any more. I wish he were more like Dawn's father or like Watson. They both make an effort to see their kids. And Mr Schafer and Dawn are separated by *three thousand* miles.

What else about me? I think boys are dweebs, except for Bart, Logan (Mary Anne's boyfriend) and the boys I sit for. I even think my fifteen-year-old brother Sam is a dweeb. I like animals and we have a puppy named Shannon (after my friend Shannon), and an old cat of Watson's named Boo-Boo. Sometimes I think my house is a zoo, but I like the activity.

So there you are. You have just met my friends and me. I know I'm lucky to have such good friends. I also know I'm lucky to have a family, even a mixed-up one. I knew that when Emily came into the study holding out a trainer I'd lost and said proudly, "Soo." (Shoe.) I gave her a big hug.

# 3rd CHAPTER

"Thanks, Charlie!"

"See you in half an hour," he replied.

It was almost time for a Monday club meeting and Charlie had just dropped me off at Claudia's in his car. (Now that I live in a different neighbourhood, Charlie has to drive me to and from BSC meetings. The club pays him to do this.)

I ran to Claudia's front door and straight inside, without bothering to ring the bell. There was no point. I knew Claud was probably the only Kishi at home, and anyway, we club members never ring the bell.

"Hi, Claud!" I greeted her, as I entered her room. (I am always relieved when her sister, Janine, isn't at home. Janine is nice enough, I suppose, but she's for ever correcting your grammar and vocabulary. I think that comes with being the genius that she is.)

153

"Hi," replied Claud. She was lying on her bed, reading *The Clue of the Velvet Mask,* and one of her legs was propped up on a pillow.

"I suppose it's going to rain, isn't it?" I said.

Claud broke her leg a while ago and ever since, it has hurt her when it's going to rain. It's a pretty good barometer.

"Yeah," agreed Claud. "Do you think Dawn and the others will mind sitting on the floor with Jessi and Mal today? My leg *really* hurts."

"Nope," I replied. "Is there any junk food you want me to search for?"

"Hmmm." Claud closed her Nancy Drew book with a snap and looked thoughtful.

"Try – Oh, wait a sec. There's something right here." She reached under the quilt that was lumpily folded at the foot of her bed and retrieved a bag of crisps and a packet of Jelly Babies. "These'll do," she said.

"I'll pass them round," I told her.

Mary Anne and Dawn arrived then, so I took my chairman's seat in Claudia's director's chair, put on the visor I wear at meetings, and stuck a pencil behind one ear.

"Hi, everyone," I said.

"Hi," they replied. They were already settling themselves on the floor.

Usually Claudia, Mary Anne and Dawn sit on the bed, Stacey sits in Claudia's desk chair (or sometimes Dawn sits in the chair and Stacey sits on the bed), Jessi and Mal sit on the floor, and I sit where I was already sitting, in the place of honour. (The director's chair makes me feel tall.) Today, Stacey would probably sit at the desk, and the floor would just be a bit more crowded than usual.

I looked at Claudia's digital alarm clock, which is the official BSC timekeeper. As soon as those numbers change from 5:29 to 5:30, the meeting begins, even if a club member hasn't arrived. I'm a stickler for being on time, though, so my friends are hardly ever late.

Our club meets three times a week, on Mondays, Wednesdays and Fridays, from five-thirty to six. As chairman, I try to run it professionally. But let me slow down here and tell you how the club started, before I tell you how it works.

See, at the beginning of the seventh grade, long before so many things had changed, I still lived here in Bradford Court, opposite Claud. David Michael was only six then, and since Mum worked full-time, Sam and Charlie and I took turns babysitting for him after school. (I babysat for other kids, too, though.) Anyway, of course a day came when none of us – not Charlie, not Sam, not I – could sit for our little brother. So Mum started calling babysitters. It was while I was eating a piece of pizza and watching

Mum on the phone that it occurred to me that my mother could save a lot of time if she could make just one call and reach a lot of sitters, instead of making all those separate calls. So I got together with Mary Anne and Claud, told them my idea, and we began the BSC.

The first thing we decided was that we needed another club member, so we asked Stacey to join. She had just moved here from New York and was getting to be friends with Claudia. Stacey was dying to join, and the club was a success from the beginning. (We advertised a lot – by word of mouth, with leaflets, even with an ad in our local paper.) Soon we had so much business that we needed a new member, so we asked Dawn, who was Mary Anne's new friend at the time, to join. Then Stacey moved back to New York, we replaced her with Mal and Jessi, and *then* Stacey returned to Stoneybrook. We have seven members now, and I think that's enough. Claudia's room is getting crowded.

Here's how we run the club and what our responsibilities are:

I am the chairman, as you know. It's my job to keep the BSC in good shape and fresh by coming up with new ideas. (Besides, I thought up the club in the first place.) Some of my ideas are Kid-Kits, the club notebook and the club record book. Kid-Kits are boxes (we each have one) that we've decorated with Claudia's art materials and filled with our old toys, games and books, as well as some new things such as colouring books, sticker books, Magic Markers, etc. We sometimes take the kits on jobs with us, and our charges love them. This is good business, because when our charges are happy, then their parents are happy, and when parents are happy, they call the Babysitters Club with more jobs for us!

The record book is Mary Anne's and Stacey's department, so I'll describe that later, but let me explain about the notebook. The notebook is more like a diary. In it, each of us is responsible for writing up about every single job we go on. This is a chore, but it's helpful because we also have to read the diary once a week to see what went on during our friends' recent jobs. We learn about problems our charges are having, how to solve tough sitting situations, and that sort of thing.

Now let's see. Claudia is our vice-chairman. This is because she has her own phone *and* her own personal phone number, so her room is an ideal place to hold meetings. Thanks to our advertising, our clients know when the BSC gets together so they phone us during meetings. We spend a lot of time on the phone and don't have to worry about tying up our parents' lines. Thank goodness for Claud and her phone.

Mary Anne is our secretary and she has a

pretty big job. Remember the record book I mentioned? Well, Mary Anne is in charge of it (except for the numbers section, which is Stacey's domain). In the record book, Mary Anne has noted all of our clients, their phone numbers, addresses, the rates they pay, the number of children they have, etc. More important are the appointment pages. There, Mary Anne writes down all the jobs we have lined up and who's got the jobs. She's great at this. I don't know how she does it, because she has to keep track of so many schedules – Jessi's ballet classes, Claud's art lessons, as well as doctor and dentist appointments and more. But she's great at it. She's never made a mistake. (Also, she has the neatest handwriting of any club member.)

As treasurer, Stacey collects our weekly subs on Mondays. She's a whiz at maths. (I hate to admit it, but where maths is concerned, she's almost as clever as Janine, Claud's sister.) Anyway, Stacey collects the subs, puts them in the treasury (a manila envelope), makes sure the treasury doesn't get too low, and doles out the money when it's needed. (Stacey *loves* collecting and having money, even when it isn't, technically speaking, her own – and hates parting with it.) The subs money goes to Charlie to drive me to and from meetings, helps Claud pay her monthly phone bill, buys things for our Kid-Kits when we run out of them, and every now and then covers the cost of a club pizza or pyjama party. Stacey also keeps track of how much money we earn. She does this in the record book. It's just for our own information, since we each keep whatever we earn on a job. We don't pool the money or anything.

Dawn is our alternate officer, which means that she's a sort of substitute teacher. She takes on the job of anyone who has to miss a meeting. We don't miss meetings often, but Dawn's job can be hard since she has to know everyone's duties. However, she doesn't have much to do at most meetings so we let her answer the phone a lot.

Jessi and Mal are junior officers. That means that they can only babysit after school or on weekend days. They aren't allowed to sit at night yet unless they're sitting for their own brothers and sisters. They're a huge help to us, though. Not only are they good, responsible, reliable sitters, but they free us older club members for evening jobs.

Last of all are two associate members who don't attend meetings. They are my friend Shannon Kilbourne and Mary Anne's boyfriend, Logan. Shannon and Logan are our reserves. They're good babysitters who can step in when a job is offered at a time when all seven of us usual sitters are busy. I know that sounds unlikely, but it *does* happen. The associate members don't attend meetings. Shannon because she's too busy with other activities, and Logan because he's embarrassed to sit around in a girl's room for half an hour three times a week. It's one thing for him to join us at our lunch table in the cafeteria. There, he can escape if he wants to. But when he's in Claud's room, he feels stuck.

Anyway, that's the BSC.

I had been keeping my eye on Claud's clock, and when the numbers turned to 5:30, I cleared my throat. Everyone had arrived and it was time to start the meeting.

"Treasurer," I said, "please collect the subs."

With a look of glee, Stacey handed round the manila envelope, and each of us dropped some coins in it. Most of us groaned as we did so. Even me.

Then Stacey dumped the contents of the envelope on to Claud's desk, counted it up, and announced that the treasury contained more than twenty dollars.

"Well, hand it over," I said. "I've got to pay Charlie today."

Stacey looked pained but gave me the money.

"And I need some things for my Kid-Kit," said Dawn. "The Magic Markers have dried up, and someone – I'm not sure who, but I'm betting on Jenny Prezzioso – has scribbled on every page of a new colouring book."

"Barbie's head fell off," reported Jessi. "I need a new Barbie doll."

Everyone laughed. We knew she was just teasing.

The first phone call of the day came in then, and Dawn took it.

"Hello, Babysitters Club," she said. "Oh, hi, Mrs Kuhn."

The Kuhns aren't regular clients of the BSC, but the Kuhn kids are on my Krushers team, so Mrs Kuhn does phone for a sitter every now and then. Mary Anne arranged for Mal to take an afternoon job with them.

As soon as Dawn had called Mrs Kuhn back to tell her who would be babysitting, the phone rang again. And again and again and again. It was one of our busiest meetings ever.

One of the last calls was from Mrs Pike, Mal's mother, needing two sitters (she always insists on two sitters, since there are so many Pike kids) for a Saturday afternoon. Mary Anne arranged the job for Mal and Jessi. We usually let each other sit for our own brothers and sisters, if possible. We're pretty nice about doling out the jobs. Not much arguing goes on.

At six o'clock, we took what Claudia hoped was the last call of the meeting. (If a client calls after six, poor Claudia has to deal with things on her own. That's one of the problems that comes with having your own phone number. On the other hand,

161

Claud can talk up a storm in private, while the rest of us have to hide out in box rooms during personal calls, hoping nobody is listening in on an extension.)

As soon as Dawn had put the phone down, my friends and I said goodbye to Claud and left. Charlie was waiting for me. He demanded his money before he would drive me home.

# 4th CHAPTER

When Charlie and I walked through the front door of our house, I was greeted by David Michael, who said, "Shannon phoned *four* times while you were gone! She said to phone her as soon as you get home. She says it's really, really, really important."

"What's important?" I asked my brother.

"She wouldn't tell me. She just said for you to call her."

So I did. Immediately. In case it was private I took our cordless phone into a box room we hardly ever use and called Shannon from there. The connection wasn't too good, even with the phone antenna stretched as far as it would go, but at least we could hear each other.

"Shannon?" I said when she got on the phone.

'Kristy? Is that you?"

*Crackle, crackle.* (Static.) "Yeah. What's going on?"

"You sound as if you're calling from a tunnel."

"I'm on the cordless phone in the box room. David Michael made your phone message sound so mysterious I thought I'd better hide, just in case."

"Oh. Well, listen. You won't believe this. I forgot to get our post until really late this afternoon." (Shannon's parents both work, so it's up to Shannon and her sisters, Tiffany and Maria, to get the post after school. Sometimes nobody remembers until after *dinner*.) "Anyway, it was a lucky thing *I* got the mail, because there was an envelope in it for you."

"So?" I said, puzzled. "The postman stuck it in the wrong box."

"The postman didn't deliver it," said Shannon, with some satisfaction. "There's no stamp or postmark on it. There's not even an address. It just says 'Kristy', and there are heart and flower stickers all over it."

*Crackle, crackle.* "You're kidding," I said in a hushed voice.

"It looks like a love letter," Shannon added tantalizingly.

"A" (*crackle*) "me? No way. No one has" (*crackle*) "love" (*crackle*).

"Kristy, would you get out of that room or off that phone? I can't understand a word you're saying."

"I'm not leaving this room." (*Crackle*.)
"If my brothers hear about—"

"Kristy!" It was Mum calling me.

"Shannon, I've got to go. Can you" (*crackle*) "over after supper?"

"Can I bring the letter over after supper? Of course. I don't know how long I can stay, but I'm dying to know what's in this envelope. . . That is, if you'll let me see. You will let me see, won't you?"

"I suppose so." (*Crackle*.) "I mean, it'll de—" (*crackle*) "what the letter, or whatever it is, says. It might be very personal."

"KRISTY!" That time Sam was calling me. He's got the world's loudest voice. It's like a sonic boom.

"I really have to go now," I told Shannon. "See you later. And thanks."

Shannon and I hung up. I pushed down the antenna on the cordless phone, burst out of the box room, and flew into the kitchen. I knew I was late for dinner.

"Sorry," I said, as I slid into my place on the bench. (We eat at a long table with a bench at either side and Emily's high chair at one end.) "I *had* to talk to Shannon. She's going to come over after dinner. She won't stay long," I added quickly. "We've both got homework." We hadn't said that over the phone, but we always have homework, so why should that night have been any different?

Somehow, I got through dinner. I really

165

don't know how I did it. All I could think of was the envelope and the hearts and flowers.

I am not the hearts-and-flowers type.

At seven-thirty, our bell rang.

"I'll get it!" I screeched. I half expected Watson to say, "Indoor voice, Kristy," to me, which is what we have to say to Karen a lot. She tends to get noisy.

By now, David Michael was as curious as I was about what was going on. He'd taken the messages from Shannon. He knew I'd phoned Shannon from inside the box room, and now he saw that I couldn't *wait* for Shannon to come inside. So he was right next to me when I answered the door.

"Hi," I said breathlessly.

There stood Shannon. She's got thick, curly blonde hair (similar to Stacey's) and blue eyes, but I wouldn't call her gorgeous like Dawn or even attractive like Stacey. She's more . . . interesting-looking. I once heard someone say that being called "interesting" is practically a curse. It's the word people use when they don't want to say someone's ugly. But I don't agree. At least not in Shannon's case. She really *is* interesting-looking. She has high cheekbones, like that actress Meryl Streep, and wide eyes. Her lashes are very pale, but she's allowed to use make-up, so she puts on black mascara every morning. And she has a ski-jump nose, the kind that's almost too cute. (Shannon told me once that she wants a nose job – to straighten it out – but her parents say no. They aren't strict. They just think she should wait until she's an adult before she makes a decision like that.)

I let Shannon inside. She was still wearing her Stoneybrook Day School uniform. Shannon, Bart and about half the kids in our neighbourhood go to Stoneybrook Day School. Karen, Andrew and a lot of other kids go to another private school called Stoneybrook Academy. My brothers and I are practically the only kids around here who go to a state school.

"So?" I said eagerly to Shannon.

She pulled the envelope out of the pocket of her school uniform and handed it to me. I was so excited I could hardly breathe. Then I realized that David Michael was at my elbow.

"Let's go to my room," I said hastily. Shannon and I thundered up the stairs. David Michael was at our heels.

When we reached the door to my room and I realized that we were still a trio, I had to say, "David Michael, this is private. You can't come in." (I couldn't help being blunt. I was nearing hysteria.)

"But I want to know what's going on," he said.

"Maybe I'll tell you later," I replied. "*Maybe*. Anyway, this is girl stuff." I knew that would get him.

167

"*Girl* stuff. Gross. Forget it. I don't want to know after all."

I grinned at Shannon. David Michael had gone off like a shot.

Shannon and I darted into my room and I closed the door behind us. We flopped on to my bed, and I let the envelope dangle between my thumb and forefinger.

Then we examined the envelope together. The front said simply KRISTY. The word was typed but the "I" had been dotted with a tiny heart sticker. A flower sticker had been placed carefully in each corner of the envelope.

"Maybe it's not for me," I said. "It doesn't say 'Kristy Thomas'. It just says 'Kristy'."

"Well, there aren't any Kristy's at my house," Shannon replied. "And I can't think of any other Kristys in the neighbourhood – and I know practically everyone around here."

I turned the envelope over. On the back were more hearts and flowers. All I could do was stare at the envelope.

"Well, open it before I die!" cried Shannon.

I ripped the envelope open. Suddenly I felt shy. "Let me read it first," I said to Shannon. "It might be embarrassing."

Shannon understood. "Okay." She rolled over and closed her eyes.

I read the note inside. Compared to the

envelope, it was very plain. It was type-written (or maybe word-processed) on white paper. The note said, "Dear Kristy, I think you are beautiful. And you're the nicest girl I know. I would like to go steady with you. I wish I could tell you this in person. Love, Your Mystery Admirer."

I sat up. "Well, it's not too bad," I said. "Here." I handed the note to Shannon. "What do you think?"

Shannon read the note and smiled, saying, "You've got a *mystery* admirer! That is so romantic."

I was surprised. Shannon is almost as sophisticated as Stacey. She's had millions of boyfriends and gone out on plenty of dates. Plus she gets to wear make-up. It's hard to believe we're the same age. And here she was, all gooey over a little note.

"I bet it's Sam," I said. "It's one of his practical jokes."

"Why would he put the note in *our* letterbox?" asked Shannon.

"To throw me off the track," I replied. "That's why he couldn't use his own hand-writing."

"You are such a dweeb," she said. "You know it's from Bart."

"Bart! Why wouldn't Bart tell me those things in person?"

"They aren't so easy to say," Shannon told me. She sounded as if she was speaking from experience.

"But you just said I have a mystery admirer. Why are you so excited if you think you know who the mystery admirer is?"

"*Because.* It's still romantic."

"Okay. Then why are there hearts and flowers all over the envelope? Stacey McGill is the only person I know who dots 'I's' with hearts. Boys don't do that. This looks like it's from a girl."

"A girl who wants to go steady with you? Kristy, grow up. Bart just wanted to make the envelope look nice."

"All right. What about *this*? Why did Bart, who knows perfectly well where I live, put the envelope in your letterbox?"

Shannon frowned. "That one I can't answer. But anyway, who else would send you a note like this? Can you think of anyone?"

I couldn't. Except for Sam.

"Listen, I have to go," said Shannon. "I have a huge history exam next week. Why don't you phone Bart? Maybe he'll drop a hint about the note."

"Okay," I answered. I walked Shannon downstairs. Then I got on the phone in the kitchen. I thought that if I made another secretive call, it would arouse suspicion.

Bart's little brother answered the phone. When I asked for Bart, he yelled, "BART!" and dropped the phone and walked away.

"Sorry about that," said Bart. "We've got to work on Kyle's manners. What's up?"

"Not much," I replied. "How's the band?"

"It's fine. We still don't have a place to practise, though."

Bart and I talked for about fifteen minutes. We talked a lot about his band. Then we talked about a teacher at my school that I don't like much, and about a couple of other things.

But Bart didn't mention the mystery note and neither did I. When we got off the phone, I wasn't at all convinced that Bart was my mystery admirer, even if Shannon thought so. But if he wasn't, then who was?

# 5th
# CHAPTER

Tuesday

Today the Krushers held a practice, and
I was babysitting for the Perkins girls,
so I took them over to the field. Myriah
and Gabbie helped me push Laura in her
buggy. They are so good with their baby
sister -- and with each other. I don't see
too many brothers and sisters who are
as close as they are. It makes me wish
I had a sister.

Anyway, there's not much to say about
the afternoon. It was pretty uneventful
Kristy was in charge of the Krushers,
which included Myriah and Gabbie, so I
just sat with Laura. We sat in the shade
because it's not good for babies (or
anyone, really) to get too much sun.
Laura took a long nap while she slept,
I talked to Shannon, who had turned

172

up to watch softball practice. Then I
took the girls home. That's about it,
you lot!
  Oh, yeah -- Shannon is really nice.

What a day Tuesday was for me. Stacey's
afternoon was pretty tame, judging from
her notebook entry, but my whole day was,
well, surprising.

It started when I leaned out of our front
door very early in the morning to bring in
the newspaper and found another envelope
addressed to me. It was lying on the door-
mat, right next to the paper. (We have a
very accurate paper girl. She hits the front
steps every time. Either she has fantastic
aim, or she *walks* the paper to the door.)

I grabbed the paper and the note,
dropped the newspaper on the kitchen
table, and then ran to my room with the
envelope. I wasn't even dressed yet, but I
read the letter straight away, then thought
it over while I got ready for school.

The envelope wasn't as fancy as the first
one had been. It just said KRISTY on the
front, and the back flap was sealed with a
pink heart sticker. I sort of wished that the
"I" in my name had been dotted with a
heart again. Anyway, inside was another
typed note. This one said, "Dearest Kristy,
I can't stop thinking about you. Maybe
I'm in love with you. I don't know. I've

never been in love before. You are as beautiful as a snow-covered mountain. Love, Your Mystery Admirer."

Well, that last part was a little flowery (over-written, my English teacher would say), but I didn't care. I'm not sure anyone has ever called me beautiful, except maybe Mum, and that doesn't count, because all mothers say their children are beautiful.

Of course, I told my friends about the notes while we ate lunch in the canteen that day. And, like Shannon, they were all sure Bart was my mystery admirer. I seemed to be the only one with any doubts.

Okay, so I had got a letter in the morning. Imagine my surprise when I found *another* one in our postbox that afternoon. It said simply, "Dear Kristy, I love you, I love you, I love you. Love (get the picture?), Your Mystery Admirer."

I was floating on air by the time Shannon and I got to the ball field for the Krushers practice that day. And that was only the beginning of my excitement.

Stacey, meanwhile, went straight to the Perkinses' after school. She was greeted at the door by an exuberant Myriah and Gabbie. (Myriah is five-and-a-half and Gabbie is almost three. Guess what? Their family moved into our house when *we* moved into Watson's house!)

"Toshe me up, Stacey McGill! Toshe me up!" cried Gabbie. (That's Gabbie-talk for

174

"Pick me up and give me a hug.") So Stacey toshed her up. When she put her down, Myriah grinned and said, "I'm learning how to ride a bike with no stabilizers!"

She was very proud of herself.

A few minutes later, Mrs Perkins left.

"Ready for your Krushers practice?" Stacey asked Myriah and Gabbie.

"Yes!" they cried. They were wearing leggings, trainers and their special Krushers T-shirts.

"You need hats," Stacey reminded them. "You're going to be in the sun all afternoon." The girls dutifully found two old baseball caps, while Stacey tied a little pink hat on Laura and put her *very* distant fedora on her own head. Then they set off.

Gabbie and Myriah took turns helping Stacey push Laura's buggy. When they reached the practice field, the older girls ran to me. Stacey took Laura to a grassy spot under a tree and sat next to the buggy.

"Do you want to sit on my lap?" she started to say to the baby, when she realized that Laura was fast asleep. Well, thought Stacey, *this* will be an easy sitting job.

She was settling down with a book she'd brought along in case this happened, when I left my Krushers and ran over to her.

"Stacey!" I cried. "I got a *third* note this afternoon." I told her what it said, and Stacey just grinned.

"Hey, Kristy," a voice said.

Stacey peered around me and saw Shannon Kilbourne. She'd met Shannon a few times, so she knew her slightly. "Hi!" said Stacey.

"Hi," Shannon replied. "Listen, Kristy, your kids are getting a little restless. I think you ought to start the practice."

So I did. I left Shannon and Stacey together under the tree with Laura. I hoped they would talk. I wanted Shannon and the other BSC members to know each other better.

They did talk.

"I've never seen you at a Krushers practice before," said Stacey amiably to Shannon. (She checked on Laura, who was still asleep.)

"I usually don't have time to come," Shannon replied. "Just like I can't come to the Babysitters Club meetings. I'm either at school in the afternoons – I'm in a lot of clubs – or I have to watch Maria, my youngest sister, or I'm babysitting somewhere else. But today I'm *free*! So I thought I'd come and support the Krushers. A lot of the kids I sit for are on the team. Kristy's great with them."

"How old is Maria?" Stacey asked. "Is she on the team?"

"Maria's eight. And no, she's not on the team. She hates anything athletic. Can you believe it? She *likes* doing homework."

Stacey smiled. "I know someone like

that. Charlotte Johanssen. She's eight, too. But she's one of the Krushers cheerleaders, so she'll try athletic stuff sometimes. She's over there." (Stacey pointed.) "I love that kid. She's almost like a sister to me."

Practice had begun and it was going well, from the actual playing to the cheerleading. Jamie Newton even put his hand out when the ball sailed towards him instead of ducking. He didn't catch the ball, but at least he tried. Claire struck out and didn't have a tantrum. All in all, the kids on both of the teams into which I had divided the Krushers, hit very well. Plus, the two main pitchers, David Michael and Nicky Pike (one of Mal's brothers), were really improving.

When practice was over, Stacey and Shannon stood up and cheered, along with Charlotte, Vanessa and Haley.

"Good game," said Shannon to Stacey and Mal (who was sitting for the Kuhn kids).

I trotted over to my friends as the Krushers started to leave. "You know what?" I said breathlessly. "I think we could beat the Bashers again – even *without* handicaps."

"The kids are improving, that's for sure," said Stacey, as Gabbie and Myriah ran to her and checked on their little sister.

"Ooh, she's sleeping," said Gabbie in a hushed voice. "Quiet, everyone."

I could tell that Stacey and Shannon

and Mal wanted to laugh (I did), but instead we just lowered our voices.

"I'd better get going," said Shannon. "I'm supposed to cook dinner tonight."

"I'm glad you two had a chance to talk," I said.

"Me, too," replied Stacey. She smiled at Shannon. Then she left with the Perkins girls, Gabbie tiptoeing across the grass so as not to disturb Laura.

Later that afternoon, Stacey received a phone call from me.

"Hi," I said. "How was the rest of your sitting job?"

"Oh, fine. The girls were angels," Stacey reported. "Laura woke up on the way back and Myriah and Gabbie entertained her with songs until we reached their house. Mrs Perkins was already at home, so I left then."

"Well, guess what. Just as you lot were heading away from the field, Bart appeared. He walked me home again. And you'll never guess what we've decided to do."

"Elope?" said Stacey.

"No!" I was horrified.

"I was just kidding. I mean, because of the mystery admirer stuff."

"Oh. Well, anyway, we decided to hold a *World Series* between the Krushers and the Bashers."

"Really?"

"Yeah."

"How many games will you play?"

"Well, we had a bit of a row over that," I admitted. "I wanted to play three games, but Bart said one was enough for little kids. He thought three would be too much pressure, especially for kids like Claire Pike. I still don't agree with him, but I gave in. At least our row is over."

"*That's* good," said Stacey. "Did Bart give away anything about being your mystery admirer?"

"Not a thing. That's why I'm so sure he's not the one."

"But he *has* to be," said Stacey.

"You sound like Shannon."

"I can't help it. Bart makes the most sense." I started to tell her all the reasons why I knew Bart *wasn't* my mystery admirer, but I was tired of repeating them. Instead, I said, "I did something you won't believe."

"What?"

"I asked Bart to the Hallowe'en Hop at our school and he said he'd come." That announcement was greeted by such a long silence that I said, "Stacey. . . ? Stacey. . . ? Are you there?"

Finally she burst out laughing. "I'm here," she replied. "I really *can't* believe you did that! That's great. The Hop's coming up in just a couple of weeks – but you'll have to find something to wear, and do your hair and. . ."

Stacey was off and running. I think she was more excited than I was.

# 6th
# CHAPTER

"This," I said, "is completely gross." I poked at something yellowy-brown on the plate of food I'd just bought in the hot-lunch line in the school canteen.

"Then why," said Claudia, "did you buy the hot lunch? You could buy a sandwich or a salad, you know."

I shrugged.

Claud, Stacey, Mary Anne, Dawn, Logan and I were sitting at our usual table in the canteen. (Mal and Jessi eat during another period since they're not in our grade.)

"Besides," I said, stabbing the unrecognizable thing with my fork, holding it up, and letting it dangle in front of me, "I like winding Mary Anne up." I aimed my fork in her direction.

"Put it *down*!" shrieked Mary Anne, and Logan gave me a dirty look, which wasn't really very dirty.

"Of all the people at this table," said Dawn, "who would think that *she*" (Dawn pointed at me) "would have a mystery admirer?" Dawn looked as disgusted as Mary Anne.

"Or that she'd be the chairman of the BSC," added Stacey. "Kristy, either put that thing down or eat it."

I put it down. I certainly wasn't about to eat it.

We talked about babysitting for a while. Mary Anne said that prissy Mrs Prezzioso had actually bought Jenny a pair of trousers. Until now, it had been hard to distinguish Jenny from lace curtains. Then Dawn said that Matt Braddock was going to be in a play in his special school. The entire performance would be done in sign language. It was going to be a Hallowe'en play.

Hallowe'en reminded me of the Hallowe'en Hop, and we began to talk about who was going with whom, and who was just going to go and hope for the best. Mary Anne and Logan were going together, of course. Claudia was hoping that this boy, Woody Jefferson, would ask her. Stacey was trying to get up the nerve to ask a new boy in her English class to go with her, and Dawn said she would go alone.

"A lot of kids do that," she added defensively. Then she said that she thought I was really brave to have asked Bart. (By that time, everyone knew what I'd done. Secrets don't last long in the BSC.)

"Speaking of Bart," said Mary Anne. "Have you received any more notes?"

"Another one this morning!" I replied.

"And you didn't *tell* us?" cried Claudia. (You have to have a loud voice to be heard in our cafeteria.)

"Sorry," I replied. "It was the fourth one. I suppose I'm getting used to them."

"*Used* to them!" repeated Dawn, awed.

"Boy, if I had a mystery admirer who was sending me love letters—" Stacey began loudly.

"SHH! Keep your voice down!" I said.

"If I keep my voice down, you won't be able to hear me," replied Stacey.

That was true, but I had noticed that Cokie Mason and her snobby little crowd – Grace Blume and two other girls, Lisa and Bebe – were sitting at the next table. They were being awfully quiet.

"You lot," I whispered, and my friends leaned forward to hear me.

"Is this going to be girl talk?" Logan whispered back.

"Sort of," I replied.

"See ya." Logan stood up abruptly and left.

He hates it when our conversations become too "girlie".

"I brought the letters with me. Look." I spread the notes out on the table. I had even saved the envelopes because I liked the stickers on them.

Mary Anne, Dawn, Claud and Stacey huddled over the letters.

"'I love you, I love you, I love you,'" Mary Anne read. She sighed. "That is so, so romantic."

"Distant," added Claudia.

"But you don't really think they're from—" I stopped. We had an audience. The boys at one table were watching us with great curiosity, and at the next table, Cokie Mason was peering rudely at us. Then she turned to Grace and sniggered.

I put the letters away in a hurry.

"Don't pay any attention to Cokie and that lot," said Stacey.

"Yeah. They're probably jealous. I bet none of them has ever had a love note from a secret admirer," said Mary Anne.

"I wonder why the letters are all typed," Stacey was saying.

"SHH!" (I hissed it.) "I've already told you. It's so the mystery admirer can disguise his handwriting."

"Then they *must* be from Bart Taylor. Who else would *need* to disguise his writing?"

"Sam," I said.

Cokie and her friends got up then and left the cafeteria. They didn't even bother to clear the table they'd been sitting at.

"What pigs," I said.

As you can tell, we don't like Cokie and her group very much. And we have good reason not to.

"Remember Hallowe'en?" said Mary Anne, just as I was about to say the same thing. I suppose that's a sign of being best friends.

"Boy, do I ever," said Claudia.

"What? What happened at Hallowe'en?" asked Stacey. (She'd been back in New York then.)

"Mary Anne started getting these weird, threatening notes. Someone even sent her a bad-luck charm. And then, we really did have bad luck. We thought we were . . . well, I'm not sure what we thought," said Claudia falteringly, "but anyway, it turned out that Cokie and her friends were behind everything. They wanted to make us look like jerks, because they liked Logan and wanted him to hang around with them — not with jerks."

"So what happened?" asked Stacey.

"*We* made *them* look like jerks. And we did it in the middle of the graveyard at midnight on Hallowe'en."

"Don't ask what possessed us." Dawn giggled. "Get it? *Possessed* us?"

We laughed.

"I really don't know where we found the courage to do that, but we did," I said. "Mal and Jessi were with us. The BSC sticks together."

The five of us were silent for a few moments, thinking, I suppose, about Cokie and Logan and Hallowe'en. Then the bell rang. Lunch was over. *We* cleared our table before we left the cafeteria.

That afternoon I babysat for David Michael and Emily. As usual, Mum and Watson were at work, Charlie and Sam were at after-school sports, and Nannie had bowling practice. Nannie is in a senior citizens league. They play really well. Nannie even has a trophy in her bedroom.

Nannie is a character and I love her. We all do. Emily Michelle is particularly attached to her. In fact, she cried as she and David Michael and I stood at the front door and watched Nannie drive off in the Pink Clinker. (That's Nannie's old car, and it really is pink. Nannie had it painted pink on purpose because she likes the colour.)

"Come on, Emily," I said as I closed the door. "Nannie will be back soon. She has to practise her bowling."

"Yeah, you want her to be a champ, don't you?" asked David Michael.

"Biscuit," Emily replied pathetically.

"Boy, she certainly learns fast, doesn't she?" I said to my brother. "Okay, one biscuit, Emily. Just one."

"Can I have one, too?" asked David Michael. He made a sad face. "I miss Nannie. A biscuit will make me feel better."

I punched him playfully on the arm and he grinned.

The three of us were just finishing our snack when the doorbell rang. "I'll get it," I said. "David Michael, keep an eye on Emily, okay?"

My brother nodded.

I ran to the front door, opened it, and saw nobody. But a note was lying next to the mat. My heart began to pound. Another letter from my mystery admirer! I grabbed it and read it before I'd even closed the door. When I'd finished, my heart was still pounding, because this note was . . . weird. It said, "I love you, I love you, I love you, but beware. Love is fickle. So are friends. Watch out for your mystery admirer."

Of course I called Shannon immediately, praying that for once she'd be home after school and able to come over. She was and she did. While David Michael and Emily played and watched TV, Shannon and I discussed the note. We examined every angle. We read it and re-read it.

"I hate to admit it, but maybe I was wrong," said Shannon shakily. "This couldn't be from Bart. This note is sort of . . . *twisted.*"

"What if it *is* from Bart?" I asked. "Maybe he's gone mad."

"He's not mad! I go to school with him. I ought to know. Maybe somebody else sent it."

187

"No. It looks just like the others."

"How come you're so willing to believe Bart is your mystery admirer all of a sudden?" asked Shannon.

"I'm not. I mean, I don't know. But if he is, then I've invited a psycho to the Hallowe'en Hop."

# 7th CHAPTER

Saturday

Today Jessi and I sat for my brothers and sisters.
And, boy, is Hallowe'en in the air!

I'll say. That's all we heard about this afternoon.
But it was fun, wasn't it?

Yeah. I sort of wished I could still make a costume and go out trick-or-treating, collecting sweets.

You're off the track, Mal.

Oh, yeah. Anyway, the kids spent the entire afternoon on Hallowe'en projects. They're going to set up a haunted house in our basement.
And charge money for it, I might add.

Oh, well. But this will interest you, Kristy. Vanessa got an idea that involves the Krushers, their World Series and Hallowe'en....

189

Mallory and Jessi *did* have a good afternoon. It started just after lunch, as Jessi was arriving at Mal's house, and Mr and Mrs Pike were leaving.

Claire was running around with a clown mask on her face, calling everyone a silly-billy-goo-goo, when Margo said, "Maybe I'll be a clown for Hallowe'en this year."

"Oh, that's so ordinary," retorted Vanessa, who's nine and plans to be a poet one day.

"Well, what are *you* going to be?" asked Margo. (Margo is seven.)

"A poet," replied Vanessa in a superior voice.

"What does a poet look like?" wondered Nicky. (He's eight.) But he didn't wonder for long. "I'd better think of a costume," he added.

"We'd all better," said Byron, one of the ten-year-old triplets.

"I'm going to be a giraffe," said Claire.

"In your dreams," replied Jordan (another triplet). "How could you be a giraffe? How could you see? You'd have to stretch your neck out about ten feet to get your head under a giraffe mask."

Mal and Jessi laughed. They were sitting with the kids in the Pikes' TV room. The day was dreary and no one felt like going outside.

"I will wear the giraffe neck on my head," said Claire haughtily. "I'll make

190

little eyeholes in the neck so I can see out."

"You have to admit that's clever," said Adam, the third triplet.

The Pike kids looked impressed.

"I'm going to be a tramp this year," spoke up Nicky.

"Boring," said Jordan. "I'm going to be a mummy."

"I suppose no one's ever been a mummy before," said Mal, eyeing her brother.

Jordan made a face. Then he brightened. "I know. I'll be a *headless* mummy. Now *that's* original!"

"I wonder what I can do to look like a poet," mused Vanessa.

"Dress up like a pen?" suggested Margo.

"No, I want to look like a poet. I mean, a poetess." She paused. "Mallory? Do poetesses wear berets on their heads and look raggedy?"

"Nope. Those are starving artists," replied Mal.

The triplets began to rifle through the Pikes' box of dressing-up clothes and props. They pulled out hats and masks and a doctor's bag. Then Adam found a spool of thread. A simple spool of thread.

"What's that doing in there?" asked Jessi.

"I don't know," Adam answered, "but I've just had a *great* idea."

"What?" asked the others.

"Listen, we should make a haunted

house in our basement. We'll set it up on Hallowe'en – that's a Saturday – and during the day, kids can come through it. We'll have ghosts and moving things and lots of scary stuff. We can use the thread for cobwebs. We'll charge ten cents or maybe twenty-five cents each. Everyone will get their money's worth!"

"That," replied Jordan, "really *is* a great idea."

"Can we all help?" asked Nicky. (Sometimes the triplets do things on their own. And they often leave Nicky out, even though he's the only other boy in the Pike household.)

But— "Of course, you can all help," said Adam surprisingly. "We'll need lots of people. We'll need someone to answer the door and take kids down to the basement. We'll need someone else to lead each kid through the haunted house. And we'll need dressed-up people, like ghosts and *headless mummies* to walk around. Real people are scarier than fake ones."

"You know what else?" said Vanessa. (She was about to make a very un-Vanessa-like suggestion.) "There should be a part of the haunted house where we blindfold people. Then we make them put their hands in peeled grapes and cold spaghetti and stuff. We'll tell them the grapes are eyeballs and the spaghetti is brains. That'll really scare them!"

"Vanessa, you're a genius!" exclaimed Jordan.

"Not really," she replied modestly. "I saw it on TV."

"Well, anyway, we'll definitely do that," said Jordan.

"And we'll play a haunted-house sound effects tape," added Adam. "The kids will hear moaning and groaning and screaming and doors slamming and the wind howling and thunder and everything!" Adam was all worked up.

Claire looked a bit scared, but she covered up her feelings. She didn't want to be left out of the family project.

The Pike kids fell into silence. Their thoughts must have drifted from Hallowe'en, because the next thing that was said was, "Do you think we can really beat the Bashers?" (That was Nicky.)

"In the World Series?" asked Margo.

Nicky nodded. "What do you think, Mallory?"

"I don't know. You beat them before, but I think you'll have to try very hard not to be nervous during the big game."

"And the cheerleaders will try very hard to . . . to, um . . . to lead the Krushers to victory," said Vanessa dramatically. "Hey! I've got an idea. Since the World Series game will be played right before Hallowe'en, Charlotte and Haley and I should wear costumes. I mean, Hallowe'en costumes."

193

"That would be cool," said Nicky. Then he looked out of the window. "It isn't raining, Mallory. Can Claire and Margo and I practise catching and hitting in the back garden?"

"Of course," replied Mallory.

The kids split up then. The three younger ones went outside. The triplets began planning the spook house. And Vanessa got on the phone with her fellow cheerleaders to discuss costumes. She phoned Haley first.

"Hi, Haley. It's Vanessa. Listen, I've got this idea." She explained her plan to Haley, who must have liked it. Then she said, "What? A group of three? Oh, I see what you mean. All right. I'll think about it. You phone Charlotte, then call me back, okay?"

Vanessa hung up. She returned to the TV room, where Mallory was giving the triplets a hand with their haunted house. (Jessi had gone outdoors to help Claire, Margo and Nicky.)

"Haley says that cheerleaders should dress alike," Vanessa reported to Mal. "So we have to be the Three Somethings, only we don't know what."

"How about the Three Little Kittens?" suggested Adam, sniggering.

"Or the Three Little Pigs?" said Jordan.

"*No!*" cried Vanessa.

"They're just teasing you," Mal told her gently.

194

The phone rang then, and Vanessa dashed for it, crying, "That's probably Haley! I bet she and Charlotte have a good idea for our costumes."

"Big deal," muttered Adam.

A few moments later, Vanessa reappeared. "Charlotte and Haley are coming over."

"Great," said Jordan. "Just what we need. More girls."

"Enough," Mallory told him warningly.

The cheerleaders holed up in the bedroom that Mal and Vanessa share. They talked for almost an hour about costumes. At last they ran down to the TV room, looking very excited.

"We know what we're going to be! We know what we're going to be!" cried Charlotte, who doesn't usually get very noisy.

"What?" asked Mal, quite interested.

The girls looked at each other and grinned. Then they said in unison, "The Three . . . Stooges!"

Mal tried (successfully) not to laugh. "The Three Stooges?" she repeated.

"Yup," said Haley.

"*And*," added Vanessa, "we're going to go trick-or-treating together. The Three Stooges costumes will be for Hallowe'en, too. Now I don't have to worry about what a poetess looks like."

"Boy," said Adam enviously. "*We* should

have thought of that. The Three Stooges would be perfect costumes for triplets."

"You can be The Three Stooges, too, if you want," said Vanessa generously.

"No way!" exclaimed Jordan. "Not if the idea is already taken by *girls*."

The girls ignored Jordan's comment. They found the *TV Guide* and began looking through it to see if any Three Stooges programmes were going to be on soon. They wanted to copy the costumes of Larry, Moe and Curly. The triplets returned to their spook-house preparations.

In the back garden, Nicky yelled, "Home run! All *right*!"

The afternoon was, Mal and Jessi agreed, a fun one.

# 8th CHAPTER

At first, I couldn't work out why my friends were looking so astonished. Finally Mary Anne stood up and whispered in my ear, "The *clock*, Kristy."

It was Monday afternoon. The seven BSC members were gathered in Claud's bedroom. As usual, I was sitting in the director's chair, visor in place, pencil behind one ear. What had astonished everybody was that the clock had changed from 5:29 to 5:30 and then to 5:31 – and I hadn't said a word. I hadn't called the meeting to order. I was just sitting in the chair, staring into space.

"Oh. Oh, um. Order, everybody," I said hastily. I paused.

"Kristy, are you all right?" asked Stacey.

"Yeah. I just forgot to start the meeting, that's all."

"You forgot to tell me to collect subs,

197

too," said Stacey. "It *is* Monday. And what do you mean you forgot to start the meeting?"

"Oh, nothing. . . Stacey, it's subs day."

"No kidding." Stacey made us fork over. Then my friends just gaped at me.

"What?" I said.

"Well, what is *wrong*?" asked Mary Anne. "You've never sat by the clock and not noticed when it said five-thirty."

"Yeah. Maybe you shouldn't be chairman after all," teased Dawn.

I tried to laugh, but it was an effort.

"Kristy?" said Claud. "Come on. Get on with it."

I sighed. "Okay. I was too embarrassed to tell you all this, but I've received four more notes from the mystery admirer."

"So? You weren't embarrassed about the first fifty or so notes," said Stacey, smiling. I could tell she was trying to get me to smile, too.

"The last four notes," I began, "have been . . . weird."

Everyone immediately looked interested, and I could tell that we weren't going to have a normal meeting.

"What did the notes say?" Jessi wanted to know.

"Well, the first one wasn't *so* bad. Just a bit odd," I replied. "It said, 'I love you, I love you, I love you. But beware. Love is fickle and so are friends'. Or something like that. Then the second note said, 'Violets are blue, blood is red, I'll remember you when you are dead'."

"*What*?" screeched all my friends.

"Yup. That's *exactly* what that note said. I'll never forget it. Then the third note was about, let's see, blood again, but I didn't memorize that one. And anyway, today, just before Charlie drove me to the meeting, I got this note."

I pulled a piece of paper out of my pocket. My friends jumped up and leaned over me, peering at the note. They surrounded my chair, and I felt smothered.

"Ugh," said Stacey. She took the paper from me and read aloud. "I want to be with you for ever – eternal togetherness. So I am coming to get you."

"Aughh!" shrieked Mary Anne. "He's coming to *get* you?"

"*Now* are you all so sure the notes are from Bart?" I asked.

"No," replied everyone else.

"They must be from Sam," added Claudia.

"That's what I said in the first place and no one listened to me!" I cried. "Now that the notes are weird, you think they're from my brother after all. But even Sam wouldn't go this far. I know him and his jokes too well. He'd stop after about two notes and find some way to let me know he was behind them. Sam likes to take credit for his work and he can't wait very long for it."

"Well, who *are* the notes from then?" Mal wondered. (Everyone was settling back into their places.) "They can't be from Bart."

"I'm not so sure," I replied. "Maybe he's really twisted or something. I read this book once about a fourteen-year-old boy everyone thought was really normal and nice, and it turned out he was . . . a cold-blooded killer."

"Kristy!" exclaimed Stacey. (She sounded like my mother.)

"Well, that's what the book was about."

"Was it a true story?" asked Stacey.

"No," I answered. "But it could have been."

Stacey looked as if she were about to say, "See?"

"Before you say anything," I rushed on, "remember the notes. They're real. *Someone* is sending them."

The room was quiet. No one knew what to say. I felt that I had to remind my friends about one small point.

"I invited Bart to the Hallowe'en Hop, don't forget," I said.

"Aughh!" shrieked Mary Anne again. "You're going with a psycho!"

"Oh, my lord," whispered Claudia.

"Now just a second," said Mallory calmly, "you don't *know* that the notes are from Bart."

"I don't know that they *aren't* from Bart, either," I pointed out, "and I don't want to take any chances."

"What are you saying?" asked Dawn.

"I'm thinking of un-inviting Bart to the Hop."

"Oh, Kristy!" exclaimed Stacey.

But the phone rang before she could go on. (I'd almost forgotten that we were having a club meeting.)

We took the calls that came in for the next few minutes, arranging jobs with the Rodowsky boys, the Kuhns, the Perkinses and Jenny Prezzioso.

Then Stacey immediately said, "Kristy, you can't un-invite Bart to the dance, especially when you don't even know if the notes are from him. I think you should confront him. Ask him straight out if he's your mystery admirer, and if he is, why he would write such awful things." She shivered. "I can't help thinking about that 'I'll remember you when you are dead' poem. That gave me the creeps."

"Think how *I* feel!" I said. "And anyway, I don't know about confronting him. Would *you* confront a psycho?"

"You don't know for sure if he *is* the psycho. I mean, *a* psycho," said Jessi. "I believe in giving a person the benefit of—"

"Wait a second!" I cried. "Oh, no! Oh, *no*! I've just thought of something. You made me think of it, Jessi. You said, 'A psycho'."

"So?" said Jessi, and the rest of my friends looked puzzled.

"What," I began, "if the notes aren't from Bart or Sam or anyone else we can think of? What if they *are* from just 'a psycho'?"

"Well—" Stacey started to say.

But I carried on going. "Don't forget. I'm rich. I mean, I'm Watson Brewer's stepdaughter, and Watson is a millionaire. What if some weirdo out there is playing a cat-and-mouse game and then, when he's ready, he's going to pounce on me?"

My friends looked more puzzled than ever.

"*Kid*nap me," I explained. "He's going to scare me to death, then kidnap me and ask Watson for the ransom money. Watson could afford to pay the ransom, and he'd do it. I'm sure he would."

"You know," said Mal, "we've just read this short story in English. It was by an author named O Henry, and it was called 'The Ransom of Red Chief'. In it, these men kidnap a little boy, only it turns out that the boy is such an awful child his parents don't want him back, so they refuse to pay the ransom and the kidnappers are stuck with the boy."

Jessi, Dawn and Mary Anne sniggered. Claud and Stacey managed not to snigger, but even they couldn't keep from smiling.

"Come on, you lot. This is serious," I said. "I *have* been getting notes, Watson *is* rich and things like this *do* happen – and not just on TV either. They happen in real life. Where do you think the TV script-writers get their ideas from?"

That shut everyone up and stopped the smiling.

But then Stacey, our sceptic, said, "Oh, Kristy, this really *is* ridiculous. No one's going to kidnap you."

"Convince me," I said.

My fellow BSC members looked every-where but at me.

"The notes said he was coming to get me." I reminded my friends.

"*One* note said that," Mary Anne pointed out. "*One* note."

"I'm not convinced," was my only reply.

Later that night, I sat in my room and tried to do my homework. Needless to say, I couldn't concentrate. I couldn't think of my room as just a room. It had become a room in a *mansion*. And Watson wasn't just my stepfather, he was a *millionaire*.

I abandoned my homework. I got up from my desk, took all the notes out of their hiding place between the pages of *The Cat Ate My Gymsuit*, and spread the notes on my bed in the order in which I'd received them. I examined the paper, the typing, the stickers, the envelopes.

They were definitely the work of a lunatic. But he was *not* going to get me.

I jumped up. I ran from window to window in my room and made sure they were shut and locked. I checked the lock on my door. It worked, too. Mum and Watson tell my brothers and sisters and me not to lock our doors at night because it's a fire hazard, but I would have to risk that. I thought there was a better chance of getting kidnapped than of Watson's house (excuse me, his mansion) burning down. Why did Mum have to marry a millionaire?

Then I thought of something horrible. A lunatic could get into my room through one of the windows even if it was locked. He'd simply wrap some cloth around his hand, punch through a pane of glass, reach in and unlock the window from the inside, and open it. Of course, I'm on the second floor, but the kidnapper could climb a ladder. He could be quiet. And in the dead of night, who would notice him?

I was trying to figure out how to board up my windows when something else occurred to me: the kidnapper could get me *any* time. He could get me walking to my house from the bus stop or on my way into school or to a babysitting job. I decided that I should try to be with people as much as possible. If I wasn't alone it would be harder to kidnap me.

Should I tell Mum and Watson about

the danger I was in? I wondered. No. They might think I was crazy.

I turned on my radio. I needed to listen to reports of missing lunatics. As far as I knew, there were no asylums around Stoneybrook, but who knows what a psycho is capable of?

I tuned in just in time for the news. I heard about the President's press conference; a plane crash; a kid who was raising money to help fight drug abuse by running all the way from Connecticut to New York City, and I heard the sports and weather reports.

But the newscaster didn't say a word about a missing lunatic.

Okay, so he wasn't an escaped lunatic. He was a *new* lunatic, one who hadn't been caught yet.

I didn't finish my homework that night.

# 9th
# CHAPTER

Two days later I told Shannon my lunatic theory. She thought *I* was a lunatic for having come up with it. In fact, she had a new theory.

"I think," said Shannon, who had either read or heard about every single note I'd received, "that Bart is the note writer."

"But you said he couldn't be. You said you go to school with him and you know him and—"

"I know what I said, but listen. I think Bart's afraid your Krushers are going to beat his Bashers in the World Series, so he's trying to freak you out. He's trying to drive you crazy so you won't be a good coach and the Krushers will play badly and lose."

I was incensed. Especially considering that Shannon and I were on our way to the ball field for a game against the Bashers. (As we walked along, I kept my eye out for

206

slow-driving, suspicious-looking cars.)

Walking ahead of us were David Michael, the Papadakis kids and a couple of other Krushers from our neighbourhood. They were laughing and talking, paying no attention to Shannon and me.

"Well, if that's what Bart is doing, that's really . . . that's really *despicable*!" I exclaimed. (That was the worst thing I could think of to say.)

"I know," said Shannon. "I agree. I refused to speak to him at school today."

"Thank you," I told her.

The thought that the notes might be from Bart after all did two things for me. One, it made me less worried about a lunatic being after me, and two, it made me incredibly angry – which was good. The more angry I am the more energy I have, and the more energy I have, the better I coach the Krushers. We were going to beat the Bashers that day.

"You know what else is wrong with your lunatic theory?" asked Shannon as we reached the playing field.

"What?" I replied, even though I was tired of hearing about all the things wrong with my theory.

"If a psycho really did want ransom money, why wouldn't he kidnap Karen or Andrew? They're Watson's own children, and they're smaller and easier to capture."

I just made a face. I didn't like the way

Shannon had implied that "real" children are more important than stepchildren. And I didn't like to think about Karen or Andrew being kidnapped.

Shannon didn't see my face, though. She had spotted Mary Anne and Dawn. They were sitting under a tree. Dawn had brought the Braddock kids to the ball field (Matt as a player, Haley as a cheerleader), and Mary Anne had just come along to cheer the Krushers on. Shannon ran over to them and they began to talk. I almost joined them, but I was a little angry with Shannon for making those comments (even though I knew she hadn't meant to hurt me or upset me). Besides, the Krushers were excited and ready to begin the game, and the Bashers were nearby, looking tough.

I caught Bart's eye (he was surrounded by his team) and he grinned at me, but I just looked away. How could he smile at me like that?

The game began. The Krushers were up to bat first, and I'd placed Matt Braddock in the number-one spot in the line-up. He may be deaf, but he's one of our best hitters.

The Bashers pitcher wound up and slammed a ball to Matt.

*CRACK!*

Matt hit the ball with such force that I thought it would break a window at Stoneybrook Elementary. But it hit the ground first. An outfielder scrambled after it.

208

Meanwhile, Matt was running bases and had lost sight of the ball. He hesitated at third base.

Nicky Pike signed something to him frantically and Matt frowned. He stayed where he was, looking completely confused. A few seconds later, the third baseman was holding the ball triumphantly, and Haley Braddock had her head in her hands.

"What's wrong?" I asked her.

"Nicky was signing, 'Swim! Swim!' to Matt. I think he meant to sign, 'Run, run'. Matt could have made a home run, but he didn't know what was going on."

No wonder Matt had looked confused, I thought. Then I said to Haley, "Will you explain things to Matt later? Tell him it wasn't his fault and I'm not angry. I'll talk to Nicky. I think he needs a refresher course in sign language from you, Haley."

Next up to bat was Claire Pike. She is not a good hitter, and I wanted to get her turn out of the way as quickly as possible. Claire surprised me, though. I think she surprised herself too. Her bat connected with the first ball pitched and sailed away from her.

She hesitated for a fraction of a second, then took off for first base.

But – *SWOCK!* The pitcher caught Claire's ball as it whistled by.

"One out!" called the referee.

Claire immediately threw a tantrum. "Nofe-air! Nofe-air!"

I let Nicky and Vanessa calm her down and sent Jake Kuhn up to bat. He struck out. Two outs. Matt stood on third base with his hand on his hip, looking disgusted and disappointed. I couldn't blame him.

Jackie Rodowsky was up next. He swung and missed twice before getting a hit. But it was a low grounder, and the pitcher scooped the ball up and tossed it to the catcher, who got it just before Matt slid home. Three outs.

Matt looked like he was ready to kill someone, or maybe a lot of someones. First his chance at a home run had been ruined, then his chance to score.

"Don't worry," I said calmly to my team before they headed, discouraged, to the field. "The score is still nil to nil. Nicky, you're pitching. See if you can keep the game scoreless. The rest of you, just play your best."

Nicky did not, unfortunately, manage to keep the game scoreless. By the end of the first inning, the score was three–nil, in favour of the Bashers.

"Come on, everyone," I said cheerfully to the Krushers as the teams changed places again. "I know you can earn some runs this time. I can *feel* it. Now get out there and give it your best."

"Okay, Kristy Thomas," said Gabbie Perkins.

210

(I am always amazed at how the Krushers just keep on going. Sometimes they're disappointed or Claire throws a tantrum, but for the most part, the kids cheer each other on, don't begrudge anybody anything, and are understanding of each other and their shortcomings. Still, they must have been upset at the prospect of losing to the Bashers, after finally beating them, especially with the World Series just around the corner.)

The Krushers dutifully got into the batting order, though, and Buddy Barrett stepped up to the plate. He was nervous but trying not to show it.

The Basher pitcher wound up and let fly a fastball.

Buddy was prepared. *THWACK.* The ball sailed through the air – but it was out of bounds.

And it hit Shannon on the head.

"OW!" she shrieked.

She and Dawn and Mary Anne had seen the ball coming towards them and, in trying to duck, had got in each other's way. Shannon hadn't been able to avoid the ball.

"I'm sorry! I'm sorry!" Dawn and Mary Anne cried.

"I'm sorrier!" That was Buddy. He and I and a whole group of kids had run over to Shannon.

"Are you all right?" everyone kept asking.

"I think so," Shannon replied, patting her head cautiously. (This is why we play *softball*.)

"Are you *really* all right?" asked Buddy anxiously.

"Yes, I really am." Shannon smiled at Buddy, and he looked back at her with what can only be called love.

Bart had run over to us by this time, along with some of his team-mates.

"Are you okay, Shannon?" he asked, genuinely concerned. (Shannon was rubbing her head, even though she was smiling at Buddy.)

Shannon didn't answer Bart. She didn't even look at him. (Neither did Mary Anne or Dawn. I had a feeling Shannon had told them her suspicions about Bart.) And I focused on Shannon, feeling only mildly sorry for Bart.

When Shannon had convinced us that she really was fine (or was going to be) and had even asked to keep the ball with which she'd been hit, the assembled Krushers and Bashers finally returned to their game. Buddy lingered for a moment, though, received another smile from Shannon, then ran to catch up with his team.

The rest of the game went about the same way as the first inning. The Krushers simply weren't a match for the Bashers that day, no matter how hard they tried, and no matter how loudly the cheerleaders shouted. In the end, the Bashers beat the Krushers ten–one, and that one run was suspect, but the Bashers "gave" it to us, since they already had eight runs at the time and the game was nearing its end.

When the game was over, Bart trotted up to me and said, "Good game, Kristy. You've coached your kids well."

I glared at him. How could he try to psyche me out, then be so nice to me? Bart looked confused, but I pretended not to notice, and when he asked if he could walk me home, I thanked him but said I was busy. Then I joined Shannon, Dawn and Mary Anne.

They were talking about Bart and the letters.

"Maybe," Dawn began, "he's not trying to psyche you out for the World Series. Maybe he's annoyed with you because of that row you two had over how the series should be played. The weird letters started after the fight, didn't they?"

I nodded.

"And you know how boys hold grudges," said Shannon, sounding wise.

I shrugged. "Either way, what he's doing is wrong."

My friends agreed.

Then I had to leave. I had to help the Krushers with their equipment, see that everyone got picked up, and finally help Charlie load the car. He drove Karen,

Andrew, David Michael and me home, and I tried not to feel too depressed.

What had I got myself into? I was still supposed to go to the Hallowe'en Hop with Bart, and Bart was either crazy or malicious. (*If* he was the note writer. If he wasn't, I didn't want to think about who was.) Anyway, I had to decide whether to un-invite Bart to the dance.

Later, I was in the middle of trying to work out how to do that, not having had much experience with boys, when our phone rang. Of course, it was Bart. Great.

I didn't even bother to sneak into the box room with the cordless phone. I just took the receiver from Mum, who had answered the extension in the kitchen and said, "Hi, Bart. I'm sorry but I can't talk to you now," and hung up.

As I returned the receiver to the cradle, I could hear him saying, "Hey, Kristy," but I didn't feel too bad. Not when I thought about his notes.

However, it took me a long time to fall asleep that night.

# 10th
# CHAPTER

Tuesday

This afternoon, I baby-
sat for Buddy, Suzi and
Marnie Barrett. Since the
World Series is coming
up, it was off to the
playing fields for a
Krushers practice. Buddy
and Suzi were really
excited, especially since
they had got a tiny
Krushers T-shirt for their
little sister to wear. I
put it over Marnie's
sweater, (the weather was
too cool for just a
T-shirt) set her in her
buggy, and we were off.

Guess what. Buddy confessed that he has a crush on Shannon! Suzi teased him about that — but only until he threatened to tell on something she'd done. Apparently, Suzi has committed some sort of household crime which only Buddy knows about, and he's holding it over her, using it to keep her in line, or else waiting for just the right moment to let it fly.

Anyway, Marnie was an angel during practice. She was very interested in Laura Perkins, who slept next to us in her buggy while Mysiah and Gabbie played softball. (Claud was sitting for the Perkinses.) And the Krushers' poor practice didn't dampen Buddy's spirits because... Shannon was there again!

When Mary Anne arrived at the Barretts', she found them organized, for once. Or maybe they're generally more organized now. Anyway, they were a far cry from the way Dawn Schafer used to find them when she first began sitting for them. The children were dressed and ready for softball practice, Mrs Barrett was ready to leave but wasn't in one of her mad dashes, their house was tidy, and Pow the dog had even been walked.

"Goodbye, you three," said Mrs Barrett when she'd put on her coat. She kissed Buddy (who's eight), Suzi (who's five) and Marnie (who's two), wished Buddy and Suzi good luck at practice, and left.

"Well," said Mary Anne, "let's get going. We should leave now if you want to be at the ball field on time."

"Okay," said Buddy. He looked at Suzi. "Do you want to get it or should I?"

"I will!" Suzi cried.

Mary Anne had no idea what they were talking about, but she didn't have to wait long to find out. Suzi returned in a flash, holding something behind her back. She whipped it out and held it up proudly.

"It's a Krushers T-shirt for Marnie!" said Buddy.

"Yeah. She comes to almost all the games. She *needs* one," added Suzi.

So Mary Anne, smiling, put the shirt on over Marnie's sweater, checked to make sure everyone was wearing a hat, and led the kids out the back to the garage, where Marnie's buggy was kept.

They set off, Buddy and Suzi chattering away, and Marnie pointing at things and crying out, "Doggie! *Big* doggie!" and, "Smell flowers, Mary Anne," and "Play ball!" which made everyone laugh, because she had said it just like a sports presenter.

Then they fell into a silence, which was broken by Buddy saying tentatively, "I wonder if that girl will be there again."

"What girl?" asked Mary Anne.

"He means *Shan-non*," Suzi answered in a singsong voice.

Buddy blushed. "I hit her on the head at our last game and she wanted to keep the ball, just like a real fan."

"*Oh*," said Mary Anne, remembering.

"*Buddy li-ikes Shannon, Buddy li-ikes Shannon*," sang Suzi.

"Want to make something of it?" asked Buddy, not denying the charge.

"*Buddy and Shannon, sitting in a tree—*" Suzi began.

Buddy grabbed her arm. "Cut it out!" he yelled. "Or I'll tell Mary Anne *and* Mum about the . . . you know."

Suzi was instantly quiet.

The rest of the walk to the ball field was quiet, but Mary Anne had a feeling that everyone (except Marnie) was thinking about or wondering about whatever Suzi had done. Mary Anne felt it wasn't her business to pry, though.

At the playing field, everyone oohed and ahhed – first over Marnie in her T-shirt, and then over the cheerleaders. They'd got their costumes together and were wearing them. They'd even managed to find wigs that matched The Three Stooges' hair.

A few kids laughed, but Charlotte, Vanessa and Haley didn't care. Their costumes were funny and they knew it.

"*We* ought to pep you lot up," said Haley to the Krushers, and the Krushers agreed.

Everyone was in a good mood. I sensed that as soon as I set foot in the grounds of Stoneybrook Elementary. David Michael was with me. He had been talking non-stop about the World Series, which was fast approaching. Then there were Vanessa, Haley and Charlotte in their funny outfits, and Marnie Barrett in her little Krushers T-shirt.

I was probably the only one who wasn't entirely ready for the game. I still didn't know what to do about Bart and the dance, and then, when I was leaving the house for practice, I found another note on our front steps. Thank goodness David Michael was still inside, looking for his mitt. I didn't want him to see what I'd found.

The new note said, "Beware. I'm coming sooner than you think. And once I find you, this is all that will be left of

Kristin Amanda Thomas." I looked in the envelope and saw . . . fingernail clippings.

Oh, yuck! I almost dumped them out, but decided I might need them for evidence at some point.

"Hey, Kristy!" called David Michael then, and I thrust the envelope in the back pocket of my jeans.

"What?" I yelled back.

"I can't find my mitt."

So we had to have a mitt-search before we could leave for the ball field.

By the time we reached Stoneybrook Elementary, I was tired. David Michael and I had a fair amount of equipment to carry and no one to help us, although Charlie had said he'd pick me up after practice. So we had to carry everything ourselves. Besides being tired, my mind wasn't on the game. It was on Bart, the school dance and the notes, especially the one I'd just received. So, despite The Three Stooges cheerleaders, practice did not go very well. But it was not entirely my fault.

Even though my Krushers were their usual enthusiastic selves, they just didn't play well. Jackie Rodowsky kept tripping when he ran to bases. Jamie Newton began ducking balls again. David Michael's pitching was not up to par.

I gathered the Krushers together after two innings of mistakes. "Listen, everyone," I said, "remember the basics, okay?

All the old stuff. Pay attention to what you're doing. Keep your eye on the ball. Don't swing at wild pitches. And no fancy stuff. Concentrate on the game, not on stealing bases, okay?"

"O-kay!" chanted the Krushers.

"Do you need a break before we continue our game?"

"Maybe just a little one," replied Myriah.

"All right," I said. "Take ten."

I walked over to the trees, where Mary Anne and Claudia were sitting with Marnie Barrett, Laura Perkins . . . and Shannon!

"Hi," I said wearily, and then added, to Shannon, "When did you get here? I thought you were busy this afternoon."

"Our hockey practice was cancelled," she replied.

"Well, I'm glad you came to watch us," I told her.

"Me, too," said a voice from behind me.

It was Buddy Barrett, gazing adoringly at Shannon. (I had no idea what was going on then, because I hadn't read Mary Anne's notebook entry yet.)

"Hey, Buddy," I said, "could you go and give Jackie some hitting tips?"

"Okay," he replied, looking both pleased and disappointed. (Disappointed at not being able to stay with Shannon, I imagine.)

"Is anything wrong?" Mary Anne asked me.

I nodded. "Yeah. This." I pulled the

envelope out of my pocket and showed my friends the latest note.

Their reaction was nearly the same as mine had been:

"Gross!" (Claudia)

"Repulsive!" (Mary Anne)

"Disgusting!" (Shannon)

After that, no one knew what to say, but I had a feeling we were all wondering the same thing. Would Bart *really* do something so gross, repulsive and disgusting?

"Well," I said, "back to the game. Cheer us on, everyone."

The Krushers returned to their practice. The third inning began. And on David Michael's first pitch, Buddy Barrett swung and hit the ball with a loud *crack!* I saw Mary Anne, Claudia and Shannon duck and cover their heads. But they didn't need to worry. The ball sailed into the outfield. Buddy had hit a double.

"Yea!" cheered Shannon.

And that was the end of our good luck. Jake Kuhn fouled out. David Michael's pitching went downhill. Then Jackie hit a double himself, but tripped and fell just as he was approaching second base.

"Out!" yelled Nicky Pike.

At least Buddy made it home.

The cheerleaders went wild. "Who are the greatest? Who are the greatest?" they yelled, jumping up and down. "The Krushers, the Krushers! Yea!"

By the time they had finished, all their wigs had fallen off, and Vanessa's trousers were practically down by her knees.

"Vanessa!" hissed Haley, aghast.

"I know, I know." Vanessa tugged desperately at her trousers.

"I suppose we'll have to work a little harder on our costumes," said Charlotte.

After another inning, I called a halt to practice. Nothing was being accomplished. Margo Pike was in the outfield, blowing on blades of grass and staring into space. David Michael was paying more attention to a scrape on his elbow than to his pitching. Buddy had eyes only for Shannon, and even I wasn't concentrating. Not on the game, anyway, but I certainly couldn't keep my mind off the notes.

Mary Anne rounded up Buddy and Suzi and set off for the Barretts'. Suzi seemed gloomy as they walked along, but Buddy was in seventh heaven.

"Did you hear how Shannon cheered for me?" he asked.

"Buddy and Shannon, sitting in a tree—" sang Suzi.

"Suzi, one more word and I'll tell about the. . ."

"Okay, okay, okay."

Mary Anne smiled – then remembered the fingernail clippings and stopped her smiling abruptly.

# 11th CHAPTER

After our disastrous practice, Bart once again appeared in the schoolyard and asked to walk me home. And once again, I went home with Charlie instead.

"What's the *matter* with you?" Bart called after me as I climbed into the car. "Why won't you *speak* to me? Why won't *Shannon* speak to me? Girls are. . ."

His voice faded away as we drove off.

"Why *won't* you speak to Bart?" Charlie wanted to know, glancing at me in the rearview mirror and frowning.

But I wouldn't answer him, either.

And that night, when Bart called, I said to Sam, "Tell him I've gone to Europe," which Sam did with a certain amount of glee. Telling Bart I'd gone to Europe was as satisfying as a prank call for Sam. Considering all this, you can imagine how surprised I was when the doorbell rang the next afternoon, and who should I find on our front steps but Bart.

"Bart!" I exclaimed.

"Can I come in?" he asked seriously.

"I suppose so," I replied. Nannie was at home. Sam, too. I wasn't babysitting, and it's a lot easier to hang up on somebody (or get your brother to tell him you've gone to Europe) than it is to slam a door in his face.

Bart stepped inside and I closed the door behind him. "We have to talk," he said. "In private. Where can we go?"

"My room, I suppose," I answered with a sigh. I went to the kitchen, told Nannie that Bart was here and we were going to my room to talk, then led him upstairs. This felt weird. Bart had only been inside my house a few times, and he'd certainly never been inside my room. I fervently hoped that I hadn't left any underwear lying around and that my room was at least reasonably neat. (I'm not exactly a slob, but if anybody were ever asked to list ten things that describe me, the word *neat* would not come to mind.)

I walked into my room ahead of Bart and was relieved to see that it was presentable. (There might have been some underwear under the bed, but Bart would never know.) I looked round to see who should sit where, and decided that I should sit in my desk chair and Bart should get the armchair.

"So?" he said, trying to fold his tall body into the small chair.

"So?" I countered.

"Kristy, what . . . is . . . going . . . on?" he said in a measured voice.

"I think you know."

"I do not. If I knew, I wouldn't be here now."

"You certainly are a good liar," I said bluntly.

"*Liar!* I'm not lying. I don't know what's going on and I want you to tell me. Either you or Shannon. But you're the one I'm supposed to be going to a dance with," said Bart. He looked angry and I began to feel afraid. First of all, I'd never seen him this angry. Second, it probably wasn't a good idea to get a lunatic angry. I was glad that Nannie and Sam were at home.

But I didn't let Bart see my fear. "Okay. You want to know what's going on? I'll show you what's going on." I marched over to my bookshelf, pulled out *The Cat Ate My Gymsuit*, and removed the notes from between the pages. Then I spread them out across the bed. "There. That's what's going on – as if you didn't know."

Bart looked at the first few notes – the love letters – and reddened.

"So you did write them," I said.

"Yeah," admitted Bart. "Only I didn't write this many." He frowned and read the rest of the notes. When he was finished, he looked at me with horror. "You think *I* wrote these notes to you?" He peered into

226

the envelope containing the fingernail clippings. "You think I *sent* these to you? How could you think that? And *why* would I do this?"

"I – I don't—" I stumbled over my words. "To scare me so the Krushers would lose the World Series?" I suggested feebly.

"That's crazy!" Bart was almost shouting.

"SHHH!" I hissed.

"Well, it is crazy," said Bart, lowering his voice. "It's the craziest thing I can think of. If we play, we play fair and square." He paused. Then he asked, "Does Shannon know about these letters? Is that why she hasn't been speaking to me?"

I nodded. (I thought Bart would explode.) "Well, you did send some of the letters," I pointed out.

"Yeah, the – the, um – the *nice* ones," agreed Bart. I was melting. Bart *really liked* me. But he was still angry.

"Listen," I said, "I'm sorry for accusing you of sending the notes, especially in order to frighten me" (I didn't mention that that had been Shannon's idea), "but it was easier to believe that than to believe. . ."

"To believe what?" asked Bart curiously.

"That some lunatic was sending them. I'm afraid someone's going to kidnap me and ask Watson for the ransom money. I mean, the note does say he's going to get me. And then he keeps talking about death."

Bart sighed. "I can see why you'd be scared," he said, "but I still can't believe that *you* would believe that *I* would . . . oh, forget it."

For a few seconds Bart and I just looked at each other. I felt so confused. Finally I said quietly, "Thank you for the first notes. I liked them a lot. That's why I saved them."

"Really?" said Bart.

"Yeah. I did. I've never had" (I almost said *love letters*) "I've never had notes like those before. I felt . . . I don't know how I felt. But I know I'll never throw those letters away."

Bart smiled. "That's how I wanted you to feel. You're really special, Kristy." (I know I blushed.) Then he asked, "What about the other letters?"

"Why did I keep them, too?"

"No, I mean *what about* them? Where did they come from? Who sent them? What do they mean?"

I was relaxing. Even though I didn't have the answers to Bart's questions, I felt as if things were falling into place. Bart had written the love letters. That made sense. Then someone else had written the scary letters.

"I don't know," I told Bart. "Shannon and I have read the letters a million times and we can't come up with anything."

Bart leaned over. Just as I had done so

often, he read all the horrible letters to himself again. He even murmured the poem aloud, shivering at the "I'll remember you when you are dead" part.

"See why I'm afraid they're from a lunatic?" I said.

"Well, I can see why they frighten you, but a *lunatic*? I don't know, Kristy. That sounds like—"

"Don't say, "That sounds like something you'd see on TV.""

"Okay, I won't. . . But it does."

I sighed. "I know. Still, I haven't got any better ideas."

"Got any enemies?" asked Bart.

I shook my head slowly. "I don't think so. Not unless you count Alan Gray, but he's too much of a dweeb to think up something like this."

"Who's Alan Gray?"

"A jerk. A boy at school who's been a pest all his life and will probably remain that way into adulthood."

Bart laughed. "But he wouldn't do this?" He pointed to the letters.

"No. I don't think so. It takes brains to do that."

"What about Sam?"

It was my turn to laugh. "Poor Sam," I said. "Everyone fingers him as a likely suspect. He's going to have trouble living down his reputation. Shannon thought the notes were from Sam, my friends at school thought they were from him. Even *I* thought the first ones were from him, before I could believe that any boy would like me enough to send me lo – to send me notes like those," I said.

"Hmm," said Bart, looking deep in thought. "Kristy, how many people know about the notes?"

"Well, let's see. Just Shannon, my friends in the Babysitters Club, and now you. Oh, and David Michael was here when Shannon brought the first letter over. It was in her postbox for some reason."

"Oh," said Bart. "That was Kyle's fault, I imagine. He must have got the postboxes mixed up. I, um, I sent him to deliver the notes. I was afraid to go myself. I thought someone might see me on your street and you'd realize who was sending the notes."

I giggled. "You don't have to explain anything to me."

"So," Bart went on, "quite a few people know you've been getting notes."

"I suppose so," I replied. "But what—?" I was interrupted by David Michael yelling up the stairs. "Kristy? Phone for you!"

"Just a sec," I said to Bart. I answered the second-floor extension. It was Shannon. I told her what was going on and invited her over. I thought that with three people, we could do some real brainstorming.

So Shannon came over. After she'd apologized to Bart for having given him the silent treatment, she sat on my bed, being careful not to disturb the notes. "Any theories about the notes?" she asked us, sounding like a detective.

"No theories," I answered. "But we know there are two people responsible for them. Bart did write the first notes, the nice ones, just as you thought. But somebody *else* is writing the others. The question is *who*? And don't say Sam," I said quickly.

"Kristy doesn't have any enemies," Bart added.

"Maybe someone *is* trying to sabotage the Krushers and make them lose the World Series. Can either of you think of anybody who would want to win so badly that they'd do all this?" Shannon waved her hand across the bed, indicating the notes.

Bart and I shook our heads, and Bart added, "None of the Bashers are old enough to do something like that. And I'm sure none of their parents would do it." He paused. "You know what's weird, though? The scary notes look just like the ones *I* wrote. Who could have seen me writing the notes? I did that privately."

Neither Shannon nor I had any suggestions. Kyle was too little to think up awful letters, and Bart doesn't have any other brothers or sisters.

"It's got to be a crazy person, then," I said. "There's no other answer. He'd been watching our house, he'd seen Kyle delivering the notes, and he opened a couple before I did. You didn't always seal them," I said to Bart. "Sometimes you just stuck the flap down with a sticker. The stickers peeled off easily." I put my head in my hands. "Oh," I moaned, "there really is a kidnapper after me."

"I still think that's far-fetched," said Bart firmly. "There's another answer. I just don't know what it is."

"Me neither," said Shannon.

"Me neither," I said.

I went to bed that night thinking only of being kidnapped. Every creak or rustle in our old house made me jump. A car honked and I nearly fell out of bed. It took me for ever to drift off to sleep . . . *after* I thought I'd seen a face at my window.

# 12th CHAPTER

On Saturday, a week before Hallowe'en, and six days before Bart and I would go to the Hallowe'en Hop, I woke up without a knot in my stomach for once; without a worry about being kidnapped.

It was the day of the World Series and I could think of nothing but softball and the game that was to be played. It was going to be a big event. Both the Krushers and the Bashers had been practising hard and were geared up for the game. Parents and brothers and sisters would be sitting watching the game. So would friends and, of course, the members of the BSC. And The Three Stooges would be present to cheer the Krushers on.

There was an awful lot of excitement at my house that morning. Karen and Andrew were not spending the weekend with us, but they had come over early, and both they and David Michael (all Krushers) were racing around in a state of . . . I'm not sure what. They were certainly keyed up.

"Our T-shirts have to be clean!" I could hear Karen say as I put on my bathrobe and went downstairs for breakfast.

"And we have to have a big breakfast," added David Michael, whom I found seated in front of an enormous bowl of cereal and a stack of toast. "I need starch," he was telling Mum matter-of-factly. "So do you," he added to Karen and Andrew.

"I can't eat all that!" exclaimed Andrew. "Besides, I've already eaten breakfast."

"You three, calm down," I said. They were practically bouncing off the walls, just as they'd been on the morning of the first game we ever played against the Bashers. "Eat what you feel like eating," I said. Then I turned to Mum. "Is everything ready for the refreshment stand?" I asked her. (We were going to have a Krushers refreshment stand, just like we'd had at our first game against the Bashers. The parents had chipped in with biscuits and lemonade to sell to the fans. We were trying to earn enough money for team baseball caps. We'd almost earned enough the last time, but then Jackie Rodowsky had managed to knock over the refreshment stand with a flying bat, so we'd lost a few things. In the end, we'd earned some money for our team, but not enough for hats for everyone. We were hoping we could accomplish that today.)

"Everything's ready," replied Mum. "Sam and Charlie will bring the tables in the estate car. Oh, and I made some brownies for you to sell."

"You did?" I cried. "Thanks, Mum! You were only supposed to supply the tables. Boy, our refreshment stand is going to be great."

"Well," said Mum, "I thought you might need some extra food – in case your walking disaster has another disaster."

"Thanks," I said gratefully.

And then, just as before any big game, the phone calls started. Kids were nervous. Kids had lost their T-shirts. They'd forgotten tips that I'd given them. Jake Kuhn's younger sister was ill and wouldn't be able to play. I tried to remain calm, mostly for the sake of Karen, Andrew and David Michael, who were, by then, at about an eleven on an excitement scale of one to ten.

Our game was due to begin at noon that day. But I needed to arrive earlier, so my family left at 10:45. We set out in two cars – everybody, every single person in my family from Emily to Nannie. And we were loaded down with equipment, food and the refreshment tables.

When we reached the grounds of Stoneybrook Elementary, we were the first ones there, but I knew that a crowd would gather quickly and soon the field would be full.

I was right. By about twenty past eleven, people were streaming on to the playing field. Charlie and Sam, who had volunteered to man the refreshment stand, were already doing business. The Krushers were gathering round me, anxious, and eyeing the Bashers as they appeared. The Bashers, as usual, were impressive. They're bigger than my Krushers, for the most part, and have T-shirts *and* baseball caps. (Matching, of course, which was what we were hoping to earn enough money for that day.) Then there are the Basher cheerleaders – four girls with actual cheerleader's outfits – pleated skirts, the whole bit. The best that Vanessa, Haley and Charlotte usually do are Krushers T-shirts, matching flared denim skirts, white knee socks and trainers. On the day of the World Series, though, they were The Three Stooges. Nobody knew quite what to make of them. At least they drew attention to themselves.

I hoped their wigs wouldn't fall off. Or their trousers down.

I was just about to give the Krushers a pep talk when, for some reason, I glanced into the crowd.

My eyes landed on Cokie and her friends!

What on earth were they doing at our World Series? None of them had brothers or sisters on either softball team, and they certainly weren't friends of ours. As far as I was concerned their appearance at the game was suspicious. Why were they there? Were they going to make fun of the Krushers? Or *me*? I know I'm not as cool as they think *they* are, but that wasn't any reason to come and ruin the game.

I almost went into the stands to talk to them, but then I thought better of it. My Krushers had surrounded me. They needed me. And if Cokie made any trouble, then my BSC friends would take care of them. I hoped.

"Okay, everybody," I said to the kids. "We've still got some time before the game. I'd like you to do some warm-ups. Nicky and David Michael, practise pitching to each other. Jake, you pitch some balls to these five," (I pulled a group of kids away from the others) "so they can practise hitting."

When all the kids were busy, I grabbed Mary Anne and pointed Cokie out to her. "What do you think she's doing here?"

Mary Anne shrugged. She wasn't nearly as suspicious as I was, despite what Cokie had done to her in the past. After a moment she said, "I think Cokie's just going to watch the game. Grace and the others, too."

"Oh, you know perfectly well that's not—"

"OW!"

Mary Anne and I were interrupted by a cry. Without even looking, I knew it had come from Jackie, the walking disaster. "Oh, brother," I muttered.

I turned round.

Jackie was rubbing his elbow, but he seemed all right.

I sighed. I hoped the Krushers were *really* ready for the World Series. They could beat the Bashers again if they tried hard enough. I knew they could. Their record was poor, but they could overcome it.

"What?" said Mary Anne. "Is anything wrong?"

I hesitated. "No," I said at last.

Mary Anne returned to Shannon and Logan and Claud and the rest of my friends. I searched for Bart and found him breaking up a fight between two of his toughest Bashers. When things had calmed down, we smiled at each other. Boy, it was hard to like a boy and want to crush his softball team at the same time!

"Hi," said Bart.

"Hi," I replied.

"Are you ready?" he asked.

"As we'll ever be. Are you?"

"I think so. My team is all keyed up. They can't stop thinking about being beaten by the Krushers."

I couldn't help it. Inwardly, I gloated.

"So," I said, "same rules as before? A

238

seven-inning game, Gabbie gets to hit a foam ball and stand closer to the pitcher, and we toss a coin to see which team goes to bat first?"

"Fine with me. . . Coach," replied Bart, smiling.

"Oh, and just remind your team that we have to sign to Matt Braddock."

"You got it."

Bart was off then, in answer to a kid who'd been pestering him for help with something for at least five minutes.

I turned round, all ready to call the Krushers together for a pep talk – and ran straight into Cokie.

"Hi, Kristy," she said a bit too casually, if you know what I mean.

"Hi," I replied coolly.

"So how are things?"

"What things?" I replied.

"You know. *Things*. Life."

"Fine."

"Is your team up for the game?"

"Cokie, what are you doing here?" I demanded.

"I just want to see the game."

"Why?"

"Oh, to show my support for your team."

I rolled my eyes. "*Why?*"

"Can't you accept it, Kristy? I'm not your enemy."

Well, she certainly wasn't my best friend.

"Anyway," Cokie went on, "I thought you might need a little extra cheering. You've looked a bit depressed lately. I want your team to win."

"I haven't been depressed!" I cried. "I've even got a boyfriend. He's coming to the Hallowe'en Hop with me."

"Really?" said Cokie. "You must like each other a lot."

I drew myself up. I knew I was showing off, but I couldn't help saying, "We plan to spend our lives together."

I'd thought Cokie might screech, "You mean, you're getting *married*?" Instead she said, "Ah. That's nice. Eternal togetherness?"

Cokie caught what she'd said before I did, and she blushed. That was when I remembered. Eternal togetherness. That had been a phrase from one of the lunatic notes. "*You* wrote the scary letters!" I exclaimed.

It was too late. Cokie knew she'd given herself away. She couldn't even think of anything to say. She just began to back away from me. I may be short, but I'm strong and good at athletics. Every kid in my grade knows it.

"Just a second," I said through gritted teeth. I reached out and caught Cokie's sleeve. "You stay right here. I've got some questions for you."

Cokie looked so afraid that I knew she'd

answer anything I asked her – and answer truthfully.

"Did you send all those letters – all the frightening ones?" I demanded.

Cokie looked at the ground. "Yes." I still hadn't let go of her sleeve and she tried to squirm away, but I held on tightly.

"Why?"

"Because of . . . because of what you and your friends did to me and my friends in the graveyard. You made us look like fools in front of Logan."

"Too bad. You started the whole thing by trying to make Mary Anne look like a fool in front of Logan." Cokie didn't say anything, so I went on. "How did you know what to make the letters look like? They match Bart's perfectly. Stickers and everything."

"Well, you weren't too subtle about Bart's letters. You brought them to school and showed them to your friends at lunchtime. Practically the whole canteen saw those letters." Cokie made it sound like *her* letters were *my* fault.

I let go of her sleeve then. I was a jumble of feelings. First of all, I was relieved. There was no one after me. I didn't have to worry about being kidnapped any more. Second, I was furious with Cokie. "By Monday," I said, "the whole school is going to know what you did. And maybe everyone at Stoneybrook Day School, too. Think about that. If you felt like a fool before, it won't be anything compared to now."

Cokie ran away. She rounded up Grace, Lisa and Bebe from the crowd, and the four of them left in a hurry.

More than anything, what I wanted to do then was rush to my friends and tell them the news, but it was almost noon and time for the game. I found that I was filled with rage at Cokie, and therefore filled with energy, almost with exuberance.

I signalled to Bart. "Time to start the game," I told him, "and I've got news. I've found out who the letter writer is and we don't have a thing to worry about. I'll tell you everything after the game."

Bart grinned. "Okay, Coach."

We gathered our teams and tossed a coin. The Krushers would be batting first.

"Play ball!" shouted Bart.

# 13th
# CHAPTER

The game was off to a good start. I sent Matt Braddock out as our first batter, and he hit the first pitch with a resounding *whack*, running to third base before I signalled him to stop.

Next I sent Jake Kuhn to bat. He made it to first base and Matt made it home. One run for the Krushers! They were elated. They were also very involved with the game. Sometimes while they're waiting for their turn to bat, the little ones get fidgety and I have to recruit my friends to keep them occupied. Not during the World Series, though.

By the end of the first inning, the score was two to one, in favour of. . . The Krushers. The game was intense. I stood on the sidelines chewing gum and paying attention to every little thing that happened. I remembered which kids needed what coaching tips when. I didn't let my team members try anything fancy. I shouted encouragement – but never scolded.

Bart began to look nervous.

During the second inning, although I thought it was a little risky, I let Gabbie Perkins, Claire Pike and Jackie Rodowsky go to bat. Gabbie (with her special playing rules) hit a single, Claire struck out but didn't throw a tantrum, and Jackie hit a home run! (He lost his balance, tripped, and fell as his team-mates surrounded him to congratulate him, but I don't think the Bashers noticed. At any rate, nobody laughed at him.)

The Bashers, tough as nails, were now on their guard. There was no jeering at the Krushers as there had been during past games. They concentrated on playing a game that was as intense as I felt.

At one point during the third inning, with the Krushers still ahead (by one run), I glanced at Bart. He was looking at me rather fiercely. Oh, no, I thought. We've just got over the nasty note business, and now we're going to go back to our old competitive selves. If the Krushers won today, would Bart still go to the dance with me? I wondered. I couldn't worry about that. I put the thought out of my head and whispered to David Michael, who was about to go up to bat, "Smash it!"

When the score was six to five (still in

our favour) we took a fifth-inning break. "You're all doing a *great* job!" I told the Krushers. "'Absolutely terrific. You're playing well, you're trying hard and you're not letting the Bashers scare you."

The Krushers beamed.

I wandered over to the refreshment stand.

"You've easily got enough money for hats now," Sam told me. "People have been buying things all morning. And – and your team is playing, um, well." (It is not easy for Sam to be serious or to give compliments.)

"Thanks," I said gratefully, and bought a cup of lemonade. Then I sought out The Three Stooges. "I think you're a hit," I told them. (Their wigs and trousers were still on.)

"Really?" exclaimed Charlotte from under a fringe of black curls.

"Cool," added Haley.

I had to admit that the Bashers cheerleaders were more polished – but The Three Stooges attracted more attention.

Twenty minutes later, the game began again. And two innings later, it was over. The score was eight to seven.

*The Krushers had won the World Series!*

You should have seen the hugging and jumping up and down, and heard the whooping and cheering in the stands. The Krushers were beside themselves but had the presence of mind to join The Three

Stooges in a cheer of, "Two, four, six, eight. Who do we appreciate? The Bashers! The Bashers! Yea!"

Almost too soon the crowd had emptied and I found myself helping my brothers dismantle the refreshment stand. Around us milled a few stray ball players, my family, the BSC members . . . and Bart.

I was afraid to look at him. My team had beaten his. Was he angry with me all over again, but for a different reason? We've always known how competitive we are. Now, I wondered, could we *really* coach opposing teams and go out together, too? Let alone – maybe – be boy- and girlfriend?

I put off finding out by running to my friends and telling them what Cokie had done. They were all properly incensed.

"*Cokie* wrote the notes?" exclaimed Claudia.

"That – that sewer rat!" said Stacey, who still thinks in New York terms half the time.

"You should get back at her," said Jessi.

"I think I already have," I replied. "I told her I'd make sure that by Monday everyone at SMS and Bart's school will know what she's done. That's enough for Cokie. Besides, I don't want to continue this war with her."

Slowly my friends began to leave then, until only Shannon remained.

"Anything wrong?" she asked me.

"I don't know. I have a feeling Bart's

upset. Do you think I should have let the Bashers win? I could have done that, you know."

"No way!" exclaimed Shannon.

"But will he still want to come to the Hallowe'en Hop with me?"

"Go and find out," said Shannon.

Reluctantly, I walked across the field to Bart, who was tossing equipment into a canvas bag.

"Hi," I said.

Bart glanced up. "Hey!" He grinned. "Good game."

I paused. He didn't sound angry. "So. Are you still up for the Hop?"

"Can't wait. Now tell me about the letters."

I did, after breathing a huge sigh of relief.

"Kristy!" called Charlie then.

"Bart!" called Mr Taylor.

And then in unison they said, "Time to go!"

"See you Friday," whispered Bart, "but I'll probably talk to you before then."

"You got it, Coach!"

Later that afternoon, when I was recovering from the game, Shannon surprised me by coming over unannounced. She walked into my room, where I was lying on the bed.

"I'm dead," I told her.

"Too dead for some tips?"

"What kind of tips?"

"Oh, make-up, stuff like that."

"I don't wear make-up," I told her.

"Not even to dances?"

I rolled over. "Hmm. I'm not sure."

"You want to look good for Bart, don't you?"

"I just want to look like myself. And if I'm going to look good, I'll look good for me."

"Okay. So what about make-up? And what are you going to wear?"

"Wear? I don't know."

"You do own a dress, don't you?"

"Of course I do . . . I think." I got up and went to my wardrobe. "There must be a couple here somewhere." I pawed through my collection of shirts and sweaters. "Oh, here's one. I wore it when Mary Anne's dad and Dawn's mum got married. And here's another. This is the one I wore when my mother and Watson got married." I held it up.

"Well, you can't wear that one to the dance," said Shannon. "It's much too dressy. It's a *long* dress for heaven's sake. Let me see the other one."

I put the fancy dress away and showed Shannon the more casual one. "Of course, Bart and I could go in costume," I pointed out. "A lot of kids do go to the Hop in costume."

"But don't you want to look special for Bart?" asked Shannon. "And that dress is perfect. Who helped you choose it?"

248

"Stacey did," I admitted.

"Well, it's great for a dance. Okay, put it on.

"How come?"

"Because I can't decide on your make-up and nail varnish until I see you in the dress."

"*Nail* varnish? No way! I'll wear make-up – a *little* make-up – but no nail varnish."

"Okay, okay. Calm down."

Luckily, before we had got too far into the make-up ordeal, Watson stuck his head in my room and told me that Bart was on the phone.

"Thanks," I said, but as soon as he'd left I moaned to Shannon, "I just know he's decided he doesn't want to go to the dance after all. I should have let the Bashers win the game today."

"*Kristy*," said Shannon sharply, "you should not have. Go and see what Bart really wants. I'm sure he's not backing out."

I picked up the phone as if it were a dead snake. I barely touched it. "Hello?" I squeaked. "Bart?"

"Hi, Coach," said Bart cheerfully. "Listen, you won't believe this. I have the greatest costumes for us to wear to the dance. I know we didn't say anything about costumes, but I was just up in our attic and I found – I *know* you're not going to believe this – but I found two *lobster* costumes. My parents wore them to a party once. A long time ago. I think my mum's costume would fit you. Do you want to wear it?"

Did I want to wear it? Of course I did! Then I wouldn't have to wear a dress. Or paint my nails. "Oh, yes!" I cried. "Definitely. That's terrific, Bart. You know, they're giving out prizes for costumes this year. Scariest, funniest, that sort of thing. Hey, do these costumes have masks?"

"No," replied Bart. "We'll have to wear a little make-up. Is that okay?"

"It's great!" I said. "Thanks. I'll talk to you soon. Bye!" I hung up and ran back to my room. "Shannon," I said, "that was Bart. Guess what. I'm going to do my own make-up. Watch this." I smeared my entire face with liquid blusher. I looked as red as a you-know-what.

Shannon gaped. "Kristy! That's not a make-up job."

"It is when you're going to be a lobster."

I explained to Shannon about the costumes. Then I gleefully took off my dress and put it back in the wardrobe.

"Kristy?" said Shannon.

"What?"

"You're weird."

"Thank you."

Shannon grinned at me. "You and Bart are going to have a great time," she said.

"I hope so," I replied.

# 14th CHAPTER

It was Friday night, the night of the Hallowe'en Hop.

I stood in front of the full-length mirror in the bathroom.

I was wearing a lobster costume.

"Not bad," I murmured. I certainly did look like a lobster – if lobsters were able to stand up and walk on their tails with their legs waving around in front of them. I had antennae, the proper number of legs and even claws. (The claws fitted over my hands, like mittens.) The other six legs were stiff with wire and were fastened to the body of the costume.

I was just applying the last of the blusher to my face when, "Aughhh!"

"Aughhh!" I shrieked back.

Karen was standing behind me. My costume had scared her, and she'd scared me. "Is *that* what you're wearing to the dance tonight?" she asked, incredulous. "I thought when girls went to dances they wore beautiful gowns and ribbons or maybe pearls in their hair. And jewellery, lots of jewellery."

Karen moved beside me and gazed in the mirror. I'm sure she was picturing herself at a "big girl" dance, jewel bedecked and gorgeous.

"No, silly," I said, fluffing her hair. "I mean, usually people do get dressed up for a dance, but this is a Hallowe'en dance, so Bart and I are wearing costumes. How do I look as a lobster?"

"Fine. Is Bart your boyfriend?"

"Maybe," I answered. "I'm not sure."

"How come you're not sure?"

"I'm just not, that's all." Usually, I like having Karen and Andrew live with us every other weekend, but sometimes Karen asks too many questions. So I asked her one instead, hoping she'd forget about Bart. "Is *your* Hallowe'en costume ready?"

"Yup." (Karen, Andrew, David Michael, Emily and a group of their friends were going to go trick-or-treating the next day as characters from *The Wizard of Oz*. Mum had hired me to take them around the neighbourhood.)

"Well, I suppose I'm as ready as I'll ever be," I told Karen.

"Are you nervous, Kristy?"

"A little." Actually, I was very nervous,

but not for any reason Karen could imagine. Here are the reasons I was worried:

1. I'm not a great dancer, and it was hard enough to *walk* in my costume, let alone dance in it.

2. This was basically my first true date. I'd gone to dances before, but only with dweebs like Alan Gray, so those didn't count. And Bart and I had gone to the cinema and things before, but usually on the spur of the moment, and definitely only as friends. I had a feeling tonight would be different.

3. Nobody at SMS, except my friends (and some enemies, who shall remain nameless) had seen Bart. Kids didn't bring dates from other schools very often, so Bart and I would have stood out as a couple even if we weren't dressed like lobsters. I was afraid that some kids might give Bart a hard time.

"Kristy!" called Watson from the front hall. "Are you ready to go? We told Bart we'd pick him up in ten minutes."

"Coming!" I called back. "Are you sure I look okay?" I asked Karen.

"Okay for a lobster," she replied.

I grinned. Then I gave her a goodnight kiss. "See you in the morning."

"You're going to be out that late?"

"Pretty late. Oh, and guess who will be here when you wake up tomorrow?"

"Who?"

"Shannon, and Mary Anne, and all my friends from the Babysitters Club. We're going to have a sleepover after the dance."

"Goody!" said Karen.

"Kristy!" Watson called again.

"Okay, coming!" I ran downstairs. Watson drove me to Bart's house, we picked up the second lobster, and before I knew it, Watson was dropping us off in front of SMS.

"Charlie and I will pick up you and your friends at ten-thirty, okay?" said Watson, as Bart and I struggled out of the car.

"Okay," I replied. "And thanks."

The Hallowe'en Hop was a dance for all grades at SMS. Mary Anne and Logan were going to be there. Claudia was ecstatic because Woody Jefferson had asked her to go. Stacey had worked up the nerve to invite Kelsey Bauman (the new boy she liked). Dawn and Jessi were going alone. And Mallory was going with Ben Hobart!

"Well," I said nervously to Bart as we entered my school, "this is SMS."

"It's *big*," said Bart. "I mean, it's not like I've never driven past it, but when you're this close up, it seems so much bigger than Stoneybrook Day School." Bart looked quite nervous himself.

"Come on," I said, taking his claw, which was difficult to do.

I led Bart inside. We were entering the back way, near the gym, where the dance would be held. The BSC members (with or without dates) had agreed to meet there. I was relieved to find Stacey and Kelsey, Dawn, Mary Anne and Logan already there. As soon as the others arrived, we entered the gym in a big group.

Straight away, people began staring at Bart and me.

"Everyone's looking at us," I whispered to Mary Anne.

"It's just your costumes," she whispered back. "They're so unusual. Don't worry. No one's laughing."

But Bart and I gripped claws even more tightly.

"Come on," said Bart. "Let's get some punch."

So we did. After we'd stood around for a while, and people had got used to us, Bart said, "Do you want to dance? This band is *good*."

"Hey!" I exclaimed, as we headed for the dance floor, "maybe one day your band could play here. We're always looking for bands."

"Maybe," replied Bart, sounding excited at the prospect.

And so we began to dance. I soon realized that Bart couldn't tell if I was a good dancer or a rotten one. *Neither* of us could dance well with all the legs and claws and tentacles.

I relaxed and looked around the gym. It

was decorated with black and orange streamers and balloons. And the chaperones (our teachers) were all in costumes! Bart and I whirled by Mary Anne and Logan, who were dressed as a witch and Frankenstein's monster. We danced by Stacey and Kelsey, who were just dressed up. (Karen would have approved.) We passed by Dawn, dressed as Alice in Wonderland, who was dancing with a hunchback. (I didn't recognize him.)

And then we danced by Cokie Gray and Austin Bentley.

I prepared myself for remarks, but Cokie pretended not to notice Bart and me – even though I *know* she saw us. Good. Maybe our war was over. I didn't mind being ignored by Cokie. Anyway, a lot of kids at school were furious with her for sending the notes. I felt satisfied.

Bart and I took a break after a while, had some more punch, and then returned to the dance floor. The first slow dance began. Yikes! A *slow* dance. Bart put his arms around my neck and we swayed back and forth, back and forth, in time to the music. Somehow, though, I had a feeling that I wasn't getting the full effect of things, what with those layers of foam between us. It didn't matter, though. A slow dance felt pretty nice.

When the band stopped for a break of their own, one of the teachers (Ms Mandel, who was dressed as Snow White) stepped up to a microphone. "While the members of the band are taking a rest," she began, "I would like to present the prizes for the best costumes."

Bart and I glanced at each other, hopeful.

"Scariest costume prizes," said Ms Mandel, "go to Donny Olssen and Tara Valentine, our space monsters. Funniest costume prizes go to Danielle Pitchard and Marcus Brown, the surfing dinosaurs. The prizes for the most unusual costumes go to our lobsters, Kristy Thomas and . . ."

I didn't even hear the rest of what Ms Mandel had to say. "We won!" I exclaimed to Bart. "I wonder *what* we won." And then I added, "You don't think most unusual really means strangest, do you?"

"No," Bart assured me. "Besides, who cares? We won a coupon for a free large pizza at Pizza Express."

"You're kidding!"

"Nope. That teacher just announced it. Come on. We're supposed to go and collect our prize."

So Bart and I joined the other winners, who were surrounding Ms Mandel. As our pizza coupons were handed out, everyone clapped.

Then the band members returned and the dancing began again. Bart and I danced until Bart looked at the clock on the wall and said, "Kristy, it's ten-fifteen. We'd better find your friends and get going."

"Oh," I said in disappointment, but I knew he was right. "Let's just finish this dance first, though." (It was a slow dance.)

So we did. And when the music ended, Bart leaned towards me and kissed me very gently on the cheek.

Ooh, I thought. So this is what it's like to be in love.

# 15th
# CHAPTER

"All right, I want to know *every*thing," said Shannon.

She and I, and Jessi, Stacey, Mary Anne, Mallory, Dawn and Claudia were sitting around my bedroom. The dance was over. Scattered about the room were pieces of our costumes – Dawn's Alice in Wonderland dress, Mal's clown feet (she'd had a lot of trouble dancing at the Hop, and had had to take the shoes off and dance barefoot), Mary Anne's witch hat and my lobster suit. The suit was huge and was standing in a corner, the tentacles waving ever so slightly.

My friends and I had all changed into our nightdresses. Shannon, Stacey and I were lying on my bed on our stomachs with our feet in the air. Mallory, Dawn, Mary Anne and Jessi were propped up in various places on the floor of my room. Dawn, in fact, was leaning against the bed, and Shannon was plaiting her hair from above. Claudia was sitting at my desk, painting her nails.

"Why *are* you painting your nails *now*?" I asked her, looking at my watch.

"So I won't have to do it tomorrow," she replied simply.

"Come on, I want to hear about the dance," said Shannon again.

"All right," said Jessi. "I'll start. The gym was beautifully decorated. There were streamers and balloons everywhere—"

"Not that kind of stuff!" Shannon interrupted her. "The good stuff."

"The good stuff?" repeated Jessi. She and Mallory hadn't been to too many dances. They weren't sure what sort of information Shannon wanted.

"How about this?" said Stacey. "Cokie Gray was all dressed up. I mean, not in a costume, just really *dressed up*. She was wearing a lot of make-up, too, including false eyelashes." (I began to laugh. I knew what Stacey was going to say. I'd seen what had happened.) "And she leaned over the punch bowl and one of her lashes fell off and landed right in the punch."

"And Miranda Shillaber was standing there and she made the teacher who was in charge of the refreshments get a fresh bowl of punch because she said the first bowl had been contaminated by the eyelashes. I thought Cokie was going to kill her. She gave her a Look," I finished.

Shannon laughed. "So what else? Did you all dance?"

"Yup," answered Dawn. "No wallflowers here."

"Ben is a great dancer," said Mal dreamily.

"I danced with about eight different boys and they were all clods," announced Jessi, with disgust.

"That's because you're used to dancing with boys who take ballet," said Mal. "They're graceful."

"No, Jessi's right. Sixth-grade boys are clods," said Shannon knowingly. "Trust me. I remember. Half of them are all gangly, kind of like spiders, and the other half are so short you can hardly see them."

"When does it change?" asked Jessi.

"It's slow. A – a sort of – what's the word?" said Claudia, without looking up from her nail polish pursuits.

"A metamorphosis?" suggested Mary Anne.

"Yeah, that's it. A metamorphosis," said Claud. She held out one hand, examining her fingertips critically. "Not bad," she murmured. "One day I'm going to go to the nail salon and get a French manicure."

I was about to ask what that was when Shannon said, "Come on. More details! More details! I can't stand not knowing what happened."

"Kristy and Bart won the prize for the

261

most unusual costumes," said Dawn. She reached up to pat her head and feel how the plaiting was coming on.

"Great," said Shannon. "What'd you win?"

"A coupon for a free large pizza with everything," I answered.

"Ugh," said Jessi. "Even anchovies?"

"Bart and I happen to like anchovies," I replied. "We've got a lot in common."

"*Yeah*," said Stacey slyly.

Shannon peered across Stacey's back and over at me. "What does she mean?" she asked with interest.

"I – I—" (I couldn't get the words out.) "Bart *kissed* her!" exclaimed Mal, unable to contain herself. "He kissed her at the dance right in front of everyone!"

"He kissed you?" cried Shannon. She dropped the plait she was working on. "*How* did he kiss you?"

"It was just a kiss on the cheek," I said. "And how did you know about that, Mal?" I asked.

Mary Anne giggled. "We all know," she said. "Everybody saw. He kissed you in the middle of the gym."

I tried to be embarrassed, but I don't think I even managed a red face. I was quite proud that my friends had seen Bart kiss me.

Mary Anne began to giggle.

"What?" I said.

"Bart is better than Alan Gray with M&M's in his eyes, isn't he?" she said.

We all laughed, except for Shannon, who didn't understand the true extent of Alan's pestiness.

"Alan," I began explaining to Shannon, "will do anything for attention. Once we gave Mary Anne a party," (I said that part quickly because Mary Anne had hated the party; we should have known better than to surprise her) "and Alan walked around with yellow M&M's squinted between his eyes, telling everyone he was Little Orphan Annie."

"I can assure you," said Shannon, "that Bart will never do that. At least not in public." She returned to Dawn's hair.

"Kristy?" Jessi spoke up softly. "Are you in love?"

I hesitated, knowing that by hesitating I was giving myself away. If any of my brothers had been in the room they would have teased me for about a year. But my friends wouldn't do that. They all just glanced at me and let the subject drop.

"Well," said Dawn, "tomorrow's Hallowe'en."

"No . . . it's today," said Mal in a low voice, looking at her watch. "The time is twelve-oh-three."

"I'm taking Karen, Andrew, David Michael, Emily and some of their friends trick-or-treating later," I said. "They're going to dress up as characters from *The Wizard of Oz*." I hoped I'd be able to keep my mind on the task. At the moment, all I could think of was Bart's kiss.

"That's a good idea," said Shannon. "Going as characters from *The Wizard of Oz*. They must be really excited."

"Half scared, too, I think. Remember how scary we used to think Hallowe'en was?" I asked everyone.

"Definitely," said Mal. "I thought ghosts and vampires and things really did come out on Hallowe'en night. The year I was six, I wouldn't even go trick-or-treating because I was afraid I wouldn't be able to tell the real spooks from the kids in costumes."

"We were all pretty scared just last Hallowe'en," pointed out Mary Anne. "Thanks to Cokie and Grace and their friends."

"That's for sure," said Jessi.

"I'm sorry I missed all that," said Stacey.

"No, you're not," Claud told her. "It was *really* scary."

"I'm glad Cokie gave herself away at the game last weekend," I said. "Can you imagine how we'd feel now if I was still getting those notes?"

And at that very moment, a scream ripped through the air. I froze. Then I thawed out and looked at my friends. They were all looking at each other. None of *us* had screamed.

"Yikes!" I said. I tiptoed on to the landing – just in time to hear another scream. It came from Karen's room.

The door to Mum and Watson's bedroom opened then, and Watson rushed out. "Don't worry," he told me. "I think Karen's having a nightmare."

With a sigh, I returned to my friends. "Just Karen," I said. "Bad dream. Watson's taking care of her."

We began to get ready to go to sleep. We put away our nail varnish and hairslides, shoved our junk into a corner of the room, and my friends rolled out their sleeping bags. I was going to sleep in my bed. Even so, seven sleeping bags made the floor of the room pretty crowded.

*Scritch, scratch. Scritch, scratch.*

Mary Anne jumped a mile. "What was that?"

"Just branches scraping my windows," I said carelessly. I wasn't going to let Hallowe'en spook *me*. "A storm must be blowing up."

I waited until everyone was settled in their sleeping bags. Then I pulled back the covers on my bed and found . . . a kidnapping note on my pillow. It was all I could do not to shriek, but I didn't want Watson to come dashing into my room. Instead I just gasped.

"What? What's wrong?" asked Dawn.

"This is," I whispered. I held up the

note. It was made of letters cut from magazines and newspapers and said, "I am coming for you tonight. I will be there at 3:00 AM There's no way to escape me."

Everyone crawled out of their sleeping bags and was reading the note wide-eyed, looking ready to scream.

Everyone except Shannon. She began to laugh.

"Shannon! Did you do this?" I demanded.

Shannon couldn't control herself. "Yes," she said, giggling. "I didn't know what to do with myself all evening while I waited for you all to come back from the dance. So I wrote that letter. It took hours."

"I'll treasure it always," I said sarcastically.

"You aren't angry, are you, Kristy?" asked Shannon.

"Nah. In fact, you've just given me an idea."

"I'm afraid to ask," groaned Mary Anne.

"Come on. I'll show you."

If any of us had been sleepy before, we weren't now. Shannon's note had given us a second wind. So everyone jumped up and followed me out of my room, across the landing, down the stairs and into the study, where our computer is set up. I slipped a disk into the drive and typed out:

My dearest, darling Cokie,

You are the light of my life. You make the sun rise every morning. You make the flowers grow, yellow-dappled and dewy. Every day I watch you. I watch you in the halls and the cafeteria and science class. You are a creature more gorgeous than a goddess. Please accept this heartfelt invitation to dissect a frog with me.

Always and forever,
Your Mystery Perspirer

Everyone was howling, and Shannon asked, "What are you going to do with that note, Kristy?"

"Stick it in Cokie's locker on Monday morning."

"Don't you think she's going to know who wrote it?"

"Yes," I replied, "and I don't care. I know I said I didn't want to continue the war with Cokie, but I can't help it. This is too good an idea to pass up. Come on, everyone. Let's go to bed."

And so, note in hand, I led my friends back to my room, where we promptly fell asleep and didn't wake up until eleven o'clock the next morning.

# POOR MALLORY!

This book is for
Bonnie Black,
who keeps things running smoothly.
Thank you.

# 1st CHAPTER

*"Underwear! Underwear!"* I sang. *"How I itch in my woolly underwear. Oh, how I wish I'd gottennnn,"* (I held the note for as long as I could) *"a pair of cotton, so I wouldn't itch everywhere."* I turned to Jessi Ramsey, my best friend. "Hit it, Jessi!" I cried.

Jessi picked up the song. *"BVDs make me sneeze, when the breeze from the trees hits my knees."* (We were beginning to giggle.) *"Oh, I'm itching!"* Jessi managed to continue. *"Oh, how I'm itching, in my gosh-darn, bing-bang woolly underwear-hey!"*

"That's it! You've got it!" I said. "That's the whole song."

"Your brothers know the weirdest songs," commented Jessi as we walked along. School was over. We had survived another day of the sixth grade at Stoneybrook Middle School (or SMS).

I am Mallory Pike, better known as Mal.

273

And Jessi is really Jessica, except she's *only* known as Jessi. Most days, when school is over, we walk home together, but just part of the way. After a couple of blocks we branch off, Jessi going in one direction and I in another.

"Want to come over this afternoon?" I asked Jessi. "The triplets," (they're three of my four brothers) "will teach you the song about Johnny Rebeck and his sausage-making machine."

"I'd *like* to come over," replied Jessi, "but I'm babysitting for Charlotte Johanssen. I'll see you at the Babysitters Club meeting at five-thirty, though, okay?"

"Okay," I replied.

We had reached our parting place. Jessi pretended, as she always does, that we were parting for ever. She put the back of one hand to her forehead and began to moan. "Parting is such sweet sorrow," she said in a wispy voice.

"Will we ever pass this way again?" I asked her.

"Yeah, tomorrow," Jessi answered, and we laughed. "See you later," she said.

"Later!" I called to her.

I walked the rest of the way home by myself. Under my breath I sang, *"Oh, Mr Johnny Rebeck, how could you be so mean? I told you you'd be sorry for inventing that machine. Now all the neighbours' cats and dogs will never more be seen – for they've all been ground to sausages in Johnny Rebeck's machine.*" Suddenly, I realized just what, exactly, I was singing about. "Ugh, gross!" I said out loud. And then I wondered where my brothers had learned their weird songs. Probably at day camp when they were little.

When I reached my house, I shifted my book bag from one hand to the other and ran across our front lawn. We live in a medium-sized house in an average neighbourhood in Stoneybrook, Connecticut, a small town. Sometimes I wish our house was just a little bigger. That's because I have seven brothers and sisters. We could really do with the extra space. My brothers share one bedroom (two sets of bunk beds), my sister Vanessa and I share another room, and my two youngest sisters, Claire and Margo, share a third room. (My parents have the fourth bedroom. It isn't very big.)

"Hi, Mum!" I called as I opened the front door of our house. I took off my jacket and hung it on the coat peg. "Mum?" I called again. "Mum?"

"She's upstairs," said Claire, emerging from the kitchen. Claire is only five and goes to nursery school in the mornings, so she comes home from school before the rest of us do. "She's lying down," Claire added.

"Is she ill?" I asked in alarm.

"Nooo, but. . ." Claire trailed off.

"But what?" I asked her.

"We came home from school and the

phone was ringing and Mummy answered it and she kept saying, 'Oh, no,' and then she hung up and she said she had a headache and she went to her room." Claire said this in a small explosion of words.

"Hmm," I replied. "Well, I'll go upstairs and see what's wrong." I wasn't too worried. If something really awful had happened, like if one of my grandparents had died or if Dad had been in an accident, Mum would be racing around *doing* things, not lying on her bed.

"Mum?" I called. I was standing in the upstairs hallway and the door to her room was ajar.

"Mallory?" Mum replied. "You can come in, darling."

I pushed open the door. Mum was sitting on the edge of her bed.

"I was just getting ready to come downstairs," she said.

"Oh. . . Mum, what's wrong?"

Mum sighed. "I might as well tell you. And we should probably warn your brothers and sisters this afternoon, too."

Warn them? About what? This sounded dangerous. I replayed what Claire had told me. My mother had obviously received bad news over the phone. Had her *doctor* called? Was she ill? Maybe she'd heard those awful words: We've got your test results, Mrs Pike, and they don't look good.

"Are you ill?" I cried.

"Oh, no," said Mum. "It's nothing like that. Look, I'll tell you first, and then you can help me tell the others when they come home from school."

"Okay," I said.

"Well. . . well, it's the company your father works for," Mum began. (Dad is a corporate lawyer for a big company in Stamford, Connecticut, which is not far from Stoneybrook.) "You know that it hasn't been doing well."

I nodded. Dad had been talking about that lately.

"Apparently this morning the chairman announced that half of the employees will be asked to leave."

"You mean sacked?" I exclaimed. "That won't happen to Dad."

"Your father thinks it might," said Mum. "Pink slips have been appearing on desks ever since the announcement was made."

"Pink slips?" I repeated.

"A pink slip is notification that you're being asked to leave your job," Mum explained.

"Oh. . . but Dad hasn't had one yet."

"No. He thinks he will, though. He hasn't been at the company as long as most of the top executives have."

"And I know what that means," I said. "It means he doesn't have seniority."

"Right, smarty-pants," said Mum, smiling finally. Then she sighed. "We'd better

go downstairs. I hear voices and footsteps."
"And thuds," I added. "The triplets must be home."

I was right. The triplets were home. So was everyone else. And they were all in the kitchen making sloppy, disgusting after-school snacks. There were Byron, Adam and Jordan, who are ten; Vanessa, who's nine; Nicky, who's eight; Margo, who's seven and Claire, who's five. (I'm eleven.)

Mum waited until everyone had made a snack and was sitting at the table in the kitchen. I joined my brothers and sisters, but I didn't feel like eating.

"Kids?" said Mum.

"Yeah?" replied Byron, just as Adam flicked a Cheerio at Nicky, which made Nicky laugh and snort milk up his nose.

"Kids, this is serious," said Mum.

The giggling stopped. The eating stopped. Everyone faced our mother. Then she repeated what she had told me upstairs. I tried to help the little kids understand what she was saying.

"That's silly," scoffed Vanessa. "Dad's job is important."

"Yeah, he won't get sacked," said Jordan.

"What's a pink slip?" asked Claire. "I don't get it."

Mum explained again, patiently.

"I *want* Daddy to get a pink slip!" exclaimed Claire. "If he didn't have to go to work, then he could stay at home and play with me."

"Stupid," said Adam. "If he doesn't work, how are we going to get money?"

"Yeah, we need money to buy food and clothes and stuff," said Nicky.

Claire finally began to look worried, so I said, "But we've got a savings account, haven't we, Mum? We could use the money that's in the bank."

"We do have a savings account," Mum answered, "but there's not very much in it. We'll run through it pretty quickly trying to pay the mortgage and other bills every month, and putting food on this table for ten people. Besides, the money is supposed to be a college fund for you kids."

My brothers and sisters and I looked at each other.

Finally Jordan said again, "Dad's not going to lose his job."

"Yeah, we don't know that, Mum," I added. I looked at my watch. "It's after three-thirty. In fact, it's almost four. Don't you think Dad would know by now?"

Mum shrugged. "Not necessarily."

"But his job is im*por*tant," said Vanessa again.

"The company has other lawyers," Mum replied, "and they're all a lot older than your father. Look, I don't want Dad to be made redundant any more than you do. I'm just preparing you for what might happen, for what we might hear when Dad comes home tonight."

"If Daddy lost his job," Claire began thoughtfully, "what would – what would change? I'm not sure. . ."

"We would have to be very careful with our money," said Mum. "We couldn't buy extras or go on trips. And your dad would stay at home and look for a new job. He wouldn't be happy about that," she added.

"Why not?" asked Margo.

"Because looking for a new job, especially when you've been made redundant, isn't easy. Dad will have to hear people say no to him a lot. He might start applying for jobs that are below the level of the one he's got now, and people still might say no. He'll phone companies and hear other people say that there aren't any jobs at all. It would be like going over to your friends' houses and hearing each one of them say they don't want to play with you."

"Ooh," said Claire softly. That had hit home.

Margo looked as stricken as Claire.

"Anyway," said Mum, getting to her feet, "this *might* not happen. Your father may walk through the door tonight as happy as a clam. But I want you to be prepared if he doesn't."

"Okay," said my brothers and sisters and I.

I retreated to my room. I needed to

think. In terms of "extras", what would those things be that we couldn't buy any more? New clothes? What would happen if we outgrew our old clothes? Hand-me-downs only last so long. And I'm the oldest. There's no one in our family to hand clothes down to me. When we went to the supermarket, what could we buy? We probably wouldn't be able to buy ice cream or biscuits or any nice things. Would we have to get food stamps? I'd always heard about food stamps but I wasn't sure what they were or how they worked – just that they were supposed to help people feed their families.

I wanted desperately to talk to Jessi. I always talk to my best friend when there's a crisis – or when something good happens. But Jessi had said she was sitting for Charlotte that afternoon. The members of the Babysitters Club (I'll explain about the BSC later) try not to phone each other when we're working. We take our sitting jobs seriously.

But I decided that this was an emergency.

# 2nd CHAPTER

I went into Mum and Dad's bedroom, sat in the flowered armchair, and dialled the Johanssens' number.

Jessi answered the phone professionally. "Hello, Johanssens' residence."

"Hi, Jessi. It's me," I said.

"Mal, what's wrong?" (My voice must have given away my feelings.)

"Mum's really worried," I told Jessi. "She and Dad are pretty sure that Dad's going to lose his job today."

"Lose his *job*? *Your* father?" (I suppose I don't need to point out that Jessi was shocked.)

"Yeah," I said. I explained to Jessi what was happening at Dad's company. Then I added, "I'm really sorry to interrupt you while you're babysitting."

"Oh, that's okay," Jessi answered. "Charlotte's doing her homework. She doesn't even need help." (Charlotte is very bright. She skipped a year in school and is still at the top of her class.)

"I'm just so worried," I told Jessi. "It's bad enough losing your job. But it's especially bad when you have eight kids, a wife – and a hamster – to support."

"Listen, I know this is easy for me to say, but try not to worry. Maybe your dad *won't* lose his job."

"That's what I keep hoping," I answered. Then I sighed. "Oh, well. I'll let you go. I'll see you at the meeting."

We hung up and I went to my bedroom and flopped on my bed. I was hoping for privacy, which meant I was hoping Vanessa would stay out. Since we share a bedroom, I can't force her to stay out, but sometimes Vanessa can tell when I want to be alone, and then she stays away without being asked.

Anyway, I seemed to have the room to myself, so I closed my eyes and thought of Jessi and my other friends, all members of the Babysitters Club. If Dad really did lose his job, I had a feeling I would need my friends. I'd need them to stick by me, and I was pretty sure they would. We've stuck together during bad times, like when Claudia's grandmother died, and when Stacey's parents got divorced.

I think I should tell you about my friends, so you'll know the kind of people I'm talking about. I'll start with Jessi, since she's my best friend. Jessi and I are alike in lots of ways. First of all, we're both eleven. We're the two youngest members of the BSC. Everyone else in the club is thirteen and in the eighth grade at Stoneybrook Middle School. Jessi and I are also both the oldest in our families, although Jessi doesn't have nearly as many brothers and sisters as I do. She just has Becca (short for Rebecca), who is eight, and her baby brother, Squirt, whose real name is John Philip Ramsey, Jr. Jessi and I feel that, although we're the oldest in our families, our parents still treat us like babies sometimes. Our friend Claudia says eleven is a hard age because your parents can't decide whether you *are* a baby or not. For instance, our parents *did* let us get our ears pierced, but Mum and Dad won't let me get contact lenses yet, so I still have to wear my glasses, which I hate. Also, I wear a brace on my teeth. The plastic kind, which doesn't look too bad, but I don't think I'm particularly attractive these days. Hey – if Dad loses his job, maybe the dentist will have to remove my brace! (I knew that was a selfish thought, but it just goes to show how badly I want to get rid of my metal mouth, which is what the kids at school call it, even though it's really a plastic mouth.)

Anyway, Jessi and I both like reading, especially horse stories, and especially the ones by Marguerite Henry. And I *love* to write and draw pictures. I keep a journal in which I write down my innermost thoughts and feelings. I write stories, too, and illustrate them. One day I hope to become an author and illustrator of children's books. Jessi likes to write, too, and recently I convinced her to keep a journal like mine. But her passion is dancing. Jessi is a ballerina. She dances *en pointe* (that means *on toe*), and she takes lessons at this special school in Stamford that she had to audition just to get into. She has performed on stage lots of times and has even had leading roles, or whatever they're called in ballet.

One difference between Jessi and me is our skin colour. She's black and I'm white. This doesn't matter to us or to our BSC friends, but it's been hard to ignore since, when the Ramseys first moved here, some people weren't very nice to them. For reasons I haven't worked out entirely, they didn't want another black family in our community, which is almost all white. (Jessi is the only black kid in the whole of the sixth grade.)

Let's see. What else about Jessi? She's pretty (I think), she has long eyelashes, and long, *long* dancer's legs. She's a good pupil. And she lives with her parents, her brother and sister, and her Aunt Cecelia, who helps run the house since both Mr and Mrs Ramsey work.

Okay. On to the other BSC members. The chairman of the club is Kristy Thomas. (Jessi and I are junior officers, since we're still too young to babysit at night.) Kristy has the most incredible family. (Or as she would say, the most dibble family. *Dibble* is short for *incredible*. My friends love to make up words. Another word meaning *dibble* is *distant*. The opposite of *dibble* and *distant* is *stale*!) Kristy's family is as big as mine, but all mixed up. Kristy lives with her mum; her two older brothers, Charlie and Sam; her little brother, David Michael; her step-father, Watson; her adopted Vietnamese sister, Emily Michelle and her grand-mother, Nannie. Every other week, Watson's children, who live with their mother here in Stoneybrook, come to stay for the weekend. They are Karen and Andrew (seven and almost five) and they're Kristy's stepsister and stepbrother.

The way Kristy acquired this family is that her father walked out right after David Michael was born, leaving Mrs Thomas to bring up four kids. In those days, the Thomases lived across the street from Claudia Kishi (BSC vice-chairman) and next door to Mary Anne Spier (BSC secretary and Kristy's best friend). Mrs Thomas worked hard, finally began to go out on dates (to Kristy's dismay), and soon met Watson Brewer, whom she fell in love with – and married! Watson is a millionaire and has

286

a huge house (okay, it's a mansion) on the other side of town, so he moved the Thomases from their cramped house into his gigantic house. Kristy adjusted pretty well, considering she didn't like Watson at first. But she's used to her new neighbourhood and expanded family.

Kristy is a tomboy who loves sport. She even coaches a softball team called Kristy's Krushers. It's for kids who are too young or too scared to join Little League. Kristy dresses in a sort of tomboyish way, too. She usually wears jeans, trainers, a polo neck, and – in cool weather – a sweater. She likes this old baseball cap with a picture of a collie on it. I suppose I have to say that, although Kristy's mother and stepfather would probably let her wear anything she wants, Kristy just doesn't care that much about clothes. She's a little less mature than her eighth-grade friends, although she does sort of have a boyfriend named Bart, who coaches a rival softball team – Bart's Bashers. (Bart lives in her neighbourhood but goes to a private school. Kristy and we BSC members go to the state school.)

Kristy is the shortest one in her class, has brown hair and brown eyes, and is the only older BSC member who doesn't wear a bra yet. She can be bossy and has a big mouth, but we all love Kristy. She's funny and creative and *great* with children.

As I mentioned before, Claudia Kishi is

the club vice-chairman. She and Kristy are about as different as night and day. Claudia is also outgoing, but she doesn't have a big mouth, and she is *so dibbly* sophisticated and chic. She wears wild clothes like big hats; flowered waistcoats over long shirts that belong to her father and which she leaves untucked; short black trousers and then, something just a little off-beat like penny loafers from the 1950s with white ankle socks. And her jewellery. It's the height of dibble-dom. She makes most of it herself – ceramic-bead necklaces and big dangly earrings, but in shapes you wouldn't expect. For example, in my ears I am allowed to wear studs or *very* tiny gold hoops. That's all. Claudia might wear a monkey in one ear and a banana in the other. Also, one of her ears is pierced twice, so she can wear a hoop and a stud or something in that ear, too. (By the way, Kristy does *not* have pierced ears and neither does Mary Anne.)

How does Claud make her jewellery? She's a fantastic artist, that's how. She's *really* talented. She can paint, draw, sculpt, make collages, you name it. And she takes pottery classes sometimes. Claud's other passions are eating junk food and reading Nancy Drew mysteries, neither of which her parents approve of, so Claud hides the books as well as Mars Bars, crisps, crackers, etc, all over her room.

Claud lives with her parents and her older

sister, Janine. Janine is a certified genius. This is bad news for Claudia, since, although she's bright, she's a terrible pupil — and a worse speller. Her teachers say she could get better grades if she just applied herself, but Claud says she isn't interested. (Personally, I think that Claud is afraid to try harder because she'd find out that even if she did she still couldn't live up to Janine.)

Claudia is Japanese-American, and she is drop-dead gorgeous. She has this *long*, silky black hair, which she likes to wear in different ways. (And of course she has millions of bows and hairslides and things for it.) Her eyes are dark and almond-shaped, and her skin, despite her junk-food addiction, is perfectly clear.

Claud's best friend is Stacey McGill, who's the treasurer of the BSC. Stacey is just as sophisticated and chic as Claudia, if not more so. In fact, the other day, Claudia referred to Stacey as the Queen of Dibbleness. Stacey's family story is about as interesting as Kristy's. She grew up in big, glamorous New York City. Then, just before she was supposed to start the seventh grade there, her father's company transferred him to Connecticut, so Stacey and her parents moved to Stoneybrook. (Stacey's an only child.) The McGills had been here for less than a year when the company moved them *back* to New York. That was hard on everyone, but especially on Claudia and Stacey.

In New York, the McGills' marriage began to fail, and before Stacey knew what had hit her, her parents announced that they were getting a divorce. Not only that, Mr McGill wanted to stay in the city with his job, while Mrs McGill wanted to move back to Stoneybrook. After a lot of thought, Stacey decided to live with her mother (were we ever glad!) but she visits her father in New York pretty often. Guess what? When Stacey and her mum returned to Stoneybrook, they had to find a new house to live in. That was because Jessi and her family had moved into the McGills' old house!

As I mentioned before, Stacey is as cool as Claud. She dresses in outfits that are just as wild, *and* she's allowed to perm her blonde hair sometimes. Also, she likes to wear sparkly nail polish. And in her pierced ears, she often wears earrings that Claud has made for her.

Stacey is pretty, but as far as I'm concerned, too thin. This is probably because on top of her family problems, Stacey has a severe form of diabetes. That's a disease in which her pancreas doesn't make the right amount of something called insulin, which controls her blood sugar. Stacey can't eat sweet things, except for controlled amounts of fruit, and she has to give herself injections (ugh, ugh, UGH!) of insulin everyday. She also has to monitor her blood and eat only a certain number of calories each day. Poor Stace. Some people can control their diabetes with diet alone. They don't have to bother with injections (Ugh!), or blood tests, or calorie-counting. But not Stacey. She has to be *very* careful or she could go into a diabetic coma. My friends and I are a little worried because Stacey hasn't been feeling too great lately. But she seems to be coping.

Two more members of the BSC are Mary Anne Spier and Dawn Schafer. Mary Anne, as I said, is the club secretary and Kristy's best friend. Mary Anne has another best friend, though, and that's Dawn. Like Stacey and Jessi, Dawn is a newcomer to Stoneybrook. (The rest of us were born and grew up here.) Dawn moved to Connecticut from California in the middle of the seventh grade. This was because her parents were getting a divorce, and Mrs Schafer wanted to move back to the town in which she'd been brought up – Stoneybrook. She brought Dawn and Dawn's younger brother, Jeff, with her, and they settled into a colonial farmhouse that has an actual secret passage in it! Soon, Dawn and Mary Anne became friends, and then, guess what they discovered? They found out that Dawn's mum and Mary Anne's dad had been high-school sweethearts. Since Mary Anne's mother had died when Mary Anne was just a baby, the girls decided to reintroduce their parents. And after dating practically for ever, Mr Spier and Mrs Schafer got married – so Dawn and Mary Anne became stepsisters. And now Mary Anne, her father and her kitten, Tigger, live in the Schafers' farmhouse. One sad thing is that Jeff moved back to California to live with his dad. He never adjusted to life in Connecticut. He's much happier in California.

Although Mary Anne and Dawn are best friends, they're pretty different people. Mary Anne is shy and has trouble showing her feelings, except when she cries, which is often. She's also very romantic and is the first BSC member to have a steady boyfriend. (Her boyfriend is Logan Bruno. He comes from Louisville, Kentucky, is nice and funny and understanding, and speaks with a southern drawl.) Mary Anne's father used to be dibbly strict with her. He even chose all her clothes, so she dressed like a first-grader. Now he's relaxed a bit, and so has Mary Anne. She dresses pretty well, especially since she and Dawn can swap clothes. Mary Anne is short, has brown eyes and brown hair, and looks like Kristy!

Dawn, on the other hand, is about as gorgeous as Claudia. Our California girl has LONG blonde hair and sparkly blue eyes. She's not shy like Mary Anne or a loudmouth like Kristy. She's just herself. She's very independent and dresses however she wants, which is usually casual but cool.

Dawn is totally into health food, wouldn't touch meat with a ten-foot pole, and always refuses Claudia's sweets. (This is nice for Stacey.) Dawn likes mysteries and ghost stories (so of course she *loves* the secret passage in her house, which may, by the way, be haunted). And she misses Jeff, her dad and California. Luckily though, she likes Stoneybrook and her new family.

So – those are my friends. The ones I would turn to in a crisis. For instance, if Dad lost his job. But that, I had decided, was not going to happen.

Apparently, my brothers and sisters had decided the same thing.

"See you at dinner," I said as I left for the BSC meeting. "We're going to hear good news then, aren't we, everyone?"

"Of course," said Vanessa. "Dad would never lose his job."

# 3rd
# CHAPTER

I cycled to Claudia Kishi's house and arrived there at 5:20. BSC meetings start at five-thirty on the dot.

"Hi, Claud!" I said as I walked into her room. I sounded pretty cheerful since I'd convinced myself that my family had nothing to worry about.

"Hi," replied Claud. "What kind of snack do you want today?"

I went for the junkiest. "Mars bar," I said immediately.

"Good choice!" Claud must have been in a junky mood, too. "Now if I can just remember where I hid them. . ."

"In your hollow book?" I suggested.

"Nope. They don't fit in there. I've tried. Let me see. . . Oh, yeah." Claud opened a drawer in her desk, found a key, used the key to open her jewellery box, and produced the promised Mars bar.

"How did you fit the Mars bars in there with all your jewellery?" I asked.

"I didn't. I had to take the jewellery out to make room. And I put it. . . Hmm. Oh, yeah. In my pencil case."

I was going to ask Claud where she had put the stuff that was in her pencil case, but I decided not to. Sometimes talking to Claud makes my head spin.

Anyway, the other club members were arriving. By 5:29, Stacey was sitting in Claud's desk chair – backwards, facing into the room, her arms draped over the rungs. Mary Anne, Dawn and Claudia were sitting in a row on Claud's bed, leaning against the wall. Jessi and I were seated cross-legged on the floor, working on a paper-clip chain. And Kristy, ready to start the meeting, was sitting in Claud's director's chair, wearing a visor, a pencil stuck behind one ear, with the club notebook open in her lap.

As the numbers on Claudia's digital alarm clock changed from 5:29 to 5:30, Kristy cleared her throat. Then she said, "Attention! This meeting of the Babysitters Club will now come to order."

As you might have guessed, Claud's bedroom is the official headquarters of the BSC. We meet there three times a week, on Mondays, Wednesdays and Fridays from five-thirty until six, and we take job calls from people who need babysitters. How do people know about our meetings and when to phone us? Because we advertise. Maybe I'd better explain things a little.

The original idea for the Babysitters Club was Kristy's. She got the idea back at the beginning of the seventh grade, just after Stacey had moved to Stoneybrook. In those days, Kristy's mum had not yet married Watson Brewer, the Thomases still lived on Bradford Court across the street from Claudia and next door to Mary Anne and her dad, and Kristy and her older brothers were responsible for babysitting for David Michael after school. But of course an afternoon came when Kristy, Sam, and Charlie were all busy, so Mrs Thomas had to phone for a babysitter and she had to make a lot of calls because no one seemed to be available.

Mum is wasting her time, thought Kristy. And that's when she got her great idea. Wouldn't it be wonderful if her mother could make just one phone call and reach a lot of sitters at once? So Kristy invited Mary Anne and Claudia to form the Babysitters Club with her. The first thing the girls decided, though, was that they really needed at least four members, so they asked Stacey to join the club, too. Stacey and Claudia had met at school and were already becoming friends.

After the girls had decided when they were going to meet, they had to decide where to meet. The answer was obvious: in

Claudia's room, because she's got her own phone, and her own phone number. Then the club members began advertising. They even placed an advert in the *Stoneybrook News*. And during their very first meeting people called them needing babysitters. (Well, actually one person needed a dog-sitter, but that's a long story.) Anyway, by January of that school year, the BSC was getting so much business that when Dawn moved to town, the girls invited her to join the club. Then, at the beginning of the eighth grade (sixth grade for Jessi and me), Stacey moved back to New York. So Kristy, Claudia, Mary Anne and Dawn asked Jessi and me to join the BSC. Of course, when Stacey returned to Stoneybrook after her parents split up, we let her straight back into the club. Now the BSC has seven members and that's plenty. Claud's room is getting crowded!

As chairman of the club, Kristy runs our meetings (quite officially). She also thinks up ways to keep the club efficient – and creative. For instance, the club record book, the club notebook and Kid-Kits were all Kristy's ideas. (The record book is Mary Anne's department, so I'll describe that later.) The notebook is like a diary. It's where we write up each and every job we go on. This is something of a pain, but we all agree that it's necessary and helpful. See, each of us is responsible for reading the notebook once a week. That way we find out what happened during our friends' sitting jobs. We learn how they solved babysitting problems, and we keep up with the children our club regularly sits for. It's always useful to know if a kid has developed a fear, is having trouble at school, or anything else that's new or unusual. Then there are Kid-Kits. I just love mine. When Kristy got the idea for Kid-Kits, each of us made one. We found cardboard boxes, decorated them with paint, fabric and other art supplies belonging to Claudia, then filled the boxes with our old books, toys and games from home, as well as some new, shop-bought things, such as colouring books, Magic Markers, construction paper and stickers. When we go on sitting jobs, we sometimes take the Kid-Kits along. Children love them! They don't even care that half the toys are old. There's just something appealing about playing with toys that are new *to them*. I have to brag a little here and say that the Kid-Kits have helped make us pretty popular babysitters! Anyway, you can see why Kristy, with her big ideas, is such a good chairman for our club.

Claudia is the vice-chairman mostly because three times a week her room is invaded for club meetings, and her junk food is eaten. But she also gets stuck taking calls that, for one reason or another, come in while we're not holding a meeting. Then she has to schedule those jobs herself.

The person who's *really* in charge of scheduling, though, is Mary Anne. As secretary, that's one of her main jobs. Also, she's in charge of the record book. The record book is where we keep track of our clients, their addresses and phone numbers, the rates they pay, how much money we earn (that's actually Stacey's department), and – most important – our schedules. Every time one of our clients calls, Mary Anne opens the record book to the appointment pages and checks to see who's free to take the job. Poor Mary Anne has to remember an awful lot of things, such as when Jessi has ballet classes, I have dental appointments, or Kristy has a Krushers practice. But Mary Anne is organized and precise (she has neat handwriting, too), and she's great at the job. No one could do it better than she does.

As club treasurer, Stacey records the money each of us earns. (This is just for our own information. We don't divide up our earnings or anything.) She also collects subs from us each Monday. The subs go into the club treasury (a manila envelope), and Stacey doles it out as needed: to pay Charlie Thomas to drive Kristy to and from club meetings now that she lives on the other side of town, to help Claudia pay her phone bill, to buy supplies for the Kid-Kits when things run out or get used up, and for fun things such as club parties or sleepovers! Stacey is a very good treasurer. She's a whiz at maths, and she loves money, even if it's really club money. Sometimes we even have a bit of trouble getting her to part with it. But she always does in the end.

Dawn is our alternate officer. Her job is to be able to fill in for anybody who might miss a meeting. In other words, she has to know how to schedule jobs, keep track of money, etc. She's like an understudy in a play. Since most of us don't miss meetings very often, though, she doesn't usually have anything special to do, so we let her answer the phone a lot.

Jessi and I are junior officers, which simply means that we're too young to take evening jobs, unless we're sitting for our own families. But we're still a big help to the club. Taking on a lot of afternoon and weekend jobs frees the older members for the nighttime ones.

Guess what? Technically, there are two other club members. I haven't mentioned them yet because they don't come to meetings. They're our associate members, and they're people we can call on to take a job if none of the rest of us can take it. Believe it or not, that does happen sometimes. Our associate members are Shannon Kilbourne, a friend of Kristy's (she lives across the street from Kristy), and . . .

Logan Bruno, Mary Anne's boyfriend! He's a terrific babysitter.

Our Wednesday meeting was underway. I found that, for short periods of time, I was able to forget that bad news might be waiting for me at home. I tried to concentrate on the meeting.

"Any club business?" asked Kristy.

"Jenny Prezzioso's going to be a big sister!" announced Dawn. I could tell she'd been holding that secret in for a long time, probably since Monday night when she had sat at the Prezziosos'.

"Mrs Prezzioso is going to have a baby and you didn't even tell *me*?" exclaimed Mary Anne. (Mary Anne is the only one of us who tolerates Jenny very well. Jenny is a four-year-old spoiled brat. I wondered how she would react to being a sister and having to share everything – including her parents.)

"It was worth keeping the secret to see the expressions on your faces," Dawn said. "And guess what? The Prezziosos already know what the baby will be. Mrs P had a test done. The baby's going to be a—"

"Wait! Don't tell!" I cried. "I don't know about the rest of you, but I want to be surprised."

"Me, too," said everyone except Mary Anne.

"I'll tell you at home tonight," Dawn said to her stepsister.

"Okay," agreed Mary Anne.

The phone rang then and Dawn answered it. "Hello, Babysitters Club. . . Oh, hi! . . . For a whole month? . . . Oh, okay. I'll check with Mary Anne and call you back." Dawn hung up the phone. "That was Mrs Delaney," she said. (The Delaneys live in Kristy's posh new neighbourhood, right next door to Shannon Kilbourne. There are two Delaney kids — Amanda, who's eight, and Max, who's six. Kristy used to call them the snobs, since they were so bossy and mean when the club first began sitting for them, but now she's changed her mind. She can handle the Delaneys.) "Mrs Delaney wants to go back to work," Dawn told us, "so she's taking a refresher course in property management. She needs a sitter on Mondays, Wednesdays and Fridays from three-thirty till five for the next month."

"Boy, that might be hard to schedule," said Mary Anne, looking at the appointment pages in the record book. "No, wait. You could do it, Mal, and so could you, Kristy."

"You take it, Kristy," I said immediately. "It makes much more sense since you live in the Delaneys' neigbourhood."

So Kristy took the job. I knew she considered that particular meeting a huge success.

# 4th CHAPTER

When the meeting was over, the BSC members trickled out of Claud's house.

"Any word?" Jessi whispered to me as we unchained our bicycles from the Kishis' lamppost.

I shook my head, glad that Jessi hadn't said anything about my dad's job at the meeting. She's a good enough friend to know when to keep quiet. "Dad should be back by the time I get home, though," I said. "I'll phone you tonight to tell you whether the news is good or bad."

"Okay," replied Jessi. "I'll keep my fingers crossed. I'm *sure* the news will be good. Talk to you later."

"Later!" I called as we both rode off.

I pedalled along in the semi-dark. Good news, good news, good news, I said to myself in time to the pedalling.

When I reached my street, I picked up

303

speed. (Good-news-good-news-good-news.) And when I reached my drive, I picked up even more speed. (Goodnewsgoodnewsgoodnews.) I was cycling so fast that I nearly crashed into Dad's car as I sped into the garage.

Calm down, just calm down, I told myself.

I entered our house through the garage door. The TV room was silent and empty. So I ran upstairs to the living room. Everyone was sitting there, either on the couch or chairs, or on the floor.

Nobody needed to tell me what the news was. I could see for myself.

"Oh, Dad," I said, letting out a breath.

"I'm sorry," said Dad simply.

"Hey, you don't have to apologize," I told him quickly. "It wasn't your fault."

"He got a pink slip," Claire spoke up. She was sitting on the floor, playing with Vanessa's hair. "He got it at five o'clock."

"Those stinkers!" I exploded. "Why did they wait so long to tell you? Why didn't they give out all the slips in the morning, instead of driving people mad making them wait all day?"

"I don't know." Dad sighed. "Maybe they were still making decisions about who should go and who should stay. Those aren't easy decisions."

"Well, I still think the people who run your company are really stale."

"Look," said Dad, sounding cross, "I got the sack and that's that. I don't want to spend all night discussing it."

"*Okay. Sorry*," I replied. I was taken aback. Mum and Dad don't usually behave like that. My brothers and sisters and I do sometimes, but not our parents. And especially not Dad. He's a sensitive, gentle person.

"Come on," said Mum. "Let's have dinner."

"Is it okay to eat? Shouldn't we be saving our food for when we really need it?" asked Nicky. He wasn't being cheeky. He *meant* it.

"For pity's sake, we aren't destitute," answered Dad.

"What's 'dessatoot'?" Claire whispered to me as we followed Mum and Dad into the kitchen. I felt bad for her. I knew she was whispering because she didn't want Dad to hear her and get angry with *her*.

"Destitute," I corrected her, "and it means as poor as you can get."

"Very, *very* poor?" whispered Claire.

"Right. Very, very poor. And we aren't very, very poor," (yet, I thought) "so don't worry, okay?"

"Okay."

Dinner that night was gloomy, as you can imagine. At first, no one knew what to say. So we didn't say anything. Then finally Mum spoke up. (Sometimes it's nice to have a mother who speaks her mind. Other times it is dibbly horrible.)

"Okay, everybody," said Mum. "Heads up, eyes on me." She sounded like a teacher, but I think she just didn't want us looking ashamed or embarrassed. We looked at her. Even Dad looked at her. "We've got a problem here," said Mum.

"Duh," muttered Jordan.

"I heard that," Mum said, then continued by saying, "We are a family."

"*We are the world, we are the children*," sang Jordan.

"*Jordan!*" bellowed Dad. (He didn't need to say another word.)

"We are a family," Mum repeated, "and we will stick together and work together and everything will be fine. I want you to understand what I mean by work together," she went on.

"You mean like in the garden?" interrupted Margo.

"Not exactly," said Mum. "I mean, doing what is asked of you, since we're going to have to make some changes. First of all, no extras. That means new clothes only if it's a *necessity*. If it's not a necessity, you wait, or you ask a brother or sister – nicely – if you can borrow something. It means no new toys, because we've got plenty already. It means no trips, and it means that your father or I will do the grocery shopping and we won't hear complaints about what we buy." (I knew it, I thought. This was the end of the junk food.) "Furthermore," continued Mum, "I will be going to work."

"*You* will?" cried Adam. The idea was foreign to him.

"Yup," Mum answered. "I can type and use word processors, so I'm going to register with an agency to do temporary work. That means," she said, "that I won't have a steady job, I'll just be working at companies whenever and wherever I'm needed, and that means that some days I'll be working and some days I won't, and *that* means, Mallory, that if I'm at work and your father needs to go for a job interview, I'll ask you to babysit – for free. Do you understand?"

"Of course," I replied. I was glad I could help out.

"Oh, another thing," said Mum. "I hate to tell you this, but no pocket money until we're back on our feet. We need every penny."

"No pocket money?" repeated Byron. "Aw, *man*."

"Sorry, kiddo," said Mum.

"That's okay," Byron replied, glancing at Dad.

During this whole discussion, Dad hadn't said a word (except to shout at Jordan). Now I studied him and decided he looked almost angry. Why? I wondered. I thought we were all being pretty cooperative and accepting. Mum was going to get work, I had said I'd babysit for nothing (and without any help – Mum usually insists on *two* sitters at our house), and my brothers and sisters and I had barely moaned about cutting back or losing our pocket money. I would have thought Dad would be proud, or at least pleased, but he certainly didn't look as if he *felt* proud or pleased. Which made *me* feel confused.

I was so deep in thought that when Dad said, "Kids?" I jumped a mile.

"Yeah?" we replied.

"I'll be in charge when your mother's at . . . at work," he said gruffly. "I'll expect you to listen to me and behave."

Why wouldn't we? I wondered.

"I'll probably only work a couple of days a week," said Mum apologetically.

"Right," said Dad shortly.

Next to me, Claire became wriggly. I nudged her with my elbow. For some reason it seemed important for us to be model kids, and I realized why. I didn't want to upset Dad any further.

I felt afraid.

When our torturous dinner was finally over, nobody scattered, as we usually do. Instead, we helped clear the table and clear up the kitchen. Then my brothers and sisters and I crept to our rooms, leaving Mum and Dad downstairs.

"Listen everyone," I said softly, standing in the hall, where I knew everyone could hear me. "Come into my room for a sec."

In a minute, the eight of us were jammed into Vanessa's and my bedroom, sombre-faced.

"Okay," I began. "I call to order a meeting of the Pike Club."

Claire brightened up. She likes the idea of clubs and wishes she could belong to the BSC. "What's the Pike Club?" she asked.

"It's us," I replied. "The eight of us. And we're going to meet sometimes while Dad is out of work to talk about things."

"What kind of things?" Nicky wanted to know.

"Well, ways we can help save money. . . And things we're worried about," I tossed in, off-handedly. I knew we were all afraid of things we hadn't mentioned yet.

"I'm scared of Daddy," said Margo in a small voice. "He shouted tonight. And I think he's angry with Mummy."

"He *sounded* as if he was angry with Mummy," I said slowly, "but I think maybe he's angry with himself. Or ashamed. Even though he shouldn't be."

"Well," said Byron, "let's think of some other ways to save money."

"Yeah!" cried Nicky. "Like not leave on lights when we don't need them."

"Good idea," I agreed. "We could probably cut our electricity bill right back just by being careful. Don't leave *any*thing on unless you really need it. We're always forgetting and leaving the power to the stereo on. And we can watch less TV and not use the stereo or our radios too often."

"We should use tea towels instead of paper towels," added Vanessa. "Then we wouldn't have to buy paper towels."

"And only one Kleenex instead of two when we blow our noses," said Claire.

I smiled. "These are all terrific ideas. See what happens when the Pike Club meets? We can think of plenty of ways to cut back." I looked at my brothers and sisters, who seemed relaxed. That was nice.

The first meeting of the Pike Club broke up about ten minutes later. Most of us had homework to do, including me. But instead of starting it, I phoned Jessi.

"My dad lost his job," I whispered to her. (I didn't want my family to know that I was already spreading our bad news.)

"He *did*?" Jessi squeaked. "I don't believe it. How stale." She paused. "Mal? Is there anything I can do?"

I thought for a moment. "Not really, I suppose. Just . . . just let me lean on you when I need to. My brothers and sisters are all leaning on *me*."

"Boy," and Jessi. "If they lean on you and you lean on me, I might fall over."

"Please don't," I said, giggling.

"I won't. You know I'm here," Jessi told me seriously.

"I know. Thanks, Jessi. I'll see you tomorrow. Good night."

"'Night, Mal."

# 5th CHAPTER

Friday afternoon arrived. It was time for the next meeting of the Babysitters Club. Two days had passed since the last meeting and since my dad lost his job, but the days felt more like years. Mum had registered with the temping agency, but they hadn't contacted her with a job yet. And my dad had launched right into his search for a new job. He worked so hard at it that he was making a job out of looking for a job.

However, my parents didn't seem much happier than they had on Wednesday night. Breakfast and dinner were agonizing times. Dad was gruff and cross, Mum was constantly apologizing for him, and the rest of us didn't know what to do or say, so mostly we were silent. Neither Mum nor Dad seemed to notice the money-saving campaign that my brothers and sisters and I had started, though the house was noticeably

312

quiet with the TV, stereo and radios off most of the time. Mum and Dad didn't even say anything when we washed the dishes by hand on Tuesday night, so as not to use up electricity by running the dishwasher. I think Mum and Dad were dazed.

I called Jessi regularly to report on things.

By Friday, my friends knew what had happened. Mum and Dad had not said to keep Dad's job loss a secret, and anyway, secrets don't last long in the BSC. So when I reached Claud's room that afternoon I was greeted by a chorus of, "How were things this afternoon?" and, "How's your dad doing?"

"Okay," I had time to answer before Claud's clock turned to 5:30 and Kristy called our meeting to order.

"Any club business?" Kristy asked, then immediately answered her own question. "I move that we let Mal have the job at the Delaneys', that is, if Mrs Delaney approves. You haven't sat for the Delaneys, have you, Mal?"

I shook my head. Why was Kristy giving me the job?

"I second the motion," said Claudia.

"I third it," said Dawn, and we laughed.

"Just a minute, you lot. What's going on?" I asked. "Kristy, how come you can't take the job with Amanda and Max?"

"Oh, I can take it. But I think you need it more than I do." Kristy stopped abruptly, probably wondering if she'd just blurted out something she shouldn't have said. "You're not offended, are you?" she asked.

"No," I replied. "Just, um, surprised. And – And—" I didn't know what else to say except, "Thank you, Kristy." Then I thought of something. "Wait a sec! Don't phone Mrs Delaney yet. How am I going to get to your neighbourhood every day, Kristy? I can't cycle that far, and I can't ask my parents for a lift either." (It had been Jordan's idea to save on petrol.)

"No problem. I've got it all worked out," Kristy answered. She grinned at me from under her visor. "Mrs Delaney needs a sitter on Mondays, Wednesdays and Fridays, right?"

"Right," I said.

"And those are club meeting days, right?"

"Right."

"Okay, so three times a week you'll take the bus home with me, go over to the Delaneys', and then travel with Charlie and me to Claudia's. Charlie can even drop you off at your house after the meetings, since you won't have your bike."

"I think we should let Mal have as many sitting jobs as she can handle," added Claudia. "Tuesdays, Thursdays, weekends. Whatever jobs come in."

"Yeah, Mal has first refusal on daytime jobs," said Stacey. "That's fair."

"Mal?" asked Jessi. "Mal?"

I hadn't said anything because I was desperately trying not to cry. I swallowed hard and finally found my voice. "Thanks," I managed to say. "This is – I mean, you lot are—"

"Don't! Stop!" exclaimed Mary Anne. "In a few seconds, *I'm* going to cry!"

"Oh, lord," said Claud.

"I'll call Mrs Delaney," Kristy spoke up in her most businesslike voice.

There. That was good. The meeting began to feel more normal.

Mrs Delaney agreed to the change in sitters without even asking questions. She trusts the BSC.

So the job became mine. By that time, I was more in control. (So was Mary Anne.) "This is dibbly great," I said. "I've decided I'm going to give all of my babysitting money to Mum and Dad to help with the groceries and stuff. Well, I'll give them most of it, anyway. I might save a little for myself in case I need something. Then I won't have to ask them to buy it for me."

The phone rang then. It was Mrs Prezzioso needing a sitter for the following Tuesday afternoon. Mary Anne gave me the job after saying, "Only if you really want it, Mal. I know how you feel about Jenny. I'll take the job if you don't want to go to the Prezziosos'."

"No, I'll go. I can't afford to be a baby

now. I'll put up with Jenny." I felt like a soldier volunteering to cross enemy lines or something equally dangerous.

So I got the job with Jenny. Wow! I thought. I'll be rich! Then I paused. No, I wouldn't. And neither would my parents when I turned my pay over to them. Babysitting money was not going to feed ten people.

The phone rang several more times, and several more jobs were scheduled.

After the last call, Claud waited a moment to see if the phone would ring again. When it didn't, she reached behind her pillow and pulled out a bag of Hula Hoops, which she passed around.

"Hey, Jessi, Mal," she said. "You know what happened at lunch today?"

"What?" we asked. (Jessi and I eat lunch with the sixth-graders. The other club members eat with the eighth-graders during a later period. They all sit together. Sometimes Logan joins them.)

"Dori Wallingford fainted."

"You're kidding!" exclaimed Jessi. But I wasn't listening. I couldn't help thinking about what had happened during *my* lunch break.

"Mal. . . ? Mal?" Claud was saying. "Earth to Mal."

"Oh, sorry." I must have been on another planet.

"Anything wrong?" asked Dawn.

I glanced at Jessi. *She* knew what was wrong.

"It s just that . . . well, at lunch today, um—" I began.

"Yeah?" said Mary Anne.

"Nan White – Do you know her?" I asked my friends.

"I do, sort of," said Kristy. "She isn't the nicest person in the world. She likes to put people down. Especially – don't take this the wrong way, Mal – but especially people who aren't good at fighting back."

"Well, she chose the right person," I said. "Jessi and I were eating lunch, minding our own business, when Nan came up to me and said, 'I heard your father got the sack. What'd he do? Steal from his company?'"

"I hope you denied that," said Stacey, looking astonished.

"I tried to. But Nan was with Janet O'Neal," I replied.

"A bad combination," added Jessi.

"Yeah," I agreed. "And the two of them stood there and laughed and said that *their* fathers had never lost their jobs. And then they sat down with Valerie and Rachel, and all *four* of them began talking about me. I know they were talking about me because they kept looking over at our table. They weren't very subtle. And they laughed a lot."

"I thought Valerie and Rachel were friends of yours," said Kristy.

"I thought so, too," I said.

"That is *so mean!*" cried Mary Anne. "Why would Nan White start something like that? Well, actually I can see why *she* would do that, but why would Valerie and Rachel join in and laugh and stuff?"

"I don't know," I replied. "I'm glad they're not close friends. If they were, I'd feel like a real outcast. Instead I just feel . . . hurt, I suppose."

"You have every right to feel hurt," spoke up Jessi. "They were being cruel."

"I wonder why some kids always want to hurt other kids," I mused.

"I don't know," said Jessi slowly. "I think Nan was just born that way."

"Maybe," said Mary Anne thoughtfully, "Valerie and everybody were laughing because they're afraid. You know how sometimes you tease people because you need to feel that you're better than they are? Not that you tease, Mal. I mean, just in general. Well, maybe those girls were laughing to cover up the fact that *they're* afraid *their* parents might lose their jobs some day. And they're glad it hasn't happened yet."

"Maybe," I answered. It was a good theory, but I didn't feel any better.

"Well," said Stacey, "don't worry, Mal. *We'll* stick by you."

"Definitely," agreed Claud.

"Right," added Jessi. "You all stuck by

me when I first moved here and people snubbed me. Now we'll stick by you."

"The members of the BSC *always* stick together," said Kristy from the director's chair.

"I wish Jessi and I were in your grade," I told her. "Then we could really stick together."

"Boy, I'd like to teach Nan White something," said Kristy. "And Janet and Valerie and Rachel, too."

"Don't get carried away," Mary Anne warned her.

"I won't," Kristy promised.

"You lot are great," I said huskily.

"Oh, please. Don't start crying!" exclaimed Mary Anne.

And then we laughed again. We sounded like we did at the beginning of the meeting. But I couldn't help adding, just as Claud's clock turned to 6:00, "You're the best friends ever."

And Dawn said, "You'll get through this, Mal. I know you will."

I cycled home that evening thinking that she was right, but not knowing just *how* I would get through it.

# 6th CHAPTER

"Smell this.

"Do I have to?"

"Yes. Just smell it."

"Ugh! That's so gross. What is it?"

"My gym socks. Can't you tell?"

"No. They look like—"

"Don't listen to them, Mal!" Kristy hissed in my ear.

It was Monday, the afternoon of my first sitting job at the Delaneys'. Kristy and I were sitting on her bus home, and behind us, two kids were having a dibbly disgusting conversation, which was hard not to overhear.

"Concentrate on Amanda and Max," said Kristy. "I've got to give you some sitting tips on them, anyway, since this will be your first job with them."

"Okay," I replied.

"Now," began Kristy, "this is very

important. *Don't let them get away with anything.*"

"Like what?" I asked.

"Anything they shouldn't be doing, or anything they *should* be doing for themselves. They love to test new sitters. Don't let them order you around."

"Kristy—" I interrupted.

"No, I'm serious. I know you're a good sitter, and I know you know how to control children, but Amanda and Max are a little bit different."

"Okay," I said uncertainly. I'd never met a kid I couldn't handle. However, I'd also never been given such a warning about sitting charges.

"Phone me if you have any trouble," was the last thing Kristy said to me as we got off the bus. (The two kids who'd been sitting behind us were still talking about the smell of the decaying gym socks, trying to come up with an exact description of their odour. I was glad to leave them behind.)

"I will," I called to Kristy, even though I wouldn't. "Thanks for letting me ride with you!"

"You're welcome. . . Good luck with Amanda and Max!"

Kristy crossed the street to her house and I walked slowly up the Delaneys' drive. Good luck? Would I really need luck that afternoon?

I hesitated on the Delaneys' front porch,

then rang the bell. In a few moments, the door was opened by a tall woman who gave me a smile.

"Mallory?" she said.

"Yes. Mrs Delaney?"

"Yup. Come on inside."

Now, I should stop here and tell you that from the outside, the Delaneys' house looked like any other mansion in the neighbourhood. But inside! The inside of Kristy's house is like the inside of any house, only bigger. There are a lot of ordinary-looking rooms with toys and homework papers and jackets and trainers scattered around. Inside the Delaneys' house was another story.

The first thing I saw, right in the front hall, was a *fountain*. Honestly. A fountain that was *indoors*. It was golden, and in the shape of a fish standing on its tail. The water splashed out of its mouth and down into this pool that surrounded it.

Whoa.

I looked from left to right as Mrs Delaney led me down a short hallway to the kitchen. We passed a library and a study and the living room. Oriental carpets and gilt-framed pictures were everywhere. And I didn't see a single speck of dust or anything on the floor that didn't belong there. Amanda and Max probably weren't allowed in those rooms. If they were, they must be pathologically neat, I thought. At the end of the hallway was the kitchen, which Kristy had told me looked like a space control centre. She was right. It was full of gadgets and appliances, all gleaming white, that were operated mostly by button panels that looked as if they would light up when you touched them. I hoped I wouldn't have to use any of the gadgets to make the kids an after-school snack. I'd be lucky to find the fridge.

"Okay," began Mrs Delaney. "Amanda and Max should be home from school any minute now. Their bus gets here a little later than yours does. The emergency numbers are by the telephone. Our GP is Doctor Evans. And our next-door neighbours are the Kilbournes – I think you know Shannon?" (I nodded.) "And the Winslows. . . Let's see. Did Kristy tell you about our swimming pool?"

"No," I replied. How could Kristy have forgotten to mention that? I knew the Delaneys had two tennis courts, but I didn't know they had a pool.

"Okay," said Mrs Delaney. "The pool has just been installed. It's built in, of course." (Of *course*, I thought.) "Amanda and Max are both good swimmers. They can use the pool any time they want, as long as an adult is supervising them. When a sitter is in charge, then one of the next-door neighbours must be at home – just in case of an emergency. Both Mr and Mrs Kilbourne work, as you probably know, but Mrs Winslow said she'd be at home all afternoon, so swimming is okay today. Now, a lot of Amanda's and Max's friends want to go swimming as well. The rule for them is that when a sitter is in charge, they can only use the pool if they are good swimmers – if they can swim the width of the pool without stopping to rest. Amanda knows who those children are, and that the others may not go in the water."

"Okay," I said. "And I'm a good swimmer myself, so you don't need to worry."

Mrs Delaney smiled, checked her watch, and announced, "Well, I'm off. I'll be back by five. Phone Mrs Winslow if you need her."

I breathed a sigh of relief as Mrs Delaney pulled out of the drive. Then I rummaged around the kitchen, found some fruit and crackers and put them on the table for Amanda and Max. A few moments later, I heard the front door open.

"Hello!" I called, running into the hall.

There were Amanda and Max, perfect children in tidy school uniforms.

"Are you Mallory?" asked Amanda.

"Yup," I replied. "Hi, you two. Your mum's just left. She'll be back at five. I've got a snack ready for you in the kitchen."

"In the *kitchen*!" exclaimed Amanda. "We never eat in there."

"Well, you're eating there today," I replied.

Amanda and Max didn't answer. They

just put their school bags in the cupboard and followed me to the kitchen.

"Is that our snack?" asked Max, looking at the fruit and crackers in dismay. He eyed his sister.

"We always have Coke and crisps – or whatever we want – for a snack," Amanda informed me, busily putting away the things I had put out.

I let the kids get away with this, since they had agreed to eat in the kitchen. Besides, I hadn't seen any crisps or a bottle of Coke in several days.

The three of us sat down at the table, Max and Amanda looking at me curiously.

"Are you a friend of Kristy's?" asked Max.

"Yup," I replied. "I know her whole family. I know Shannon Kilbourne, too." (Shannon often babysits for the Delaneys.)

"Where do you live?" asked Amanda.

"On Slate Street."

Amanda frowned. "I don't know where that is. Which school do you go to – Stoneybrook Academy or Stoneybrook Day School?"

"Silly," said Max. "She must go to Stoneybrook Academy. *We* go to the day school, and we'd know if Mallory went there, too."

I smiled. "Actually, I go to Stoneybrook Middle School."

"Do you have any pets?" asked Max.

"Just a hamster. We used to have a cat, though."

"We have a cat," said Amanda. "Her name is Priscilla. She's a snow-white Persian and she cost four hundred dollars."

*Four hundred dollars for a cat?* I thought. Boy, you could get one free at a shelter. And you could certainly spend four hundred dollars on better things, like groceries.

"How about brothers and sisters?" asked Amanda.

"I've got seven," I said.

"*Seven!*" squealed Amanda. "Gosh, your father must be rich. What does he do? I bet it's something really important."

I believe it's always best to be honest with children, so I said, "Actually, my dad isn't working right now. He's just lost his job."

"He did?" exclaimed Max.

"Well, *our* father," said Amanda, "is a partner in a *law firm*. He makes a lot of money. He gets Max and me whatever we want."

"Yeah," said Max. "We have tennis courts *and* a pool."

And a four-hundred-dollar cat, I thought. But all I said was, "I know."

"Our swimming pool is huge," said Amanda. "It has very beautiful steps in two corners and it's painted aquamarine blue and it's got a slide and a diving board. Max and I go swimming all the time. Our

326

friends come over to swim, too. We have lots of friends. Is Mrs Winslow at home, Mallory?"

"Yes," I answered.

"Great."

The next thing I knew, Amanda was on the phone, inviting her friends to come to her house for a swim. Then she and Max changed into their bathing suits and ran outside. They jumped into the pool.

Of course, *I* didn't have *my* suit with me. So I sat in a lawn chair by the side of the pool and felt like a real dork.

Soon kids began to appear at the gate in the fence that surrounded the pool. The first three must have been the kids Amanda had phoned. She ran to the gate and let each of them in gleefully. I tried to watch five bouncy children and it wasn't easy, so I was alarmed when yet another kid, a girl about Max's age, came to the gate. But I felt relieved when Amanda stalked over to the girl and bossily said, "You can't come in. You can't swim yet."

My relief faded quickly when I saw the look on the girl's face, though. Chastised, she turned and walked slowly towards the drive. Amanda watched her, looking smug.

Ten minutes later, the same thing happened with a little boy.

"Amanda!" I called.

Amanda trotted over to me. "Yeah?"

"Can't you tell them *nicely* that they

can't swim today? I think you've hurt that boy's feelings."

"Well, he deserved it. He hurt mine once. Besides, he can't swim."

"Amanda, don't use the pool as a way to get back at people. Or to make friends. I think you'll be sorry."

"Huh?" replied Amanda. She wasn't even listening. She was watching Max swoop down the slide and into the water with a splash.

"Never mind," I said, and Amanda ran off.

For the next hour I sat in the hot sun in my school clothes while the Delaneys and their friends played with their new toy. I thought of Claire at home who wanted a new toy, too – a Skipper doll she had seen advertised on TV. She knew she couldn't have it. Not now.

How unfair, I thought, as I looked around at the pool and the tennis courts and the big house with its fish fountain.

I felt like a nothing.

# 7th CHAPTER

Saturday

I sat at the Delaneys' house today. The weather was gorgeous, and the kids were already in the pool when I arrived— Amanda, Max, Karen Brewer, Timmy Hsu and two kids I'd never met before whose names are Angie and Huck. (Huck isn't his real name, but that's what everyone calls him.)

Anyway, I see a little problem with Amanda and Max and the pool. You wrote about it after your first job at the Delaneys', Mal, but today it's taken a different course. This time, Amanda's feelings were hurt....

Stacey had gone on an unexpected Saturday job at the Delaneys'. Of course, the members of the BSC had offered it to me first, but I couldn't take it. I was just too busy. I was babysitting more than ever, and I felt pressured to do better than usual at school. I was going to need good grades to get a scholarship to college if Dad didn't find another job. Oh, of course, college was seven years away, but you just never know. It's always best to be prepared. Thrifty, too. I had learned a lot over the last week or so.

Anyway, that Saturday I was sitting for the Barretts for a couple of hours, and then I needed time to work on a social studies project. So Stacey went to the Delaneys'. She brought her swimsuit along, having learned from my first experience there. She didn't want to be unprepared.

Stacey has babysat for Amanda and Max before. They think she's weird. That's because when the BSC first began sitting for the Delaneys, and the kids were so awful, Stacey decided to use backwards psychology (or something like that) on Amanda and Max. When they became too demanding, she would encourage them to be more demanding (which caused them to behave). When they didn't want to clean up their playroom, Stacey made it into a huge mess – which the kids quickly cleaned up before their mother got home.

So Stacey could handle the Delaneys, but the kids thought she was a nut case.

As Stacey had written in the notebook, she arrived at Amanda and Max's to find them in the pool with four friends, one of whom (Karen Brewer) is Kristy's little stepsister. Mrs Delaney had led Stacey out to the pool area (after Stace had changed into her bikini) and announced, "Kids, Stacey's here! She's in charge until your father and I get back. Remember the pool rules!"

"Okay, we will. Bye, Mummy!" Amanda called. (Max was underwater.)

Stacey seated herself at the edge of the shallow end of the pool, where most of the kids were playing. She let her legs dangle in the water.

"Hi, Stacey!" called Karen, who knows Stacey well. "Watch this!"

Karen scrambled out of the pool, backed up several paces, held her arms up in front of her, and said, "Okay, here I am, walking along, reading my newspaper. I'm just walking along—" SPLASH! Karen pretended to fall into the pool accidentally. The other kids laughed.

Amanda eyed Stacey. "Can I have a snack?" she asked.

Stacey sensed a test. She checked her watch. "It's two o'clock," she said. "Haven't you just had lunch?"

"Yes," admitted Amanda, "but I'm hungry again. I want—"

"Gosh, if you're hungry," said Stacey, "I'd better make you a nice, healthy meal. That's the best way to make hunger go away. I'll get you some yoghurt, some fruit and maybe a small green salad."

"Oh, never mind," said Amanda. She pushed herself away from the edge of the pool, glided over to Max, and said to him (not very softly), "She's crazy. She is *so weird.*"

"I know," replied Max, but he seemed unfazed. He was diving for a penny that he'd dropped on the floor of the pool.

Amanda and Karen played together for a while. Angie practised diving off the board into the deep end. And Timmy and Huck took one joyous ride after another down the slide and into the water. Presently, Amanda swam over to Stacey again, climbed out of the pool, and sat down next to her. Stacey placed a towel around her shoulders and patted her back.

"Thanks," said Amanda. She looked thoughtful. Finally she said, "Do you know Mallory Pike? Our new babysitter?"

"Of course," replied Stacey.

"Her father . . . got *fired.*"

"I know." Stacey wondered where this conversation was going and decided to let Amanda make the next move.

"What does your father do?" asked Amanda.

"He works for a company . . . in New York."

"In *New York*? Does he live there?"

"Yes," replied Stacey. "My parents are divorced."

Amanda frowned.

"But I get to visit my dad in the city whenever I want to."

"*Really?*" Amanda was impressed. "Does your father make a lot of money?"

Stacey was insulted. But she tried not to show it, even though she wanted desperately to say, "He makes enough to buy a four-hundred-dollar cat." Before she could come up with a polite answer, however, she was interrupted by Max.

He was climbing out of the pool, penny in hand.

"Stacey?" he said. "I'm tired of swimming."

"Me, too," said Amanda, who didn't seem inclined to return to the water. "Max and I have been swimming all morning."

"Okay," Stacey answered. "Call your friends out of the pool and we'll find something else to do. Maybe we can play a game."

"Hey, everyone!" called Amanda, standing up. "It's time to get out of the pool. We're going to play a game."

"I don't want to get out," replied Huck immediately.

"Me, neither," said Angie. "I've got to practise my diving."

"Come on, Timmy!" called Max.

"No. I've just got here."

"*Angie!*" Amanda whined.

"I'm diving," was the reply.

"I'll play with you, Amanda," said Karen, hoisting herself on to the side of the pool.

"Thanks," Amanda answered. Then she looked from the kids in the pool to Stacey. What was Stacey going to do about the situation? she seemed to be asking.

Clearly, Stacey had to do something. There was only one Stacey. She couldn't watch Timmy, Angie and Huck in the pool, and Amanda, Karen and Max somewhere else.

So Stacey stood up, too. "Okay, everybody out of the water!" she announced.

"I don't *want* to get out!" said Huck vehemently.

"And I have to practise," added Angie.

"I thought you kids came over to play with Max and me," said Amanda, looking wounded. Her lower lip trembled ever so slightly.

"Well . . . well. . ." began Angie.

And Timmy said, "It's so hot today."

Max had said very little up until this point. Now he said, sounding almost afraid, "Huck? *Didn't* you come over to play with me?"

"I—" began Huck. He paused. Then he said, "Yeah. You and your pool."

"You lot are jerks!" Amanda shouted suddenly.

"No, we aren't. You are!" Angie retorted.

"Jerk, jerk, jerk!" chanted Max.

Timmy looked haughty. "I'm rubber, you're glue, and whatever you say bounces off me and sticks to you. So *you're* the jerk, Max."

"Okay, okay, okay," said Stacey firmly. "Enough. I'm in charge here. And I'm mostly in charge of Amanda and Max, and they don't want to play in the pool any more. So, everybody out!"

Heaving great, exaggerated sighs, Huck, Angie and Timmy got out of the pool. Max and Amanda brightened up.

"Let's play dressing-up," Amanda said to Angie and Karen.

"Let's play dinosaurs," Max said to Huck and Timmy.

But Huck and Timmy were heading for the gate in the fence. "No, thanks," said Huck.

And Angie was gathering up her towel and a sundress. "I'm going to the Millers'," she informed everyone. "I'll practise in *their* pool."

Huck, Timmy and Angie left.

Stacey looked at the distraught, confused faces of Max and Amanda. She wasn't sure what to say to them. So she was relieved when Karen piped up.

"Do you have any new dressing-up clothes?" Karen asked Amanda. Then she added, "It doesn't matter if you do or not. You know what? We haven't played Lovely Ladies in a long time. Do you still have your Lovely Ladies clothes?"

Amanda nodded, trying not to cry.

"Well, then," said Stacey brightly, "why don't you two go upstairs, take off your wet suits, and turn yourselves into Lovely Ladies? Max, what do you want to do? You could invite another friend over."

Max shook his head. He and Stacey were following the girls into the house.

"Would you like me to read to you? Stacey asked him.

"I suppose so." Max shrugged.

"Okay." Stacey waited for Max to get dressed. Then she settled down with him in the Delaneys' immaculate white playroom and read him book after book. Max only half listened to the stories.

And from the sounds of things in Amanda's room, the game of Lovely Ladies was only half-hearted too.

# 8th
# CHAPTER

At home, our days fell into a pattern that was different from (but also similar to) the one we'd had before Dad lost his job. Our family continued to get up at six-thirty in the morning on weekdays. My brothers and sisters and I got up then so we would arrive at school on time. Mum got up then so she would be ready if the agency called and said she had a job somewhere that day. And Dad got up then in case Mum *did* have a job. Then he would help to make breakfast and get us kids off to school.

When we came home in the afternoon, Dad would be looking for a job. He spent a lot of time poring over Situations Vacant in the paper and even more time on the phone. I looked at the situations vacant section once after Dad had been through it. Some of the little boxes were circled in pencil, some were circled vigorously in ink, and others had been circled with a red felt-tip pen. Phone numbers and names were scribbled all up and down the margins of the pages.

Claire complained, "Daddy never plays with me after he picks me up from school. He just sits in the kitchen and works."

"He's trying to find another job," I told her. "That's very important, remember? He needs a job so he can earn money again."

"So I can get the Skipper doll?"

"So you can get the Skipper doll."

Meanwhile, Mum had gone out on lots of jobs. I couldn't tell if she liked what she was doing or not. Most of the jobs were secretarial. Mum said she would type letters for people and file papers and answer telephones. She made the work sound boring, but to me, it sounded better than changing sheets and ironing clothes at home, although not better than the volunteer work my mother does. Mum said she liked word processing, though. She likes computers, which I hadn't expected, and seems to know a lot about them, which I also hadn't expected.

After about two weeks of this routine, things changed slightly. Mum was working three or four days a week. But Dad seemed to have slowed down his job hunt.

"Why?" I asked him.

"Because I've exhausted most of the possibilities," he replied. "I'm beginning to see the same jobs listed over and over again in the paper. I've sent out copies of my cv, I've made phone calls. Now there's nothing left to do except wait for people to call and say they want to arrange interviews."

Dad looked discouraged – and right when I thought he should be feeling good. He'd done all the hard work. Now he just had to sit back and wait for the phone to ring.

One Tuesday, not long after Dad said he'd "exhausted the possibilities", I came home from school earlier than usual. I had no sitting job that afternoon, and school had come to an abrupt end ten minutes before the final bell because we'd had a false fire alarm. I parked my bike in our garage and ran inside, expecting to find Dad in the kitchen with the paper.

Instead, I found him sprawled in an armchair in the TV room. He was wearing jeans, a T-shirt and these awful old slippers that the triplets tease him about. Next to him was a box of crackers, half empty, and in his hand was a glass of something. The TV was playing – a game show was on, I think – but Dad didn't seem to be paying attention to it. His eyes were aimed in the direction of the TV set, but I could tell he wasn't trying to come up with the answer to the clue "favourite clothing of idiots". (The answer was "dunce caps".)

And I hoped he hadn't been watching TV all day. He would make our electricity bill too high.

"Dad?" I said. "Where's Claire?"

"Huh?" I realized that although I had not been quiet about coming home, Dad hadn't been aware of my presence until I spoke. "Oh, hi, Mal," he said absently.

"Hi. Where's Claire?" I repeated.

"Claire? She was here a while ago." Dad glanced around the room until his eyes settled on the TV screen again.

"Claire? Claire!" I called. I dropped my books on the floor and ran upstairs to the kitchen. On the way, I imagined two things. 1. Claire was missing. 2. Claire had taken advantage of things and made a huge mess somewhere. I decided the second possibility was more likely. But I was wrong. Claire was neither missing nor a mess. She was sitting on her bed in the room she shares with Margo, playing with two old baby dolls.

"Bad!" she was saying to one of the dolls. "Bad girl. You put that back. You can't have it. Daddy is sacked now."

She turned to the other doll. "Stop it!" she cried. "Stop pestering me. I've just told you – you *can't* have a new Skipper. And that's final!"

"Hi, Claire," I said.

Claire dropped the dolls and glanced up, looking somewhat guilty. "Hi," she replied.

"Have you been playing up here all afternoon?" I asked her.

"Pretty much," said Claire. "I went

downstairs three times to ask Daddy to play with me, and he just said, 'Not now'."

"Did Daddy give you lunch after school?"

"He said I could have whatever I wanted."

"What did you want?"

"Twinkies, but we didn't have any." Claire's chin was trembling.

"So you haven't eaten?"

Claire shook her head. "Daddy is an old silly-billy-goo-goo."

I sat down on the bed and put my arms around my sister.

I don't know for sure what Dad did the next afternoon, because it was Wednesday and I sat at the Delaneys' and then went to Claudia's for the BSC meeting. I think Dad did pretty much the same things as he had the day before, though. At any rate, when I came home from the meeting, he was wearing the T-shirt, jeans and decrepit slippers again. But at least he was in the kitchen helping Mum cook dinner.

On Thursday afternoon, I came home loaded with schoolwork. My social studies teacher had assigned another project, I had a French test coming up, and both my maths and science teachers had given us more homework than usual. Ordinarily, I would just have done the best I could in whatever amount of time I had. But now I was determined to get straight A's. (I'd need them for that college scholarship.) So I planned to shut myself up in my bedroom and study until bedtime, only taking time off for dinner.

But Dad ruined my plans.

After school, I found him once again parked in front of the TV, wasting electricity, this time wearing his bathrobe and pyjamas. And the slippers, of course. A soap opera was on TV. Dad has always said soap operas are silly, but he seemed rather interested in this one.

"Hi, Dad," I said wearily. "Where are Claire and Margo and Nicky?" (Mum was working that day. I knew Margo and Nicky were home from school because their bikes were parked in the garage.)

"Upstairs," replied Dad vaguely.

"Dad? Are you okay?" I asked. I had been angry with him on Tuesday. Today I was worried. Maybe he was ill. Maybe that was why he was in his bathrobe and pyjamas.

"I'm fine," Dad answered, not taking his eyes off the television.

"Are you sure?"

Dad came to life. "I'm *sure*. I just wish everyone would stop asking how I am and leave me alone."

"Okay, okay, okay," I said. I thought that Margo, Nicky and Claire must have asked him the same thing and been yelled at, too. Then it dawned on me. Claire. If Dad was still in his pyjamas, and Mum was at work, how had Claire got home from the nursery? Had Dad gone out in public in his pyjamas? Had he let Claire *walk* home from school? She'd never done that before.

"Claire? Claire?" I shouted. I bounded upstairs. I didn't need this problem today. Not before my French test on a night when I had at least two nights' worth of studying to do.

"Yeah?" Claire replied.

She and Margo and Nicky were in the living room, sitting in a row on the couch. They looked as if they were in a doctor's waiting room.

"What's going on, you lot?" I asked. Then, before I gave them a chance to answer, I said, "Claire, how did you get home from school today?"

"Myriah's mummy picked me up."

"Mrs Perkins? Why did she pick you up?"

"Because Daddy phoned her and asked her to."

I didn't pursue the subject. It would have to wait until Mum came home. "So what *are* you lot doing here?"

Margo and Nicky glanced at each other. "Daddy yelled at us," said Margo.

"Did he tell you to come up here and sit on the couch?" I wanted to know.

Nicky shook his head. "Nope. We just felt like being together."

"And Daddy said, '*Leave me alone!*'" added Claire.

Great, I thought. Dad wasn't going to look after the kids. So I would have to. But how could I revise? In the end, I encouraged Margo and Nicky to go to friends' houses, and the triplets to play baseball in the back garden. Then I parted with some of my hard-earned babysitting money to pay Vanessa to watch Claire.

When Mum came home late that afternoon, she was not happy to hear about any of this – particularly the part about Dad asking Mrs Perkins to bring Claire home from the nursery.

She confronted Dad in the TV room, where he had become, I decided, an official couch potato. "This is—" she started to say loudly. Then she seemed to change her mind. She also lowered her voice. "I cannot," she said, "work all day, come home, make dinner, *clear up the house*," (I looked around and saw that the TV room had become a real mess) "*and* help the children with their homework."

"Mum," I said, feeling guilty, "I'm sorry about the house. I should have cleared it up this afternoon, but I—"

"It's not your fault," my mother interrupted me. "And it's not your job, either. You have homework and babysitting." She turned to Dad. "It's *your* job," she said flatly. "When I go to work and you stay at home, then you keep house, just as I do when I'm at home."

"*Excuse* me?" replied my father.

A row was coming on. I could tell. I glanced up at the stairs, saw my brothers and sisters huddled in the kitchen, watching, and led them to their rooms.

We couldn't eavesdrop on the row – it wasn't loud enough – but my mother must have won. By the following Tuesday, Dad had taken over Mum's old role completely. He wasn't much of a cook, but dinner was ready when I came home from the Friday and Monday BSC meetings. The house grew neater and cleaner – and so did Dad. He started getting dressed again.

And on that Tuesday, when I returned from school, loaded with homework again, I found Dad and Claire together in the kitchen, working on a project together. Dad was up to his elbows in glue and macaroni.

For some reason, that scene scared me more than the couch-potato scene had. That night, I called another meeting of the Pike Club.

# 9th CHAPTER

It took me a while to realize why the sight of Dad and Claire had scared me. I should have been dibbly happy to see my father so cheerful. And wearing shoes. I should have been happy to find a neat house, clean bathrooms, and Bolognese sauce simmering on the stove. I should have been happy that Dad had picked up Claire from school himself and had thought of an afternoon art activity for her. But I wasn't.

Why? Because, I realized after almost twenty minutes of thinking when I should have been doing my homework, Dad looked as if he was enjoying himself. What if he didn't find another job? What if he didn't *care* that he didn't find another job?

That was only one reason why I called an emergency meeting of the Pike Club.

The triplets, Vanessa, Nicky, Margo,

Clare and I gathered, once again, in my bedroom. Nobody else was as worried as I was. My brothers and sisters liked the club meetings, so they didn't care why I'd called one.

"So," I began, when we'd all settled down, and Nicky had stopped pulling Margo's hair, "how are you lot doing?"

"I still want Skipper," said Claire immediately.

"I know you do," I told her. "Skipper will have to wait, though."

"Yeah. Silly-billy-goo-goo." (Claire is not known for being patient.)

"School going okay?" I asked.

The boys looked, if possible, even more uncomfortable.

"You know what's happening to me at school?" I said.

"What?" asked Byron with considerable interest.

"These girls are teasing me about Dad. Nan White and Janet O'Neal started it. They're awful anyway. But then Valerie and Rachel joined them. Nan passed around this note in the cafeteria – I found the note later, I think Nan *wanted* me to find it – and Janet and Valerie and Rachel were all laughing like mad."

"Valerie?" spoke up Adam. "Wasn't she the one who used to come home from school with you sometimes last year?"

"Yup," I replied. "And Rachel and I were

science partners in the fifth grade. We always had fun together."

"What did Nan's note say?" asked Vanessa.

"It said, 'Mallory's going to be on welfare'," I replied. "First of all, that's not true," (I hope, I thought) "and secondly, if it was true, it's not something to tease about. Besides, a lot of people go on welfare."

Claire opened her mouth then and I *knew* she was going to ask what welfare was, so I was relieved when Jordan started speaking before she could.

"Michael Hofmeister won't play football with Byron and Adam and me any more," he said, looking at his brothers.

"How come?" I asked, frowning.

"We aren't sure," said Byron. "One day he was teasing us because we couldn't bring in money to go on a field trip with our after-school baseball team, and the next day we asked him over and he said no and we've asked him two *more* times and he still says no."

"People can be pretty mean," I said. (Byron looked as if he wanted to cry.)

"But some people are nice," said Vanessa, which, fortunately, saved Byron from crying.

"Oh, yeah?" I replied. "Who?"

"Becca Ramsey. She gave me some money yesterday when I wanted an ice lolly really, really badly."

"Well, that *is* nice," I said, smiling.

"Boy, I'd like to *get* Michael Hofmeister," said Jordan.

"Me, too," said Adam. "I'd like to open his lunch one day and put crushed-up spiders in his peanut butter sandwich."

"Ugh, gross!" squealed Margo.

"I'd like to accidentally hit him in the head with a baseball," said Jordan.

"Jordan!" I cried.

"*I'd* like to get *his* father sacked from *his* job and *then* Michael would see how it feels," exclaimed Byron. "And I'd laugh at *him* when *he* couldn't go on a field trip."

"I," said Vanessa to me, "wish you would write mean notes about Valerie and Rachel, but especially about Nan White and Janet O'Neal, and put the notes up all over school where everyone could read them."

"Okay, you lot. Enough," I said gently. "We have other things to discuss."

"What other things?" asked Nicky.

"Money," I replied.

"Money? Again? That's all we ever talk about," complained Margo. "We've been trying and trying to save money."

"I know. And you've been doing a great job," I told her. "But now we need to work out some ways to *earn* money."

"How come?" asked Claire.

"Because Dad isn't earning any money now, and Mum is earning some, but it isn't even *close* to what Dad used to earn.

349

I bet that maybe – *maybe* – it pays for food each week. And necessities."

"What are necessities?" Claire wanted to know.

"Necessities, dumbbell," Adam replied. "They're things you really need, like soap and toothpaste and toilet rolls."

"Toilet rolls!" hooted Claire. (You just never know what will make her laugh.)

"Anyway," I went on, "so Mum's probably paying for food and stuff, but we *still* have to pay the mortgage—" I glanced at Claire.

She was looking at me. "I'm sorry," she said. "I don't know what a mortgage is, either. I can't help it."

"That's all right," I told her. (I was betting that most of my brothers and sisters didn't know what a mortgage is, any more than Claire did.) I tried to think of how to explain that term. "You see," I began. "We don't own our house ourselves yet. The banks owns part of it."

"The bank?" Nicky asked. "Which part does the bank own?"

I sighed. "No particular part. It's just that when Mum and Dad bought our house, they didn't have enough money to pay for the whole thing. So they borrowed money from the bank. Most people do that. Now we have to pay the bank back, a little each month. Well, not a *little* – I don't know how much exactly. Plus, we have to pay the electricity bill, the phone bill and the gas bill. And all those bills are high since there are ten people in our family. So I bet Mum and Dad are using the money in our savings account already. I just keep wondering: When the money in our savings account is gone, what will happen to our family? What will we do?"

Byron looked concerned. Then he said, "Dad'll probably have a job before we run out of money."

"Maybe. But maybe not," I said. "I think we should be prepared."

"How?" asked Vanessa and Margo at the same time.

"Well, we could earn money to put in the savings account. I've been hoarding all my babysitting money since Dad lost his job. I'll give it to Mum and Dad soon."

"We could earn money, too!" Jordan cried.

(I'd been hoping someone would say that.)

"Yeah!" said Vanessa, inspired, "and I know exactly what I could do."

"What?" I asked, feeling suspicious, but I wasn't sure why.

"I could sell my poems to magazines!"

Vanessa is an aspiring poet. She has notebooks and notebooks filled with her poetry. Sometimes she even speaks in rhyme, which is annoying.

"Vanessa—" I started to say. (The triplets were sniggering.)

"No, really. I could," said Vanessa. "Don't laugh."

Of course, Adam laughed even harder. Then he added, "Don't worry. We're not laughing at you . . . we're just laughing near you."

Vanessa smiled at that. Then she said, "I really am going to try it, though. Writing poetry is what I do best."

"Hey!" cried Margo. "You know what I saw in a magazine the other day? Wait a sec. I'll go and get it."

"I bet she saw one of those ads to draw 'Blinkie' or whatever it is," said Jordan. "Now she thinks she can become a famous artist."

But what Margo returned with was a page from some magazine that said: If y cn rd ths, y cn bcm a secy and gt a gd jb.

"That says," Margo began proudly, "If you can read this, you can become a secretary and get a good job.' Well, I can read it, and I'm only seven. So I can *certainly* get a good job."

"As an after-school secretary?" said Byron, teasing.

"Well, you never know. Maybe I could sign up at that temporary place where Mummy works."

"Margo, I'm not sure about that," I said.

"Me, neither," added Jordan. "I'm going

to do something I know will work. I'm going to mow people's lawns."

"I could petsit, or walk people's dogs," said Byron.

"Maybe I'll, um, I'll. . ." Adam trailed off.

"Wait! I know!" cried Byron. "The three of us could start an odd-job service. We'll call it ABJ, Incorporated."

"ABJ?" I repeated.

"Yeah. Adam, Byron, Jordan."

"Now I *like* that idea," I said. "That's using your heads, you three."

"Maybe I could get a paper round," said Nicky thoughtfully.

Before one of the triplets could jump down his throat I said, "Another good idea, Nick-o. Why don't you see if any of your friends has a paper round? Find out what you have to do to get one."

"Okay." Nicky grinned.

At this point, Margo lost her head for a moment and thought she was at school. She raised her hand.

"Margo?" I said, over the giggles of the other kids.

"If an after-school secretary isn't a good job, then maybe I could set up a lemonade stand. Claire, you could help me. Vanessa, too. *We* could be CMV, Incorporated."

"I think you'll just have to be CM, Incorporated. I'm still going to work on my poetry," said Vanessa.

So the job problems were solved. But something was bothering Byron.

"Mal?" he said. "If we don't pay our mortgage, what happens?"

"I'm not sure," I replied honestly, "but I think that, after a while, the bank can take our house away from us."

"And that," said Byron, "is probably how some people become homeless."

# 10th CHAPTER

Sunday

Today I babysat for Linny, Hannie and Sari Papadakis. They're such nice kids. I'm really glad that Linny and David Michael are friends, and that Hannie and Karen are friends. Maybe one day Sari and Emily Michelle will be friends, too.

The morning started out cloudy and cool, so the Papadakis kids wanted to play inside. But they invited Karen and David Michael over. Everyone, including Sari, played well together -- for once. (Usually the boys won't play with the girls.) But then the sun came out and things changed. Hannie and Linny's feelings got hurt, and guess who was responsible for that? My own brother and sister, that's who....

355

The Papadakis kids are favourite sitting charges of Kristy, in case you couldn't tell from her notebook entry. Linny is nine (a little older than David Michael), Hannie is seven and in the same class as Karen at their private school, and Sari is just two. They live on the other side of the street from Kristy, two houses away from the Delaneys. (Shannon Kilbourne lives between the Delaneys and the Papadakises.)

As Kristy wrote, that Sunday morning was cloudy and cool.

"Can we invite friends round?" Hannie asked Kristy as soon as her parents had left. She was looking forlornly out of the window.

"Of course," replied Kristy. "Who do you want to invite?"

"Karen!" said Hannie.

"David Michael!" said Linny.

"Well, that's easy," Kristy told them, smiling. "They're at home. And they're probably bored. Do you want me to phone them?"

"Yes," said Linny seriously, nodding his head.

So Kristy phoned home and invited her brother and sister over.

"What shall we do?" asked Karen as soon as she and David Michael had walked into the Papadakises' house.

"Let's play with Myrtle the turtle and Noodle the poodle," said David Michael.

"Nah. We've already done that today," Linny told him.

"Dolls!" Karen suggested to Hannie.

"Nah," said Hannie.

"Invaders from the planet Neptune?" Linny suggested to David Michael.

"Nah," said David Michael.

"Hey!" cried Karen. "I know something we've never played, *and* we can all play it together. Even Sari. Even you, Kristy."

"What?" said the boys suspiciously. (Most of Karen's games involve either dolls, witches, or dressing up, none of which interest Linny or David Michael.)

"We can play office."

"Office?" repeated Hannie.

"Yes. We'll set up one of your desks like a desk in a real office – with papers and pencils and paper clips and—"

"And that old telephone that doesn't work," added Linny, getting into the spirit of things. "It'll be good because it's a *real* phone, not a plastic one."

Kristy couldn't believe that the four kids wanted to play together, but they were already racing upstairs. She followed, holding Sari's hand as Sari climbed the steps one at a time, one at a time.

The kids chose the desk in Hannie's room, and in no time it looked pretty office-like.

"Let's make a waiting area," suggested David Michael.

"Yeah," said Karen. "All offices have waiting rooms with magazines."

So Linny dragged a chair into his sister's room, placed it next to her chair, and put a small table in between them. Then Hannie ran downstairs and returned with a pile of magazines.

"I got some Golden Books, too," she said. "For Sari. In case she has to wait."

"Oh," said Kristy, "is this a doctor's surgery?"

Hannie, Linny, David Michael and Karen looked at each other.

"I don't want to play doctor's surgery,' said Linny. "That's for babies."

"Besides, we wouldn't need desks; we'd need tables and stethoscopes and those little hammers," said Karen sensibly.

"We'll play something really grown-up, said Linny, thinking hard. "We'll play . . . we'll play job agency."

"Job agency?" said Hannie, perplexed.

"Yeah. I saw it on *I Love Lucy* once. Lucy and Ethel needed jobs, so they went to this office and a man there said, 'What do you do?' and Lucy said, 'What kind of jobs do you have vacant?' and the man said, 'What do you do?' and anyway, finally, Lucy and Ethel ended up working in a factory that makes chocolate bars."

"Wow! Fun!" cried Karen.

"What parts are we going to play?" Kristy asked.

Not until after a lot of squabbling and arguing were the parts assigned. It was decided that Karen and Hannie would own the job agency. They would sit behind the desk. And Linny, David Michael and Kristy would be people needing jobs. (Sari was going to play Kristy's daughter.)

"Okay," said Hannie. "Let's begin. Our office is open!"

"I'll be your first customer," said David Michael, "since I need a job really, really, really bad."

"Badly," Kristy corrected him absent-mindedly. She was thinking of my father.

"Badly," David Michael repeated.

He walked up to the desk. Linny, Kristy and Sari sat in the "waiting room", Sari in Kristy's lap. Linny looked at a magazine. Kristy read a story to Sari.

Meanwhile, David Michael was saying, "Hello, my name is David Michael Thomas and I need a job. Really badly."

"Okay," said Karen. "What kind of work do you do?"

"What kind of jobs do you have vacant?"

"Well, what kind of work do you do?" asked Karen again.

"It depends. What kind of jobs do you have – have open?" David Michael got the giggles then, and so did the girls, then Linny, then Kristy, and then even Sari, although she didn't know what was going on.

When the giggling died down, Hannie said, "Let me look at my list of jobs. Okay." She pretended to scan a sheet of paper. (The paper was blank.) "We need a substitute teacher. Can you teach in a school?"

David Michael shook his head.

"Do you cook? A restaurant needs a chef."

"I can make toast," said David Michael. "And chocolate milk."

"You've got the job!" cried Hannie.

"Oh, thank you, thank you," said David Michael. "Now I can feed my family again. And buy clothes for them."

The kids giggled, but Kristy found herself thinking about Dad and my family again. Would Dad be reduced to going to some agency and taking a job he was over qualified for? Would he end up as a waiter in a restaurant – when he had gone to college for his law degree?

Kristy told me later that she felt a knot in her stomach, just thinking about these things, and that she was relieved when, about an hour later, the sun came out and Linny cried, "Oh, good! We can go outside."

The game of "job agency" was abandoned, and Kristy accompanied the five kids into the back garden.

"Hey, it's warm enough to go swimming," David Michael pronounced.

"Yeah!" said Karen. "Let's go over to Amanda and Max's."

"You're going to go over to Amanda's?" repeated Hannie in dismay. Amanda is slightly older than Karen, but the girls are friends anyway. Not best friends, but friends. Hannie, on the other hand, who lives in Amanda's neighbourhood day in and day out (not just at the weekends like Karen), can't stand Amanda. The feeling is mutual. Amanda doesn't like Hannie much, either.

"Yes. Now it's a perfect day to go swimming," said Karen. "Come on, Hannie."

"No thanks," Hannie answered. "I don't like Amanda. You know that."

"But you want to go swimming, don't you?"

"Not badly enough to go over to the Delaneys'."

David Michael looked at Linny. "You'll go swimming, won't you?" he asked.

"No," answered Linny. "I don't like the Delaneys, either. And neither do you. How come you're going?"

"Because . . . I . . . want . . . to . . . go . . . swimming," said David Michael impatiently.

"Okay, go ahead," said Linny.

"Yeah, go ahead," Hannie said to Karen. "I don't care."

"Okay, we will," Karen replied haughtily.

"You lot," said Kristy warningly. "Is the pool worth arguing over?"

"We're not arguing," Karen told her.

Kristy could have supposed otherwise, as her brother and sister left, and Hannie and Linny remained behind. Hannie looked close to tears, but Linny just began to dismantle the "job agency". He was very quiet.

"That's so unfair," Hannie cried.

"I'm sorry they left," said Kristy.

"It's not just that," Hannie replied. "I know Karen wants to go swimming. And she and Amanda are friends. I wish Karen had stayed here, but I suppose Karen has a right to play with other kids. But David Michael doesn't like the Delaneys at all. I think it's unfair of him to use their pool when he doesn't even *like* them. Amanda and Max probably think he wants to play with *them*."

"Yeah," Linny spoke up finally. (He was gathering together the magazines and books.) "I would never go somewhere just to use someone's pool. It really isn't fair. Hannie's right."

"Do a lot of kids use the Delaneys' pool?" asked Kristy.

"Oh, loads," Hannie answered. "Amanda and Max think they're the most popular kids in Stoneybrook." She sounded very wise.

"How many of these kids are really Amanda and Max's friends?" Kristy wanted to know.

362

"A few, I suppose," said Linny.

"But the rest of the kids are taking advantage of the Delaneys?"

"Yup," replied Linny.

Hmm, thought Kristy. That was a problem. She'd seen it coming, but she didn't know just how bad it had got. Worse, her own brother and sister were part of the problem. At least, David Michael was. Karen really is friends with Amanda, but she shouldn't have deserted Hannie that morning.

After Kristy left the Papadakises', she phoned to tell me what was going on.

# 11th CHAPTER

I was at the Delaneys' again. It was a Wednesday afternoon, one of my usual days there. And I was sitting at the edge of the pool in my swimsuit, sipping a Coke. Behind me was a mansion with a fish fountain inside. In front of me, beyond the pool, a green lawn rolled down to tennis courts.

I felt like a princess – except that I was a paid princess. This wasn't my mansion, my fountain, my pool, my lawn, or my tennis courts. And the four-hundred-dollar cat that was dozing on the sun-warmed pavement beside me wasn't mine, either.

But I could dream, couldn't I?

So I did dream as I watched Amanda, Max, Timmy, Angie and Huck play in the water. Long before anything actually happened, though, I stopped my dreaming and started paying even closer attention to the children. I don't know why, but I could sense something brewing.

On the surface, everything seemed all right. Angie was practising her diving, as usual. And she was doing nicely, jack-knifing and tumbling off the board. The boys were taking turns whooshing down the slide into the water, calling out things like, "Bombs away!" and "Look out below!" And Amanda was floating around on a raft shaped like a turtle, her legs hanging over the end. She was reading *Superfudge*, by Judy Blume, and was lost in a world of her own.

What first made me pay even stricter attention to things, was Max's saying, "Let's be otters at the zoo instead of dive-bombers, okay? Then we can go down the slide on our stomachs."

Okay, so Max was tired of dive-bombing. Big deal.

Then Amanda closed *Superfudge* with a sigh and said, "What a great book."

"Have you finished it?" I asked her.

"Yup. And I only started it yesterday." Amanda paddled herself to the side of the pool, handed me the book so that it wouldn't get wet, and then climbed out of the pool and sat next to me.

"Hey, Angie!" she called. "I've finished *Superfudge*. Now will you play with me?"

Angie had just emerged from under water. Her hair was slicked back from her face.

"I've got a diving contest next week," was her reply.

"So are you here to play with Amanda or to practise?" I couldn't help asking.

Amanda looked at me in awe. Then she sat up straight and said, "Yeah, are you here to play with me or to practise?"

Angie blushed to the roots of her hair. "Um—" she began, but she was interrupted by Max, who had clearly tired of the pool altogether. He was standing next to me, drying himself off.

"What's up, Max?" I asked.

"I want to go and hit balls in the tennis court," he said.

"We don't!" Timmy said, apparently speaking for both himself and Huck.

"Bombs away!" added Huck as he catapulted into the water.

"How about you?" I asked Amanda gently. I sensed another scene coming on like the one Stacey had written about.

"I – I don't know," replied Amanda, not sounding at all like the self-important snob she'd been the first time I'd sat at the Delaneys'.

"Have you had enough of swimming?"

Amanda nodded.

So I was faced with Stacey's problem. I was in charge at the Delaneys'. The Delaney kids didn't want to swim. But there were three other kids in the pool. I had to do what Stacey had done.

"Okay! Angie! Huck! Timmy! Out of the pool! It's time to do something else. You can play tennis with Max or . . . or. . ."

Amanda tugged at my suit and I leaned down. She whispered in my ear.

"Or," I continued loudly, "Cabbage Patch dolls with Amanda."

These suggestions were met with groans.

"But I have a *new* doll," said Amanda.

"So what? So do I," said Angie.

"Well, everybody still has to get out of the pool," I said.

Angie, Huck and Timmy did so, with much huffing, grumbling things like, "What a rip-off," and, "Thanks for nothing!"

Even so, Amanda and Max looked at me gratefully. Amanda went so far as to say, "Thank you, Mallory."

When Huck and Timmy and Angie had dried off, Max said, "Okay, I've got extra rackets for you lot."

And Amanda said, "My new doll is upstairs, Angie."

But Huck, Angie and Timmy walked straight through the gate in the fence surrounding the pool. They did this wordlessly.

Amanda looked at me with her mouth open, while Max just watched the other kids leave.

"I don't believe it!" Amanda exclaimed. "I don't *believe* it!" She sounded both angry and bewildered.

I put my arm around her. Then I put my

arm around Max. "Come on. Let's sit down for a few minutes." I started to lead them over to some lawn chairs, but Max wriggled away.

"I'm still going to practise hitting balls," he said. And he disappeared into the house to change and to look for his tennis racket.

Amanda, however, stuck with me. She seemed to want to talk.

"How come Angie wouldn't play with me?" she asked. "I thought she was my friend." She paused. "Oops. Am I being bossy?"

Poor Amanda. She really can be bossy, and someone must have given her a hard time about it. Now she was sensitive to it.

"Not at all," I assured her. "If you were being bossy, you would have said, "Angie, get out of the pool and play dolls with me!"

"You said that!" Amanda told, me giggling.

"I suppose, I did," I replied. "Sort of."

Amanda's smile faded. "Then if I'm not being bossy, what's wrong? I mean, I want kids to come over here and play with me. And with Max. I don't want kids to play with the *pool*."

"I can understand that," I told her.

"You know what?" said Amanda.

"What?"

"I don't know if the kids really like Max and me, or if they just like the pool. I really don't know." She was beginning to cry.

"Are they our friends or not? Do they like me?"

I stroked Amanda's hair and let her cry. And all the while I was thinking, Maybe being a "princess" isn't so great. Would you always wonder whether people liked *you* or whether they liked the things you could do for them – like letting them swim in your pool or play with your fancy toys, or lending them money, or introducing them to other rich kids.

It was no picnic having an out-of-work father, but at least I knew where I stood with my friends. Obviously Jessi liked *me*. I certainly didn't have anything besides myself to offer her these days, and she had stuck around. Nothing had changed between us.

I ached for Amanda – and at the same time I coveted her pool and house and four-hundred-dollar cat.

I had also found out who my friends *weren't*.

"You know what?" I said to Amanda.

"What?" she asked.

"I learned some pretty important things when my dad lost his job."

"You did?"

"Yup. I saw who stuck by me and who didn't. The ones who stuck by me are my real friends. The others are. . ."

"Enemies?" suggested Amanda.

"No, not enemies. But people I can't trust. People who care more about what their friends have than about who their friends are."

"Oh."

"So I was thinking. Even though your family is pretty different from mine, you and I are having sort of the same problem. Now you've got a swimming pool and you don't know who to trust. Do your friends like you because of what you have or because of who you are?"

"I don't know," replied Amanda.

"I bet you could find out."

"Really? How?"

"Well," I began, "maybe you could tell Angie and Karen and whoever else has been swimming here that you're not allowed to have friends using the pool when a sitter is in charge. Tell them it's a new rule or something. Then see who will still come over to play."

Amanda wiped some tears away with the back of her hand. She actually smiled. "That's a good idea," she said.

"Thanks."

"And you know what else I'm going to do? I'm going to tell *off* the kids who *don't* come over to play! Mallory, I'm so glad you're my babysitter."

I realized it no longer mattered to Amanda that Dad was out of a job. We were conspirators. We had a plan.

I just hoped that some kids *would* play with Amanda.

# 12th CHAPTER

That night, I felt inspired. I lay in bed unable to sleep because I was thinking about my conversation with Amanda. I decided to take my own advice. And some of Amanda's.

My room was dark, the curtains were drawn, and one of the windows was wide open, so I snuggled under the covers, listening to the night-time sounds: the last crickets, a car turning into the drive of the house across the street, my parents locking our front door before they went to bed. On the other side of the room, Vanessa tossed in her sleep and made funny noises with her mouth.

What I wanted to do was confront the kids who had been mean to me. But right away, I thought of two questions. Was it worth confronting them? After all, I had my BSC friends. And if I did decide to confront Valerie and the others, how would I do it? Would I just walk up to them and say, "You're not my friends any more"? Would I say, "Friends don't treat friends this way"?

By the next morning I only had an answer to my first question. I had decided to confront my former friends. Maybe the BSC members had stuck by me, but not everyone had. Rachel and Valerie hadn't even *tried* to be understanding. They had just listened to Nan and Janet – and then they had snubbed me. They were prejudiced against me because my father had lost his job. It was the principle of the thing, and I wasn't going to let them get away with it. If nothing else, I needed to stand up for myself.

I just wasn't sure how.

So I talked to Jessi about it in the cafeteria that day. Jessi had bought the hot lunch, and I had brought lunch from home. Mum said it was cheaper to make sandwiches for us kids than to give us money. Of course, nothing very interesting went into our lunch boxes – just sandwiches and fruit – but we didn't complain because we knew we were helping our parents out, and that was important.

Jessi and I sat down at the end of a long table in the cafeteria, separating ourselves from other kids. Jessi knew I wanted to talk privately.

I looked at the food in front of us: my peanut butter and jam sandwich and apple, and Jessi's pizza and limp salad.

"Gross," I said.

"I know," Jessi replied. "So what did you want to talk about?"

I glanced around the room. Valerie, Rachel, Nan, and Janet were sitting just one table away, so I leaned over and whispered to Jessi, "I want to get even with Valerie and everybody. Well, especially with Nan White and Janet O'Neal, since they started everything."

"How are you going to do it?" Jessi whispered back.

"I don't know. That's what I need help with."

Jessi took another bite of her pizza. "Hmm," she said. "Do you want to *do* something to them? Do you want to get them into trouble?"

I shook my head. "I really don't know."

As it turned out, it didn't matter. I didn't need plans. That was because of what happened next. Jessi and I were sitting in silence, both planning revenge, when from the next table, I heard my name. The girls were talking about me.

"Jessi," I said quietly, barely moving a muscle, "*don't* look over at Nan and everyone, but they're talking about me. I think."

Immediately Jessi glanced over at the other table.

"I said not to look!" I hissed.

Jessi turned back to me. "They're looking at us," she reported.

"Well, just keep eating. But don't talk. Let's listen to them."

Jessi nodded.

I concentrated on the other table and heard Janet say, "He must have done *something*. Something bad."

"Maybe he's stupid," said Rachel, and the four of them giggled.

"Nah," said Nan White finally. "Mallory's father is just a loser."

I gaped at Jessi. She was gaping back at me. "If you don't do something to them," said Jessi, "then I will."

"Don't worry. I'll take care of them," I replied, and stood up.

"You're going to *fight* them?" squeaked Jessi.

"Of course not. There are four of them and only two of us. But watch."

I placed myself at the end of Nan's table. Nan was on my left and Janet on my right. Next to Nan was Rachel. Next to Janet was Valerie. The four of them looked up at me.

"In case you're blind or something," I began, "I just thought I'd tell you that I'm sitting right over there." I pointed to the empty seat across from Jessi. "I also thought I'd tell you that I'm not deaf. I heard everything you said about my father.

I suppose you wanted me to, didn't you?" (Nan opened her mouth to say something, but I cut her off.) "That's just the kind of thing people like you would do."

"People like us?" said Valerie uncertainly.

"Yeah. Prejudiced people. But I want you to know that you can talk about me all you want. You can make jokes about me and my family. You can tease me. I don't care. And you know why? Because you're not my real friends, so your opinions don't count. I know who my real friends are," I went on. "They're the ones who stuck by me when Dad lost his job. It didn't matter to them whether my father was employed. And by the way – not that it's any of your business – my father was not sacked because he wasn't doing his job. He was let go, along with a lot of other people in his company, because the business was failing, which was not my father's fault. So go ahead. Say whatever you want. But you two," I said to Valerie and Rachel, "are not my friends any more, and you two," (Nan and Janet) "never *were* my friends." I looked back to Rachel and Valerie. "One more thing. Nan White and Janet O'Neal probably aren't your true friends, either. They can't be. They don't know how. They're only friends with people when it's convenient for them. So watch out."

Very casually I returned to my lunch and sat down at the table. I couldn't help looking at Valerie and everyone, though. And they were looking back at me, stunned. They were literally speechless, which also meant they didn't apologize to me, but I hadn't expected that anyway.

"Mallory!" Jessi said with a gasp as I slid into my chair. "I can't believe you just did that."

"Neither can I," I replied. And suddenly I found that I was shaking. But I didn't regret what I'd done. I knew that I had made my point. Rachel and Valerie would probably never talk to me again. But I knew they wouldn't ridicule me, either.

The next afternoon, I went to the Delaneys' once again. And once again, I arrived before Max and Amanda returned from school. When they did, they burst through the front door and Amanda called, "Mallory! Mallory! Where are you? Guess what?"

"I'm right here," I called, hurrying through the hallway from the kitchen, where I'd made a snack for the three of us. "What's up?"

Amanda, grinning, flung herself at me. "Your idea worked. Max tried it, too, didn't you, Max?"

"Yup," he answered.

"We told our friends no swimming when a babysitter is in charge. And then I invited Angie and Karen and Cici and Meghan to come over this afternoon and play Snail on our drive."

"And I invited Timmy and Huck to come and play basketball," added Max.

"And everyone is coming except Angie," Amanda reported. "Even Karen, and her mother has to drive her over."

"Why isn't Angie coming?" I asked. I had helped the kids put away their school things, and now we were seated at the kitchen table, drinking milk and eating oatmeal biscuits.

"She said she didn't want to," Amanda replied. "Wasn't that rude?"

I nodded.

"But I didn't like her much anyway. And just like you said, I found out who my real friends are. Max did, too. They're the ones who *will* come over to play with us even if they can't use the pool."

"Right." I grinned.

The guests began arriving before the kitchen was even cleaned up. First came the neighbourhood kids, followed by Karen Brewer. Karen's mother dropped her off and waved to her as she drove away.

The boys had immediately separated themselves from the girls. They were at one end of the drive playing basketball, while the girls were at the other end (but not too near the street) drawing the diagram for the Snail game.

The seven kids played calmly all

afternoon. And no one said a word about the pool, except Amanda, who whispered to me, "Now that I know who my real friends are, I'll tell them the pool rules have changed again. I want to go back in our pool. I miss swimming!"

# 13th CHAPTER

Friday

Today I sat for Becca and Squirt while Aunt Cecelia went shopping. As always, we had a good time. It was a pretty quiet afternoon. Vanessa and Charlotte came over to play with Becca. Mal, do you know what Vanessa is doing at school to earn money? I suppose you probably do. When Becca first told me about it I was surprised, but now I think it's funny.

*The girls had fun playing Secret Agents (Vanessa taught them the game). And Squirt had fun with his newest activity — climbing stairs! Of course, I have to hold onto him because he's still unsteady. That meant I spent most of the afternoon climbing stairs, too. When we finally stopped I think I was more tired than Squirt was. But sometimes you have to make sacrifices, right?*

I certainly didn't know what Vanessa had been up to, and when I found out from Jessi *I* was surprised at first, too, and then thought it was funny. Here's how Jessi found out about Vanessa's "job".

It began when Aunt Cecelia was getting ready to leave for an afternoon of shopping. Squirt had just woken up from a nap, and Jessi and Becca had just got home from school. Everyone had gathered in the kitchen.

"Okay, girls," said Aunt Cecelia as she found her wallet. "Jessi is in charge while I'm gone." (Duh.) "Becca, listen to your sister." (Doesn't she always?) "I'll be at the shopping centre. You know how to reach your parents or the neighbours if there's an emergency, don't you?"

Of *course* Jessi did. She's a babysitter. But all she replied was, "We'll be fine, Aunt Cecelia. Honest."

"All right, then." Jessi's aunt left, looking uncertain.

As soon as they heard her car backing down the drive, Jessi and Becca looked at each other.

"O-*kay*!" cried Becca. "An afternoon without Aunt Cecelia!"

"Yeah," agreed Jessi. "What do you want for a snack? Since you-know-who isn't here, we can have anything we want."

Becca chose biscuits and orange juice, and Jessi cut herself a piece of chocolate cake and poured a glass of milk. Then she hoisted Squirt into his high chair and gave him a bottle of juice and some crackers.

"Ah," said Becca, tipping dangerously far back in her chair. "This is the life. I miss having you sit for me, Jessi."

"I miss it, too. But maybe when Aunt Cecelia's been in Stoneybrook longer she'll make friends and start going out more."

Becca suddenly straightened up in her

chair. She took a biscuit *out* of her mouth. "Oh, no!" she exclaimed.

"What? What's wrong?" asked Jessi. "Is there something in your biscuit? Did you lose a tooth?"

"No." Becca had replaced the biscuit on her napkin. "I just remembered Vanessa and I felt bad."

"What do you mean?" asked Jessi.

"Doh-bloo!" crowed Squirt from his high chair. His bottle was still in his mouth. Jessi and Becca barely heard him.

"I mean," said Becca, "that Vanessa *never* gets treats like this any more. You know, because of her father."

Jessi nodded. She did know.

"But maybe she will be able to have treats soon."

"Really? How come?"

"Because she and her brothers and sisters are all earning money."

"Oh, right," said Jessi. "Mal mentioned that to me. But are you saying that Vanessa is actually selling poetry to magazines?"

"Selling poetry to magazines?" repeated Becca. "No. She calls herself Miss Vanessa and styles hair in the playground."

Jessi almost spat out her milk. "Excuse me? She calls herself Miss Vanessa and styles hair in the playground?"

"Yup," said Becca.

"Is she any good?" asked Jessi, still trying not to laugh.

"I suppose so. Today she did Emma Pape's hair in French plaits. Oh, and she also did Tess Werner's hair really nicely. Tess just has this plain old brown limp hair, and Vanessa brushed it all over to one side of Tess's head and pulled it into a ponytail. You wouldn't believe what a difference it made."

"Good or bad?" asked Jessi.

"Good, silly," Becca answered, smiling.

"Well, I'm glad for Vanessa," said Jessi.

"Me, too. Some kids have been teasing her about her father. The triplets and Nicky and Margo and even Claire get teased, too."

"Yeah. So does Mallory. . . Hey, how would you like to invite Vanessa over this afternoon?" Jessi asked her sister.

"Could I?"

"Of course. Go ahead."

So Becca called my house. "Is Miss Vanessa there?" she said when my dad answered the phone, and Jessi laughed.

Vanessa was delighted with her invitation and turned up at the Ramseys' house only twenty minutes later.

"You want to ask Charlotte to come over, too?" Becca asked Vanessa. (Charlotte Johanssen is Becca's best friend.)

"Okay," replied Vanessa. "I'll teach you two how to play SAs."

"Essays?" said Becca.

"Yeah. SAs. Secret Agents. It's a really

good game. I'll explain it when Charlotte comes over."

When Jessi told me about SAs, I just groaned. I had hoped my brothers and sisters had forgotten about that game, but apparently they hadn't. SAs is something Jordan invented – a spying game. You need either real or make-believe people to spy on and then the head SA sends the others out on "secret missions". The missions start out easy and get harder. For each mission completed (there are ten in all), you earn a badge. The badges are in different colours – pink for the easiest and black for the hardest. Like a black belt in karate, I suppose. Anyway, if you earn all ten badges, you become a top agent.

Vanessa explained this to Becca, Charlotte and Jessi. Jessi tried to work out who the girls could spy on, and finally decided not to interfere, except to say, "Don't make nuisances of yourselves. I don't want you looking in the neighbours' windows or anything." Then she turned to Squirt, who was wordlessly demanding to be released from his high chair.

"See you!" Becca called as she and her friends left the kitchen.

"Have fun," Jessi answered. She put Squirt on the floor. "Okay, little one. What do you want to do this afternoon?"

Squirt couldn't answer in words, but he took Jessi's hand and led her into the front hall. He stopped at the bottom of the stair-case.

"You want to climb?" she answered.

"Up," said Squirt, and began climbing. It was a laborious process for him. One slow step at a time. Reaching the top seemed to take for ever. As soon as they'd reached the first floor though, Squirt turned around.

"Down," he said solemnly.

Step . . . step . . . step . . . step.

Jessi must be unendingly patient.

They reached the ground floor.

"Up," said Squirt.

Oh, brother, thought Jessi.

She and Squirt were halfway upstairs for the second time when Jessi thought she heard a noise behind her. Still gripping Squirt's hand, she looked over her shoulder. Nothing.

Step, step, step, step.

Another noise. Jessi looked again. This time she saw a flash of red disappear around a corner. (Charlotte was wearing a red sweater.)

"Aha," said Jessi to her little brother. "You know what? I think we're being spied on. Someone has been sent on a secret mission."

"Down," was Squirt's reply.

Jessi helped him turn round – and saw her sister disappear around a corner.

Twenty minutes later, Squirt *finally* tired of climbing the stairs. Jessi took him into the TV room to watch *Sesame Street*. She pretended not to notice when Vanessa peered into the room, wrote something on a notepad, and disappeared.

Jessi was sure that the girls – who were fairly unobtrusive – spied on her and Squirt all afternoon. Her proof came near five o'clock when Charlotte and Vanessa said they had to go home.

"*I*," announced Charlotte proudly, "earned my blue badge. I completed *three* secret missions."

"I completed four," said Becca. "I got my green badge."

"Where are the badges?" asked Jessi.

"Jordan will have to make them. He's the top agent," said Vanessa seriously.

Charlotte left then, and Vanessa looked at Jessi and Becca. "Thank you very much for inviting me over," she said. "I'm really glad you did."

I knew how my sister felt. She was relieved because she still had friends.

Jessi told me later that she'd never seen anyone look as happy as Vanessa did when she climbed on her bike. And I have to say that Vanessa was positively *beaming* when she arrived home.

Vanessa's arrival coincided with a phone call. As usual these days, Dad dashed for the telephone and picked it up after one ring.

"Hello?" he said. Then, "Speaking. . . Yes. . . Yes, I did. . . You would. . . ? On

Tuesday? Of course. That's fine. Thankyou very much. Goodbye."

"Dad?" I asked. "Who was that?"

"Only the vice-chairman of Metro-Works. He wants me to come in for an interview on Tuesday. He saw my cv and likes it. Also, he talked to my old boss. I got a good recommendation from him."

"Dad, that's fantastic!" I cried. I threw my arms round him.

Dad was smiling, but he said, "Now don't get your hopes up too high. This is just one lead on one job."

"Okay," I said. I immediately called Jessi, though. "Dad has a job lead!" I told her excitedly. "He's got an interview on Tuesday at some place called Metro-Works."

"That's wonderful!" cried Jessi.

"But we can't get our hopes up too high," I said, even though my hopes were already skyrocketing.

# 14th CHAPTER

Dad's job interview was on Tuesday. I think our entire family was as nervous as Dad was. We felt as if we were sending him off to college or something. I could barely concentrate at school that day. As soon as the final bell rang, I was out of the door. I didn't even wait for Jessi so we could walk part of the way home together. I just made a dash for my house. All the way there, I kept my fingers crossed. I was pretty sure that if I did that, I'd be greeted with good news.

I burst through our front door and dumped all my stuff on the floor.

"Dad! Dad!" I called.

"Mallory?" Dad poked his head out of the kitchen.

"Did you get it?" (I was gasping for breath.)

"Get it? The job?"

"Sure. What else?" I ran into the kitchen.

"Oh, darling, I don't know yet."

"You *don't*?" I said in disappointment. "When *will* you know?"

"I'm not sure. I have to go back for another interview on Thursday."

"Aw, man. That is stale."

Dad grinned at me. "Tired of having an unemployed father?"

I grinned back. "At least you can joke about it now."

On Thursday, Dad went to Metro-Works for his second interview. And I spent another day biting my nails. *This* time when I ran home, I burst through the front door and yelled, "Okay, when do you start?"

Dad, in the kitchen with Claire as usual, gave me a rueful smile. "Maybe sometime after the third interview."

"The *third* interview?" I wailed. "When is *that*?"

"Tomorrow."

"Why do you have to have all of these interviews? Is this a good sign or a bad sign, Dad?"

"A good one. It means they like me. They want all the top people at the firm to meet me."

"Well, why can't they do that all at once? Like the spirits in "A Christmas Carol". *They* didn't make *Scrooge* wait for three nights. They all visited him on Christmas

Eve so that he wouldn't miss Christmas Day."

Dad laughed. "Maybe Metro-Works likes to torture prospective employees."

"Are you sure you want a job at a place that tortures its workers?"

"Don't look a gift horse in the mouth," was Dad's reply.

(I had to call Kristy to ask her what that means. Kristy's stepfather is the King of Clichés. I knew that Kristy would be able to explain the gift horse thing. She said it means don't turn down an offer you really need, or something like that. So I relaxed about the third interview.)

On Friday, unfortunately, I wasn't able to rush home from school. I had to go to the Delaneys' and then to a BSC meeting. But I bolted out of that meeting before Claud's clock changed to 6:01, and made it home in a record seven minutes. The second I entered the house I knew the outcome of the third interview. My entire family was gathered in the living room.

They were all smiling.

"You got it, didn't you, Dad?" I whispered.

He nodded.

I let out a whoop. Then I hugged Dad. And the next thing I knew, everyone was hugging everyone else. And Claire was saying, "Now I can get Skipper!"

"Tell me about it," I said to Dad when we were sitting down again.

"Well," Dad began, "I'll be a lawyer for Metro-Works. The job is similar to my old one. It's not *quite* as big, and the salary is slightly lower, but I might have a chance for a promotion next year. To make up the difference in pay," he went on, "your mother may continue doing temporary work. We'll sort out babysitting arrangements some other time."

"Right now," said Mum, "we're going to have a celebration. A nice family dinner. . . Cooked by your father."

My brothers and sisters and I exchanged glances.

"Cooked by Dad?" repeated Adam.

"Hey, I'm a pretty good cook now," Dad said defensively. "Let's see. I made all your favourite things: cabbage, swede, Brussels sprouts—"

"Oh, gross!" shrieked Adam.

"Adam!" Mum admonished him.

"Really, Dad. What did you make for dinner?" asked Nicky.

"Hamburgers, baked potatoes and salad."

"And I believe we have a special dessert," added Mum.

"All *right*!" said Jordan.

Fifteen minutes later we were seated in the dining room. We never eat there except at Thanksgiving and Christmas, or if our grandparents come over. Even though the meal was just hamburgers, Mum had laid the table with silverware, our good china, a white tablecloth and white linen napkins.

When we had been served, Byron said, "Dad? When do you start your new job?"

"A week on Monday," replied Dad. "And now that I've found a job, I think I can relax a little. I really enjoy being at home."

"That's good," I said. "We were worried about you."

"We were worried about a lot of things," said Vanessa. "That's why Mallory helped us form the Pike Club. Right, Mal?"

"Right," I replied, and then had to explain what the Pike Club was. (My brothers and sisters and I decided to keep meeting from time to time.)

"Tell me what you worried about," said Mum.

"Money, mostly," said Margo. "We were afraid we'd lose our home."

"Lose our home!" exclaimed Dad.

"Yeah," said Claire. "'Cause of the baggage."

"She means mortgage," said Jordan. "Mallory said that the bank owns part of our house, and each month we have to pay the bank back some money."

"And that if we couldn't pay the bank, they'd take our house away," said Margo.

"Well, that *is* true," agreed Dad, "and

392

I'm sure that some people become homeless that way. But we wouldn't have had that problem. I was getting severance pay from the old company. Whenever an employee loses his job, his firm is required to pay him his salary for a while after he or she leaves."

The triplets shot me a dirty look.

"Well, I didn't *know* that," I said to them.

"You made me do all that work!" cried Jordan.

"I didn't make you. You agreed to."

Mum spoke up. "I want you kids to know how proud your father and I are of you. You handled this situation very well."

"Thanks," I said. "It wasn't always easy."

"I know. You worked hard to earn your money."

"Oh, it wasn't just the money. We had trouble at school."

"Yeah," said Adam.

"Trouble?" asked Dad. "You all brought home the same good grades as usual."

"Not that kind of trouble," Vanessa told our parents. "It was the kids at school. They . . . they, um—"

"They were mean," said Claire.

"They were?" asked Dad.

"Yeah. They teased us when we didn't have money for trips or to buy lunch at school. That kind of thing," said Byron.

"And some kids went beyond teasing," I added. I told Mum and Dad about Nan

White, Janet O'Neal, and Valerie and Rachel.

"Valerie and Rachel?" said Mum. "I thought they—"

"I know, I know. You thought they were my friends. So did I. But, boy, I found out who my real friends are. I found out a few other things, too."

"Hmm," said Dad. "Maybe I should lose my job more often."

"No way!" cried Claire.

There was a pause. Then Mum said, "You kids were really enterprising."

"We were what?" asked Margo.

"Enterprising. That means you had good ideas about how to earn money."

"Well, I don't think I was *terribly* enterprising," I replied. "I've been babysitting all along. The only difference was that I gave you my money."

"I think *we* were enterprising," said Byron, speaking for the triplets.

"Yeah. We got a lot of calls for ABJ." Adam looked pretty pleased with himself. "We walked dogs, we weeded gardens. We even painted all of Dawn Schafer's mother's lawn chairs."

"We're going to keep ABJ going," added Jordan.

"I'm going to stick with my paper round," said Nicky.

"I can't believe *he* got a paper round," muttered Adam.

Since I was sitting next to Adam I felt that it was okay to kick him under the table. He was just miffed because Nicky, two years younger than the triplets and working alone, had managed to earn more money than all of ABJ. And the triplets are always telling Nicky what a dweeb he is. But he had shown them a thing or two, without even planning on it.

"CM was a good idea, too, wasn't it?" Claire asked.

"It was very good," said Mum.

"We only earned eleven dollars and sixty cents, though," said Margo. "That's not too much. We sold lemonade *and* brownies. But not many people came to our stand."

"You tried, though," spoke up Dad. "That's what counts."

"Vanessa," said Mum, "you've been awfully quiet. Did you really earn all that money selling poetry? If you did, I'd sort of like to see it published. What magazines bought it?"

Vanessa blushed the colour of a tomato. As far as she knew, *nobody* was aware that she'd been Miss Vanessa at school, not even the triplets, Nicky, Margo, and Claire, who *go* to her school.

"Um . . . well . . . I – I—" Vanessa stammered.

All heads turned towards her.

"I didn't exactly publish my poetry," Vanessa managed to say.

"You didn't?" said Mum.

"No. I. . ."

I could tell that Vanessa just wasn't going to be able to tell about Miss Vanessa, so I did it for her. I tried to make her sound talented and important, but there was a lot of sniggering anyway.

Mum and Dad, however, refrained from even smiling.

"Very enterprising," said Mum smartly.

"Very . . . creative," added Dad.

"Maybe Vanessa will own a beauty school when she grows up," said Adam, spluttering in an attempt not to laugh out loud. I took the opportunity to kick him again. And that was the end of the teasing.

Dinner ended, and Mum said, "Okay, time for dessert."

"All *right*!" exclaimed Nicky.

"Is it junk food?" I asked hopefully.

"Practically," Mum replied. She disappeared into the kitchen and reappeared with a cake. A gooey, thick, chocolatey cake on which was written in bright yellow icing: CONGRATULATIONS!

Fifteen minutes later, the cake was gone. (Well, there *are* ten of us.)

When the table had been cleared and the kitchen cleaned up, Mum said, "Let's continue our celebration. How about home movies and videos?"

"With popcorn?" asked Claire.

"Of course. We can make popcorn."

So we did. Then my family – Mum, Dad, my brothers, my sisters and I – gathered in the TV room. First we ran the film projector. We watched films of Mum and Dad at their wedding, then standing in front of their first house, and then standing next to their first car. ("What an old banger!" hooted Jordan.) Then we watched films of me drooling, the triplets eating in a row of high chairs, Vanessa painting at an easel, and the five of us putting on a "fashion show". After that, we swapped to videos. There were Nicky, Margo and Claire dressed for Easter, a Christmas morning with Mum and all of us kids tearing into presents, and more.

When I went to bed that night, I relaxed immediately and slept without dreaming.

# 15th
# CHAPTER

"Par-*ty!*" yelled Stacey.

I giggled. It was a Saturday night. Stacey, Dawn and Mary Anne were standing on my front door step. I was hosting the first ever BSC sleepover at *my* house. We've had plenty of sleepovers at Kristy's house, and the houses of the older members, but never at Jessi's or my house. I felt a bit nervous about this, but mostly I was excited. Apparently Stacey was excited, too.

"Come on down to the TV room," I said. "We have to sleep there because there isn't enough space in Vanessa's and my bedroom."

Dawn, Mary Anne and Stacey followed me downstairs. They spread out their sleeping bags. (Mine was already unrolled.)

It was six o'clock. By six-thirty, all seven of us were in the TV room, sitting on our sleeping bags.

"So what's to eat?" asked Claud. "I'm starved."

"Dad's bringing us some food home. He's picking it up on his way back from work," I replied.

"Oh, yeah," said Stacey, who was emptying a bag of make-up and nail varnish into her lap. "How's his job going?"

"He likes it," I told her. "He says the people are really nice. It's not exactly the same as his old job, though."

"But he's not out of work," Jessi reminded me.

"That," I replied, "is definitely the best part. Mum's only temping once or twice a week now."

"Mal?" asked Mary Anne. "Is—"

*Squish, squish.*

"Ugh!" squeaked Kristy. "I've been slimed! Gross."

Kristy's shirt sported a streak of gooey green slime across the front.

"Adam!" I yelled.

No answer. I turned to Kristy. "Don't worry. The slime is a bit like shampoo. It'll wash out. It won't leave a stain."

"But what happened?" asked Kristy.

"Adam got you with his Power-X Slime-Master Gun," I said.

My friends laughed. But I wasn't about to let the triplets spoil my first slumber party. "Adam!" I yelled again. "Byron! Jordan!"

"Maybe it was Nicky," suggested Dawn. "No, I'm pretty sure it was Adam . . . Hey, Adam, if—"

*Squish, squish.*

"Yikes! Slimed again!" cried Claudia. "And this time it's in my hair."

"That does it," I said as Claud and Kristy headed into the bathroom to wash out the Power-X slime.

I was about to run upstairs and find Adam when the door to the garage opened and in strode Dad with—

"Food!" exclaimed Claud, emerging from the bathroom.

Dad greeted us and doled out the food before he'd even taken his coat off. Then I complained to him about Adam and the slime and Dad promised to "see to things". He sounded sort of threatening.

When we had settled down with sandwiches, pizzas and lemonade, Kristy said, "Well, I sat for Amanda and Max this afternoon."

"How are they?" I asked. (My month-long job was over and I hadn't seen the Delaneys for a week or so.)

"Fine," said Kristy.

"Any pool trouble?" I asked.

Kristy smiled. "Nope. You solved the problem. I saw it with my own eyes. Amanda invited Karen over to play, and Max invited Huck over. Karen and Huck both brought their swimsuits with them, but when they saw that Amanda and Max weren't wearing *theirs*, they didn't say a word. They behaved like perfect guests."

"Maybe they've read *Uncle Roland, the Perfect Guest*," said Mary Anne, and the rest of us laughed. (It's a really funny picture book for little kids.)

"Did any kids show up uninvited?" I asked Kristy, with a mouthful of ham and cheese. (I'll never again take junk food for granted.)

"Nope," Kristy answered. "I think there may have been a change in pool rules."

"Well, Amanda and Max realized they couldn't buy friends," I said. I paused. Then I said, "Hey, you'll never guess what happened this afternoon."

"What?" asked everyone.

"*Rachel* rang me."

"*Rachel?*" cried Jessi. "That toad-head?"

"Yes. Rachel the toad-head. You know what? She'd heard about our party tonight and she didn't exactly come out and *ask* to be invited, but I know that's what she wanted. I think Valerie might have been with her. Rachel kept covering up the phone and whispering to somebody."

"What did you say to her?" Stacey wanted to know.

"I made it very clear that the party was for my *friends*. And Rachel got all sweet-sounding and said something about our silly row and how it was all in the past. And I said,

'Because my father has a job again?' and Rachel didn't say anything, so I told her to go and phone Nan or Janet. Then I hung up on her. I actually hung—"

"Hey!" Kristy interrupted. "I've just had an idea. Let's joke call Nan White and Janet O'Neal later. They deserve it."

"Okay," I said giggling. "Should we do Sam's favourite?"

"Yes," was Kristy's immediate reply. "And then we'll do a pig farm call."

"A pig farm call?" Jessi and I repeated at the same time.

"You'll see," Mary Anne told us.

We finished our supper, cleared up our mess, and then stood round the phone in the kitchen. We all knew what Sam's favourite joke call was.

"Who should call first?" asked Dawn. "And who are we doing it to?"

"We're phoning Nan," Kristy replied immediately, "because she's worse than Janet and this is a more annoying call. And anyone except Mallory can call her first. I think Mal should make the last call."

"I'll go first, then," said Jessi, and she picked up the phone and dialled Nan's private number. "Hello, is Sissy there?" she asked. She paused. "There isn't?" she said innocently. "There's no Sissy there?" Then she hung up and we doubled up laughing.

During the next half an hour, Kristy,

Stacey, Mary Anne, Claudia and Dawn each called Nan and asked for Sissy. Dawn reported that Nan sounded especially angry after her call.

"Good," I said, and picked up the phone.

"What *is* it?" cried Nan when she answered.

"This is Sissy," I said. "Have there been any calls for me?"

"Mallory Pike," exclaimed Nan. "Is that you?"

"No, it's Sissy," I said. I hung up and exploded into laughter.

"All right, now it's Janet's turn," said Kristy. "Who'll make the pig farm call?"

To everyone's surprise, Mary Anne said, "I will." Then she added, "I've got Logan's southern accent to a T. (A southern accent seemed to be crucial to a pig farm call.)

We had to look Janet's number up in the phone book. When we found it, Mary Anne dialled it and said (in her normal voice) to whoever had answered the phone, "Hello, is Janet there, please?" A few moments later, Mary Anne put on her accent. "Hello, Mizz O'Neal?" she drawled. "This is Mizz Patterson from Atlanta Pig Farm. The two hundred piglets you ordered are ready. How would you like them shipped to you?"

Well, of course, Janet must have said something like, "I don't know anything about pigs from a pig farm."

So Mary Anne, who ordinarily is a terrible, unconvincing liar, made her voice all trembly and insisted, "But you *did* order them. I've got the form right in front of me. Two hundred piglets for a Mizz Janet O'Neal in Stoneybrook, Connecticut."

I don't know what Janet said to that, but for the next ten minutes or so Mary Anne became more and more upset, saying that her boss would fire her if she didn't put through the order and collect the two thousand dollars that Janet owed Atlanta Pig Farm. When Mary Anne finally got off the phone, having told Janet that she was sure to lose her job, she was actually crying, and the rest of us were laughing so hard we'd had to run to the TV room and get cushions to put over our faces, so that Janet wouldn't hear us.

"Well, I suppose we got *them* back," I said, referring to Nan and Janet, and feeling deeply satisfied.

The seven of us returned to the TV room.

"Make-over time!" announced Stacey.

"No, let's raid the fridge," said Claud.

"Raid the fridge! We've just eaten," Jessi pointed out.

I was about to suggest phoning Nan again and asking if there'd been any more calls for Sissy, when Dad appeared in the TV room. He handed me something. It was the Power-X Slime-Master Gun.

"Here, my enterprising daughter," he said. "I found this hidden under the basin in the upstairs bathroom. See if you can put it to good use."

I grinned. "Thanks, Dad." Then I said to my friends as Dad was leaving, "Well, I think we know what to do with this."

"Yup," said everyone.

So we staged a sneak slime attack on the triplets in their bedroom. Then we returned to our sleeping bags. We talked and ate and told each other our dreams and fears. I didn't sleep a wink.

It was one of the best nights of my life.

*Need a babysitter? Then call the Babysitters Club. Kristy Thomas and her friends are all experienced sitters. They can tackle any job from rampaging toddlers to a pandemonium of pets. To find out all about them, read on!*